T0356636

SUMMER GIRLS

Also by Jennifer Dugan

Hot Dog Girl

Verona Comics

Some Girls Do

Melt With You

The Last Girls Standing

Playing for Keeps

With Kit Seaton

Coven

Full Shift

SUMMER GIRLS

JENNIFER DUGAN

putnam

G. P. Putnam's Sons

G. P. Putnam's Sons
An imprint of Penguin Random House LLC
1745 Broadway, New York, New York 10019

First published in the United States of America by G. P. Putnam's Sons,
an imprint of Penguin Random House LLC, 2025

G. P. Putnam's Sons is a registered trademark of Penguin Random House LLC.
The Penguin colophon is a registered trademark of Penguin Books Limited.

Visit us online at PenguinRandomHouse.com.

Library of Congress Cataloging-in-Publication Data
Names: Dugan, Jennifer, author. | Title: Summer girls / Jennifer Dugan.
Description: New York: G. P. Putnam's Sons, 2025. | Summary: "A teen girl whose beachside town is being gentrified by wealthy vacationers falls in love with the daughter of a real estate developer"—Provided by publisher. | Identifiers: LCCN 2024045765 (print) | LCCN 2024045766 (ebook) | ISBN 9780593696897 (hardcover) | ISBN 9780593696903 (epub) Subjects: CYAC: Lesbians—Fiction. | Wealth—Fiction. | City and town life—Fiction. | Romance stories. | LCGFT: Lesbian fiction. | Romance fiction. | Novels.
Classification: LCC PZ7.1.D8343 Su 2025 (print) | LCC PZ7.1.D8343 (ebook) | DDC [Fic]—dc23
LC record available at https://lccn.loc.gov/2024045765
LC ebook record available at https://lccn.loc.gov/2024045766

ISBN 9780593696897 (hardcover) | 10 9 8 7 6 5 4 3 2 1
ISBN 9798217110858 (international edition) | 10 9 8 7 6 5 4 3 2 1

Printed in the United States of America

BVG

Design by Claire Young | Text set in Minion Pro

The authorized representative in the EU for product safety and compliance is Penguin Random House Ireland, Morrison Chambers, 32 Nassau Street, Dublin D02 YH68, Ireland, https://eu-contact.penguin.ie.

For anyone who's ever wondered "what if"
under a sun-kissed sky

1

Birdie

MY MOTHER ALWAYS says there are only three things you
need to be successful in life: *charisma*, which she claims I've
inherited from her in spades; *money*, which she also takes
credit for, even though she married into it; and *an interesting point of view*, which—surprising exactly no one—she *also*
feels I should thank her for.

I guess technically "extremely online child of former mom
blogger turned lifestyle influencer" *is* an interesting point of
view. Or it would be, if I was allowed to say how I really feel
about it all (which is not good) and wasn't expected to instead
toe the party line on both her streams and my own.

I'm supposed to be grateful for it all, definitely not at all
bothered that the whole world watched me potty training.
And especially not bothered by the T-shirts my mom made
when, while out at a restaurant during the potty-training process, I stuck my head under the divider to ask an unsuspecting

stranger in the stall next to me, "Are you pooping?" (My therapist has reassured me that was a developmentally appropriate question, but I would still prefer there *not* be merch commemorating it.)

It's ironic that *that* is what I'm most known for, despite the fact that my mom's mantra for me has always been: "You need to look as expensive as you are." (Read: No, you cannot go outside and play like a regular kid. You are pristine. You are elegance. You are *perfect*.)

Looking expensive and perfect is kind of my mom's thing, after all. Her lifestyle branding would probably make that other ultra-rich, ultra-blond actress turned lifestyle influencer weep—that is, if they didn't occasionally collaborate—despite making most "regular" moms laugh at her. Sometimes the hate mail outpaces the followers.

It doesn't matter to my mom either way, as long as they keep watching. After all, content is god in the Gordon house, and my mother is the high priestess.

Right now, I've been asked—read: ordered—by my mom's team to do a "behind-the-scenes" run-up to my dad's annual investor party. My mother calls it a gala, but it's not—it's just a stuffy, boring party for my dad's investors and my mom's friends.

I tried to fight her on it—laughable, really, because my streams get the most views as of late. While she's been trying to give me a good edit (as good as she can anyway), it's been obvious things have been going *a little bit* off the rails. I'm pretty sure my uptick in viewership is because both her fans *and mine* are waiting for me to fuck up in some kind of real, uneditable way.

My most recent shenanigans? Screwing up my college apps on purpose and missing two days of filming while I live streamed sneaking off to Cabo with my best friend, Ada, for a weekend. (We tried to say Ada just wanted to connect to her Mexican roots, but neither of our families bought it.) And then, of course, there was also last month when I shattered a window trying to sneak in drunk from a party. (It looked open! It wasn't my fault!)

While we're not important enough for any of the actual tabloids to care about us, we have a habit of going semi-viral often enough to keep the other bloggers talking. Whether they're portraying me as another spoiled rich white girl who doesn't know how good she has it, or as a worse, somehow more embarrassing Kardashian knockoff, or—my least favorite—a tragic example of what happens to the kids who grew up being mined for content by their parents, social media has *opinions about us.*

Opinions we can capitalize on.

Thus, the phone camera Ada is currently pointing at my face. She insisted that the temporary phone holder I stuck to the dashboard of my boyfriend's very expensive car—which I have never driven before—was not capturing my best angles.

Ada's not a content creator or anything—she actually thinks it's all ridiculous. We're polar opposites, but our inheritances keep us running in the same circles, at least for now, and I'd be lost without her. While my post–high school plans are more nebulous and influencer-y—I want to launch a line of luxury purses when I gain access to my trust on my eighteenth birthday this summer—she's heading off to an Ivy for biomedical engineering this fall. Despite that, I've still managed to mold her into the ideal Instagram husband—though we're 100 percent platonic. (She's painfully straight.)

I wasn't originally planning to film this drive, but after three texts from my mother politely (read: obnoxiously) reminding me that I promised to, I relented. Despite the fact that I'm driving Mitchell Riley's McLaren up a dangerously winding mountain road to get to the ridiculous luxury villa that my dad always hosts this gathering at.

Mitchell had begged me to grab it for him since he was running behind, and like any good girlfriend, I agreed. I chose to ignore his reasoning—that he didn't want to be "stuck at the party" any longer than he had to be, after getting caught up at the pre-gala golf match with our dads. They're all getting ready there together at the villa, and I'm really trying not to dwell on the fact that he seems to be planning to ditch me as soon as possible.

Never mind that I've only driven stick once (in a parking lot with my dad at a development he was building before it opened). How hard could it really be? And double never mind that I should still be mad at Mitchell because of some flirty comments he made on Shayna Macintyre's Insta post this morning. (He said I misinterpreted, but I don't know how you misinterpret the phrase *hottie with a body* or the five fire emojis he added afterward.)

It's not like there's really anything to do about it anyway.

Getting with Mitchell Riley took a lot of planning and scheming by both of our mothers in the first place, and mine has reminded me several times this year not to mess it up. I think my parents just like Mitchell's ties to old money—his wealth goes back generations further than mine. (My grandfather had the good sense to invest in tech early and often, changing the trajectory of our family line forever.) And Mitchell's parents like the fact that my parents seem new and hip and can help modernize their family look once we eventually get married.

And okay, yeah, I get it. I'm way too young to be thinking about getting married—but also, I'm kind of not. That's just always been the expectation. I was born a prop, raised as a prop, and now my future is as scripted as the sitcom my mom's team tried to pitch based on our story. (It never even made it to pilot.)

Ada shifts in the passenger seat beside me—wincing at the grinding sounds the car is making, because, okay, maybe this is a *little* harder than expected?—as she live streams my attempt to get up the mountain without totally ruining the clutch. I don't know *why* Dad has to always host the Gordon Development Gala all the way up here. It's convenient for exactly nobody, especially not me, right now.

No, that's a lie. I know why. Dad is proud of this place, beyond proud actually. He calls this villa—all six thousand square feet of it—his "capstone rental," having flipped it himself at the start of his real estate empire when he was only twenty-one. It boasts six bedrooms, nine bathrooms, and an indoor pool that he personally designed.

The gears grind once more as I struggle to shift into whatever gear I hope and pray is going to get me up this final hill. Ada giggles beside me, quickly turning the camera to herself. "Hope Mitchell's not watching!" she teases as my phone screen fills with hearts and laughter emojis. Someone sends a virtual crown. She bats the garish gold thing away the second it's projected onto her head and then flips the phone camera back on me.

"Hopefully not," I say, sweating through my vintage Dior gown.

"How's it going over there, Birdie?" she asks innocently enough.

I flash her a smile and then glare at the road. "I think we all heard how it's going," I say as the car bucks us forward.

"Remind your viewers again *why* you're torturing this car tonight?"

"Mitchell was running behind," I say, trying to sound more amused about it than annoyed. "You know how it is with him." I roll my eyes.

We're the cutest couple, after all, can't let them see the cracks. (Even if, like, twenty people have already screen-shotted and reposted his "hottie with a body" comment and tagged me in it.)

"Why did he even need his car?" Ada asks, quirking an eyebrow behind the camera.

What is she doing?

"Boys and their toys." I grin, even though Ada knows the truth.

It's fine, it's fine. My mom makes sure to perfectly edit

Mitchell so that he comes off like a prince instead of a frog. No one but me—and Ada—knows just how much of an absolute toad my Prince Charming really is.

"And why are we encouraging this?" Ada asks, abandoning all hints of subtlety.

To say that Ada is not completely sold on Mitchell would be like calling the California wildfires "mildly inconvenient." Which is to say, she cannot stand the man and believes he will have a devastating yet preventable impact on my life.

Like I said, she's not like us.

Her parents are both groundbreaking surgeons, from a long line of groundbreaking surgeons. They each have at least one hospital named after them, and so many medical procedures I've lost count. So while my mom is making her living off sponsored posts and a weekly stipend from my dad, Ada's family has been living their best *Grey's Anatomy* life *out* of the limelight and expecting her to do the same.

They have no idea she has, like, three finstas and more TikTok accounts than you could count on both hands. She's almost as well-known to my followers as I am.

Still, she's leaving for Princeton this August and I . . . am not.

It's not that I didn't have any encouragement. My dad wanted me to go straight to college—he even made me apply in order to keep my allowance. Thus all the fake and half-assed applications. (What do you mean they didn't appreciate me sending in a full transcript of Alexis Neiers's screaming phone call to *Vanity Fair* in lieu of an admissions essay?) However, my mom encouraged me to take a gap year while

I figured life out—although I suspect it was more so I'd be handy if she did get that television deal to come through. And like in most arguments in our house, my mom won.

My dad asked me to at least come to the Newport house with him this summer in the meantime. He was all, "You really need to find yourself, Birdie." But no thank you. Not my thing. I'd rather stay in Boston with Ada and Mitchell, and my closet full of designer dresses.

The gears crank again just as Ada's own phone buzzes in the console between us. She picks her phone up with a frown on her face, still keeping mine steadily focused on me with her other hand. Like I said, the perfect Insta assistant. I look at her out of the corner of my eye as she turns to face me, sensing an even more negative shift in her mood.

"Birdie, pull over," she says, popping my phone back in the temporary holder she literally *just said* wasn't capturing my best angles, so she can study whatever's on her phone better.

What the hell?

"Sorry, can't, babe," I say, winking at my phone and sending a new flutter of hearts flying up from the comments. "Right now, we're just fashionably late, but any more detours and we're late-late. I can't be late-late to my own party!"

I laugh, trying to save face for the two thousand and seventeen people still watching my stream. I glance at my phone, delighted to see it fill with more hearts and laughing emojis, and then go back to watching the road and the quickly approaching mile-long villa driveway.

The valets are waiting up ahead, already motioning me forward, seemingly unimpressed with my driving skills.

"Birdie—"

"Just say whatever you want to say," I reply a little too cheerfully, playing to the audience. "You all want to know too, don't you?" The screen instantly floods with thumbs-up and eyeball emojis.

"Seriously. Turn your live off for a sec," Ada says, her eyes pleading.

I put on my best Hollywood smile. "I always stream at this time of night. I can't," I say through gritted teeth. She *knows* this is a contractual obligation with my mom's company. If it's something serious enough to discuss off live, why is she even bringing it up now? Can't she wait a little longer, until I'm inside and my mom's camera crew has taken over?

"Dude," she says, sounding annoyed.

"Don't mind Ada." I laugh, swooping even closer to the valet area. "She's a little camera shy ever since she got into Princeton."

"Birdie," Ada says, grimacing at her phone. "I have to tell you something quick, before we go inside. Can you seriously just stop streaming for a—"

She reaches for my phone to click it off, and I try to smack her fingers away, sending the car jerking dangerously close to careening off the driveway as I come around the final curve at too fast a speed.

"What is up with you?" I snap, steering us back on track quickly. I frown when I notice my phone has fallen to the floor and unbuckle my seat belt to pick it up, but Ada kicks it under her seat. "What are you doing?! You know this is my job!"

"It's Mitchell," Ada says. "He's here."

"I know he's here. He asked me to bring his car, remember?" I shake my head.

That? That's the important thing she had to tell me?

"He's . . . Look." She turns her phone toward me, showing me the text she just got from our friend Carly. The same Carly whose life revolves around figuring out all the latest gossip and drama. If we were going to have someone narrating our life à la Gossip Girl, it would be her.

Omg, can you believe it? Poor Birdie. ☹

I crinkle my forehead at the text. *Poor Birdie? Why poor Birdie?* And then I drop my eyes to the grainy night mode photo, squinting at what seems to be my *perfect* boyfriend hooking up with one of the waitresses catering the party. There are glass jars of dried goods and canned food all around them in what looks to be a fully stocked pantry—each item no doubt chosen to be the ideal background aesthetic for every investor poking around the place—which serves as a jarring frame for his almost comically shocked face. He looks ridiculous. This picture is ridiculous.

My mother is going to flip out when she finds out my boyfriend is fooling around with a server next to her aesthetically placed cans of confit de canard and expensive dried mushrooms.

"Mitchell is seriously cheating on me with a *waitress*?" I screech.

Ada doesn't get to respond because this is followed almost immediately by the loudest crunching sound I've ever heard as we both fly forward in our seats. We were going slow, but my head still smacks the edge of the steering wheel, grinding one of the bobby pins into my tender skin, and *oh. Oh no.*

Ada and I both slowly face each other, realization setting in that I have just rammed Mitchell's McLaren into someone else's Bentley. My eyes go huge as the valets run over shouting and guests begin to pour out of the house to see what the commotion is.

"Birdie," someone calls, and I look over to see my parents standing in the doorway, matching looks of horror on their faces as my mom's camera crew zooms in on me.

She redirects them back inside—the hostess extraordinaire as usual, still hamming it up for her sponsorship deal with a new cookware company, which I may have just permanently fucked.

"Mom?" I say, not sure if I should apologize or scream, as the cameras twist toward me again, recording the worst moments of my life, as usual.

A few seconds later, Mitchell runs out, his hair disheveled, Taylor Swift–red lipstick still smudged on the corner of his mouth. He practically dies when he sees his car, and rushes down the steps, frantically rubbing his hand over the hood, like that will somehow smooth it all out. He looks like he's going to cry. Nope, he *is* crying. Him. He has someone else's lipstick on his skin, and I just embarrassed my whole family on camera and cost us a lot of money, *again*, and he's the one who's crying.

He's the one who's going to get sympathy when someone screenshots my life and posts it on the internet for everyone to gawk at.

Him.

"Oh god," Ada says beside me, and I tear my attention away from Mitchell long enough to look at her.

She's picked up my phone at some point during this disaster, and to my abject horror, I realize that I'm still streaming. I guess it didn't turn off after all when Ada knocked it down. The screen is filled with shocked and laughing emojis, my dazed face taking up all of the remaining space. Ada tries to hit end, but I gently push her hand down and go back to studying myself in the camera. There's a tiny rivulet of blood dripping down my hairline dramatically from the bobby pin, and I watch it fall with interest. It's possible I might be a little concussed.

"This is so fucked up," I say into the camera.

This declaration seems to spur everyone into action because seconds later everyone is shouting over one another and rushing to the car. I can't help the laughter bubbling up in me, even as Ada looks at me with an increasingly concerned expression.

2

Cass

THERE IS NOTHING I want to do less during the precious first weeks of summer than leave the beach to come out here to this stupid landlocked ski "villa" and work as a cater waiter. But still, here I am, plastering on my most butt-kissing smile to reassure all the way-too-rich people in the room that they're not horrible, actually. A monstrous feat, since every time I look at them, all I can think about is how they've been hoarding wealth for generations and, for fun, gentrifying the last affordable housing within an hour of my hometown. Screwing over townies like me and my family and the little old lady who owns the bodega down the street.

I kind of hate that me and all my Pell Grant–qualifying friends are fighting for our lives out here, trying to earn enough money to go to college, just so we can maybe, *maybe*, someday work as their accountants or their kids' teachers or something like that, in between our second jobs as DoorDashers or baristas to cover the rest of our inevitable student loan payments.

Yeah. I'm a little salty.

Speaking of salty, I would give anything to be in the water right now. I don't even have to be surfing—just sitting on my board out in the ocean, seeing the occasional fish, or watching the waves break on the rocks would be good enough to remind me what's real. I would even take a lifeguarding shift in a pinch.

Instead, I spin the little bracelet my best friend, Bentley, made me around my wrist until the silver wave is right side up. If I can't get on the water, at least I can pretend.

I would leave, I would. It's just that George—Mr. Gordon tonight since I'm being proper—is the host of this little soirée, and he dragged me here under the guise of doing me a favor. The same Mr. Gordon who has been my dad's boss for most of my life. It started with the occasional handyman job before I was even born, my dad never one for a nine-to-five, according to my mom. He's good at what he does, obviously, and so over the years, there has been a lot less fixing steps or mowing lawns. At this point, he's managing pretty much all of George's dozen-plus rental properties and Airbnbs in town. Ironic, given that my dad is the head of the Affordable Housing Coalition, and literally called gentrification his "evil enemy" once in casual conversation.

If I'm being real about it, I didn't mind when George first started snatching up all the foreclosures and short sales in my neighborhood. It was great to be riding bikes past new picket fences instead of over broken glass in the middle of the street, and I liked how pretty he made the houses and landscaping. Plus, at that point, I think I saw him more as a family friend than a boss figure; he used to come over for dinner a couple times a week even then. But then I started to realize some things . . .

Like that my dad had to work more and more to be able to afford *our* apartment in the same neighborhood, and that my friends started moving out, their parents accepting too-cheap offers from George or his friends that still somehow seemed too good to be true, only to see him resell the houses months later for a massive profit. That's when I realized "Mr. Gordon" wasn't just trying to fix up the neighborhood—he was trying to take it over, to reshape it into something more palatable.

Less than a mile from the beach, my corner of town was the last bastion of affordable housing. It's where everybody went after being driven from the better parts of town by tourists and wealthy summer people. And he's ruining it.

It's not like our little coastal town was a stranger to grossly rich people, and the Gordons certainly *weren't* the first ones to take a vacation and overstay their welcome. There's a neat little row of historic mansions overlooking the water proving otherwise. But George and his friends *were* the first ones to say, *Hey, let's leave the mansions and all the little neighborhoods full of nice, overpriced properties alone. Let's go farther inland, to where the chain-link fences and broken glass bottles live, where rent is still reasonable and you can buy a house without hitting mid-six figures. That's where the profit lies.*

And it does. Damn, it does.

But that's the thing about islands. They're only so big. Once you price people out, they can't just keep moving a little farther away and living their best lives. They just . . . leave.

I guess you could say George has sort of became a reverse Robin Hood—robbing from the poor to give to the rich, whether he means to or not. I guess he's probably not so special in that regard. It's kinda the secret to how the rich stay rich, right?

My dad, god bless him and his fight against his "evil enemy," started the Affordable Housing Coalition about eighteen months ago when George's company bought out a close family friend of ours who was struggling to make ends meet . . . but he never stopped working for George.

I asked once how he justifies it, and he said, "You can hold two things in your hand at one time," which was vague and confusing and didn't really seem to make sense in that context. I don't see how he can keep their friendship and work relationship separate from the damage George is doing. It all feels a little hypocritical to me, on both sides of the equation.

I used to wonder why George would keep Dad on even with all the trouble he makes. Mom suspects that George just wants to keep him close, to keep an eye on what he's up to with our coalition—which frequently takes over town hall to protest the development of new mansions and the destruction of old affordable communities to make way for them, and to fight against various housing authorities granting zoning exceptions to companies like Gordon Investments.

But I don't believe that. I think he just sees the same thing in Dad that he sees in me.

We're clever, my dad and me. We're clever in a way the rich

appreciate. We instinctively know the best way to be efficient and save them money. We're hardworking. We think outside the box . . . except we're honest and loyal in a way that people in the Gordons' tax bracket don't seem to be.

I mean, just look at his disaster of a daughter. She *pretends* she's all loyal and kind and whatever else on her live streams—*not* that I watch her live streams—but she dropped me like a hot potato the second she was old enough to understand that our dads weren't *coworkers* and that our tiny apartment wasn't a weird little summer project, but where we lived year-round.

Whatever.

Sometimes I wonder if George just likes to keep me around as a little pet project of his, an avatar for him to imagine what his life would have been like if he had been born into the wrong family, one that ate boxed mac and cheese instead of prime rib in the evenings. Like he fully sucks? But he's also stupidly nice? I'm not sure he even realizes how screwed up what he's doing is. I kind of hate it.

But what I hate most of all is that we need George, me and my dad both. He pays well and offers excellent benefits, something basically unheard-of for positions like my dad's. And he's not just focused on profit when he's in town, although I'm sure he is tonight and whenever he sees his investors. But, like, he'll also take the time to help my dad hang Sheetrock if a contractor is running behind, or debate the merits of different weedkillers and their impact on the environment.

Once I even caught them sipping on matching cans of cheap Narragansett beer, sitting on the porch of a recently flipped house. I stood there in the shadows, listening to my dad talking to George about how projects like that one were outpricing the average family from living here anymore. That George was making things worse instead of better. I was shocked to see him listen thoughtfully, even adding some insight of his own for ways my dad could streamline things at the coalition . . . but then he proceeded to snatch up the next short sale he could find anyway.

Still, he's not a horrible man, I guess. And, as my dad loves to point out, he's a great connection for me to have. I'm studying business at MIT this fall—thank god for "meets needs" schools or I'd be screwed—and we both know that an internship with Gordon Investments, not to mention a recommendation from George himself, will probably help me land any job I want when the time comes.

In fact, when George asked me to come work this event for him, I didn't hesitate to say yes for that very reason. I knew he would sneak me around to give me advice about schmoozing these people. He loves to point out the various movers and shakers in his orbit and then introduce me and tell them that I got into MIT in the fall so they know that I'm "going to be someone." And if I bristle a little at the idea that I'm not *already* someone, it's okay. Because he's nice, in his own extremely awful, out-of-touch way.

I refill my tray with champagne flutes and walk through the crowd, nearly losing my balance when George's wife yanks two off my tray without even giving me a chance to stop. I fight the urge to glare at her—she's lucky she's not wearing this champagne—but she's already turned back around, effectively dismissing me like I'm an annoying gnat instead of someone she's watched grow up.

Verity Gordon—no, I don't know if Verity is even her real name or just a stupid stage name—has spent all night prancing around like she's god's gift. She thinks she's the second coming of Kris Jenner, shoving her camera in everybody's face and constantly yapping about content and appearances. I swear to god, she's secretly trying to cast *The Real Housewives of New England* or something. I would laugh *so* hard if that ever happened.

George would probably die of embarrassment too.

I glance around the room. I don't know where their daughter, Birdie, is. She must be running late or something. Usually, she's following her mother around like a little lost puppy, mugging for the camera and acting desperate for her second in the spotlight too. I would love to not bump into her tonight. Even though we haven't talked in, like, over a decade, it would still smart to see her standing there in a fancy dress while I'm looking like one of the penguins in *Madagascar* in this horrible cater waiter uniform.

I hand my final glass of champagne off to some rich guy's too-young-for-him date, and then head back to the kitchen to get my next tray. Or I almost do, because before I get there, the sound of giggling catches my attention. I'm supposed to be shoving past the other cater waiters refilling their trays to get the oysters that George suggested I might bring to the state senator in the other room, but I pause, trying to figure out where the sound is coming from.

Curious, I set my tray down on one of the fancy hutches

dotting the too-long kitchen hallway and creep quietly, following the noise. More laughing and the sound of something falling has me pulling open the door to the model pantry—the same one I painstakingly set up just that morning with goods hand-selected by Verity Gordon herself—to find one of the other waitresses in full make-out mode with one of the rich boys from the party. He looks vaguely familiar. I'm sure his parents are out there in the other room, kissing asses with the rest of them, but I can't quite place him. I don't really care either.

"Gross," I say, and start to shut the door, but an arm stops me. I spin to face the person behind me, expecting to see another waiter or, I don't know, maybe even Verity or George, but instead I'm met with the cruelest smile I've ever seen, painted on overly glossed pink lips.

I'd recognize her anywhere.

It's Carly Whitmore, another recent high school graduate like me, except one who was blessed with a private school education and a ticket to an Ivy where her family's name is on half the buildings. She's filmed enough with Verity and Birdie for me to know who she is, even though I wish I didn't. She's as horrible as Birdie and her mother, the meanest of mean girls.

"What did you find?" she teases, shouldering past me to rip open the pantry. "Oh, this is lovely!" She laughs, after snapping a picture with her phone.

"Carly?" the boy in the closet calls out, clearly panicked. The waitress scurries past us, bolting into the kitchen as she adjusts her shirt. I'll have to check in with her later, make sure everything was on the up and up. I probably should have warned her about how much the boys at these kinds of parties love to let loose with the little townies their parents hire to cater to their every need.

I should probably go have that check-in right now—I mean, god knows I'm not needed here—but curiosity leaves me rooted in place. The boy steps into the hallway. He's got about a foot on my five-foot-four frame, and I have to tilt my head up to meet his eyes. He swallows in the harsh hallway light, his Adam's apple bobbing in distress as he runs his hand through his mussed-up hair.

Which fuckboy even is it? I flick through the usual suspects in my mind. Honestly, they all look the same, with their floppy dark hair and their perpetual tans and their clothes tailored just right to show off their muscles.

And oh. Whoops.

I think I do know this particular fuckboy, after all. It's Mitchell Riley, Birdie's boyfriend.

"You better not be texting Birdie," he says, grabbing for the phone just as Carly hits send.

"Relax, I wouldn't do that," she says, stepping just out of his reach.

He calms down for half a second, blurting out a half-hearted "I can explain," before she adds, "I texted Ada. They're streaming, so I knew Birdie's phone was tied up anyway." She smiles coolly and walks back to the party, leaving us to stand awkwardly in the hallway.

"That was cold," I say finally, just trying to break the tension, because, oof, Carly definitely just blew up his relationship and looked like she enjoyed doing it. I might be enjoying the show too, but I'm trying not to be a *total* monster.

"Shut up," he says, stepping around me right as the loudest bang I've ever heard in my life comes from outside. I swear the house shook, although maybe that was just how high I jumped from being startled.

I step back into the ballroom right as the crowd begins to rush out, sweeping me up with them. They propel me through the door and we spill across the grand carved staircase at the front of the house. Below us, I see good old Mitchy boy wailing over the smashed-in hood of what I'm assuming is his own super expensive car. Birdie is now crying in the driver's seat, while her friend alternates between wincing at the crowd and hugging her.

I roll my eyes. *Typical rich people drama.* It's not like they don't insure their cars to the hilt, and I don't know why Birdie's even crying. I'm pretty sure cheating is a daily occurrence among the crowd Birdie and her family runs with.

With a sigh, I push back inside, heading to the kitchen with the other waiters to reload our trays before the inevitable onslaught of gossip-infused snacking. It will be all anybody wants to talk about now, and I'm sure they'll have worked up an appetite with all their gawking.

I'm proven right as I make my way through the ballroom a few minutes later. Everyone has grown bored of the scene out front, happy to devour the little oysters and mini crab cakes and complain.

I do my best to avoid Verity, who is currently dabbing her eyes in the corner, faking tears and pretending to be desperately worried about her makeup. I wonder where Birdie is for half a second, before I get sucked into the gossip of the room, which is practically pulsating in excitement over this new morsel of misery. They seem especially scandalized by the fact that Birdie was streaming when it all went down, because of course she was.

"They need to rein her in. She's too wild for her own good."

". . . making out in the pantry! I bet he'll . . ."

"How embarrassing for them both. Crying over . . ."

"She's just like her mother. Poor George being saddled with both of them."

"Cassandra," George says, grabbing my attention. I try not to bristle at the name. I like to go by Cass, but he feels it's "beneath" me. He's spent the entire evening introducing me as Cassandra, like the extra syllables somehow indicate class.

"Huh?" I say, and then catch myself. He hates when I say huh. "I mean . . . hi. Fun party, right?" I'm trying to break the awkwardness. I don't think it's working.

"It's certainly been eventful," he says, beckoning me into the study and away from everyone's curious eyes. "Thank you so much for your help today. If you'd like to head back—"

"There are still three hours."

"I know," he says, holding his hands up. "But I also know you still have that Rotary Club scholarship essay to write, and your dad hates you driving back too late. We've got plenty of help. I'll give you full pay, though, don't worry."

"If you're sure." I shrug. I'm not about to look a gift horse in the mouth.

"I am," he says, taking a deep breath as he crinkles his forehead.

"What?" I ask, because I know his thinking face by now. I've been seeing it practically since I was born.

"I may have another job opportunity for you, actually."

"I have lifeguarding, and no offense, I like that way more than waiting on your horrible friends."

He laughs. "I don't blame you there," he says. "But no, this is something a little different. I think you'll have fun. I promise it won't interfere with your lifeguarding duties. Why don't you come over to the Newport house Monday morning, say, around ten a.m.? We'll talk then and see what you think."

"Does it pay well?" I ask, tapping my chin. I'm kidding, but I'm also not and we both know it.

He smiles. "Exceedingly well."

"Then I'll see you Monday morning," I say, with a mock salute.

3

Birdie

I'VE BEEN EXILED.

My dad says that's a very dramatic way of describing spending time with him at our summer house, but I don't know what else you would call being shipped off by your parents to sit abandoned on an island in the middle of nowhere. (Okay, fine, I'm only an hour from home, and we do have a great ocean view, but still.)

My phone, webcam, laptop, and ring lights were all confiscated by my father the second I stepped inside the house dragging my Prada luggage behind me. No more streaming, no more socials, I'm officially on lockdown. Watching him put parental controls on my phone, blocking every social media app, felt way more tragic than just being sent away in the first place. All I can do is text and call. After some debate, he let me keep Apple Maps and rideshare apps, mainly because aside from my driving the Audi to the island for him, I'm not going to be driving again anytime soon. I tried to be stoic, I did, but there were tears. Lots of them. (Some of them were even real.)

My father didn't care, and for once my mom agreed with him.

She was mortified, not over what I had done, but over the fact that I had been live streaming as it happened. She said I had "broadcasted to the entire world" that the family she was trying to partner with for a new spin on her web series had "a lying, cheating son."

I pointed out that that was good for television, no? She yelled back that our streams were supposed to be a highlight reel, not the second coming of TMZ, and now she'd have to "spin it somehow."

My dad had simply hugged me after the accident and sent me to my room at the villa for the rest of the night after offering me a Band-Aid for my injury. (Sure, it looked dramatic, but it turned out to literally be a scratch.) He even hugged me again when Mom got done yelling at me some more the next morning, even though I could tell he was upset too. Normally, he doesn't get too worked up about what I'm up to, but I guess crashing a McLaren isn't good for business for anyone, even my dad.

I should be glad he was so nice about things, but now that I'm lying here in our Newport house, listening to the horns of the boats waiting for the last of the fog to burn off in the morning sun, I almost wish he had yelled too. This? This methodical dismantling of my life? It's way worse.

I pick up my phone, instinctively going to check my socials

and record a new GRWM video to post—except the nearly empty home screen staring back at me feels like a punch to the gut. No, worse than that, like my life is literally over.

I flop back on my bed and sink deeper into my pillows, trying to decide next steps. Ada texted me already that Mitchell was being sent to Italy with his grandma for a couple weeks, so at least we've both been shipped off. It wouldn't be fair if I was the only one getting in trouble for this when it's all his fault. Just thinking about him sends a burning, jealous rage coursing through me.

I know this was probably not the first time he screwed around on me, but the fact that he couldn't even keep it in his pants at my dad's own event just adds insult to injury. We are so over, even if I suspect that my mom is hoping for a different outcome. Whatever. If I focus on that whole thing, I'll drive myself mad. I am not about to spend the summer festering away in here, even if my dad thinks I need to.

I do a quick run-through of people I know who summer here, and smile. If I'm remembering right, I think one of Mitchell's friends docks their family boat here this time of year—which seems ideal for the revenge partying I'm going to have to do to get over Mitchell. My mom always said, "One peg drives out the other," when I would cry over boys when I was younger. Maybe it's time to test that theory.

"Birdie," my dad calls, knocking twice on the bright white door before turning the knob and stepping inside. That's another thing about my room here—everything is bright white. Too white.

Crisp and clean, complete with generic ocean pictures and

what I hope is a fake starfish pinned to the wall. It's sterile and uncluttered, the complete opposite of my room at home, which is constantly a mess of clothing and half-finished products people have mailed me to try on camera. It's lived-in and scattered, the way I really feel most days. It's also a huge part of why Mom insisted on renting some studio space. She wanted to style a bedroom for me that was always clean, always perfect. In retrospect, she could have just come out here—it probably would have been cheaper—but then again, I think Dad likes having his own space. One not invaded by cameras and live streaming.

I stretch out with an exaggerated yawn as he comes over and sits on the edge of the bed. "What time did you go to sleep last night?" he asks, and I'm surprised. Generally, my parents don't care what time I do *anything* as long as it doesn't inconvenience them.

"Around three a.m.," I answer honestly, rubbing the sleep from my eyes. "I got sucked into *Love Island*, and you know how it goes." I shrug, even though I know he probably doesn't.

"You knew you had to be up early today," he says, furrowing his brows, and I swear he looks almost . . . disappointed?

"I am up, see?" I say, waving my hand in front of my body as if to say ta-da! He looks unimpressed.

"Yes, but I said we had things to do today, and now you're going to be exhausted."

I look at the clock. It's barely past nine. He's got a point, though; I'm a bear with anything less than my nightly eight hours, but six should at least have me somewhat functional.

Wait. What does he mean *things to do*? He'd better not be expecting me to help him and Mr. Adler with the houses. I know he just picked up a new one last week. I swear, if he even tries to make me paint again . . .

"I'll be fine." I smile, giving him my best puppy dog eyes. The same puppy dog eyes that had him upgrading my car last year from a Mercedes-Benz to a Mercedes-Maybach.

He sighs and looks away. "I hope so. Either way, you need to get up. You have an appointment in an hour."

"An appointment?" I ask, but he just shakes his head and stands up to leave.

"You'll see. Meet me in the office in an hour, Birdie, and make yourself presentable. We have an important guest joining us."

"Ohhhhkay," I say, grabbing my phone to fire off a text to Ada the second he's gone, only to find she's already beaten me to it.

Ada: How is day one of the banishment going?

Me: ☺ Dad's acting even more off than yesterday!!!

Ada: Off how?

Me: I don't know. He seems annoyed with me??

29

Ada: Well, you did crash a $200K
car last week. So . . .

                                    Me: Don't remind me.

          Me: Apparently, I have an "appointment"
          soon with a special guest? Idk what he's
          up to. Gotta go get ready though.

Ada: Appointment?

          Me: I stg if he's trying to make
          me paint again . . .

Ada: There are worse things!

          Me: Like what?

Ada: Trust me, you don't want to
know. Just be glad your parents
aren't making you go pre-med.

          Me: You could try talking to them,
          you know? It's your life.

Ada: Says the girl who streams whenever her mommy says to.

          Me: . . .

I set the phone back down on my side table, frowning as I get up. She's not wrong—we both know it—but it's not something I want to think about right now.

Say what you want about Ada's parents, but at least they're around and invested—even if they are divorced. Sure, Ada feels like she's disappointing them sometimes— like that time she got an A- on her bio midterm—but she doesn't realize how lucky she is that they hold her to such high standards.

Which is why this whole punishment thing is weird! It's not what we do! Ever! What could my dad have to be upset about? Yes, I crashed a car, but we have plenty of cash to fix that. I'm sure the money's already been transferred. He definitely doesn't care about the streaming stuff the way my mom does, so I know he's not mad that I blew a sponsorship deal or messed up a storyline. He's got his houses and a life all his own, separate from Mom's.

Sometimes I feel like he's just humoring Mom by sticking around, but that's too bleak to even really consider. If it's not the streaming, and it's not the money, then what is it? Why now, when I'm a month away from turning eighteen, does he suddenly decide to start grounding me and acting like a dutiful father? It doesn't make sense.

Curious and more than a little nervous, I rush through getting dressed. I throw on a pair of linen shorts and a fitted tank top in a nice beachy peach that looks great against my perfectly (fake) tanned skin, and then I pull my long, wavy brown hair into a low pony—high ponies are so out right now, even if my mom insists otherwise. (Once the elder millennials are doing it, it's pretty much over. I don't think she's come to terms with that yet, though.)

I take my time brushing my teeth and doing my makeup, trying to calm my nerves by organizing my toiletries in my equally bright white bathroom next to my bedroom. It's large enough for most people to consider it a main bath, but we use it as a guest bathroom because my dad swears the lighting is better in his.

I look at myself in the mirror and sigh. I look exhausted. I add a quick eyeliner wing to make me look a little more put together, and dot a little white eyeshadow in the corners of my eyes to give the illusion that I'm not as exhausted as I feel. One final quick swipe of gloss across my lips and I'm bouncing down the stairs, ready to see what Dad is up to.

I hear voices as I come around the corner to his office—it sounds like he's got a girl in there talking to him. I'm startled when I realize it's Cass. We were friends once, before she became my dad's protégé. I really can't stand her and the holier-than-thou attitude she has about things these days. Dad would not shut up about her getting into MIT like she was god's gift or something, when I was *right there* trying to talk to him about getting my own business off the ground once he releases the trust Grandpa left me. It didn't help matters that my college rejections were pouring in from my half-assed applications.

I hang back a little before they notice me, trying to make sense of the situation. They seem to be having an argument of some sort, and I'm all too happy to watch it unfold from here.

"No, absolutely not," Cass says, shaking her head.

"Cassandra, you need this. I know MIT is covering most of your expenses with grants, but there are going to be costs you and your family are not anticipating. Your father never went to college; he doesn't—"

"My father is doing just fine." She scoffs. "Plus, I get paid quite well as a lifeguard, thank you very much."

"Please, be reasonable. We can really help each other out here."

I slink back closer to the wall to stay out of sight. Is *this* the special guest he was talking about? Isn't it bad enough that I have to see her lurking around all of our events in her stupid little waiter uniform? Why does she have to be in my house too?

It feels like an enemy invasion, and on day one! I know her father is my dad's right-hand man, despite running the Affordable Housing Coalition that's looking to put Gordon Investments out of business, but I never could figure out his fixation on helping John Adler's daughter.

Mom said once that Dad only keeps Mr. Adler and his family around to keep an eye on what he's up to, but I don't know. Mom doesn't really believe in friendship anyway, so I can't trust her judgment. Dad and Mr. Adler sure look friendly to me anytime I see them together.

Whatever he's trying to rope Cass into, though, seems like a whole new ball game. I study her face—the not-so-subtle curl of distaste on her naturally plump pink lips, the way her short, jagged hair frames her face in a sort of angry way that shouldn't work but definitely does. Cass has always been pretty in that unaffected way that you have to fight not to notice. It makes me hate her a little more. I doubt she spends much time (maybe not even any) worrying about contouring or lip injections or painful skin treatments to draw out that youthful, dewy glow that my mom insists I'm somehow lacking despite my only being seventeen.

"I am being reasonable!" Cass says. "I have a good job already. This one sounds like more trouble than it's worth."

"Is lifeguarding going to get you that internship you're after? The letters of recommendation?"

"Oh, come on, we both know you're doing that anyway. I can't believe you'd pretend to bribe me into—"

"Hi!" I say, suddenly bounding into the room looking far too chipper for the conversation happening in front of me. Because if Dad is dangling letters of recommendation and personal favors, then I want in. Seeing as how my dad is one of the most respected developers and investors in New England, those things could open a lot of doors for me, even for the line of purses and bags I'm hoping to launch. I'll be damned if he's helping someone else's daughter instead of his own.

"Hi, Birdie," Dad says, cheerfully matching my energy even though I'm not sure the current situation calls for it.

"What are you up to in here? I thought I heard shouting," I say, as if I wasn't just spying on them.

Dad flicks his eyes to Cass, who just laughs.

"Your dad is trying to hire a babysitter," she says.

"For what?" I snort because I know damn well that Mom has the dogs. Dad hates the little Pomeranians since neither of them is housebroken . . . Unless Mom is sending them here for the summer too, dumping even more of her responsibilities?

"For you," Cass says, speaking slowly, like she thinks I'm a small, confused child or something.

"What are you talking about?" I ask, scrunching up my face as I spin toward my father. "What is she talking about?"

"Birdie, calm down," he says, holding up his hand, trying to placate me and doing a bad job of it. "She's not your babysitter."

"Right, because I'm not taking the job. I'm glad you've finally come to terms with that, *Mr. Gordon.* Now, if you'll excuse me—"

"Cassandra, please," he says, and that makes her stop in her tracks. "I'm asking for a favor here."

I watch the two of them, the strange, casual way they act around each other, and it hits me—she's probably grown up with him more than I have. He spends so much time here, most of it, actually, when he's not stuck in the Boston office. We're the same age, she and I. Dad always loved that—he used to try to get us to play together. But she loved sandcastles and swimming and playing in the dirt. She was too loud and swam out too far, and I needed to stay clean and quiet, and always ready for Mom to go live on a moment's notice.

Eventually, Cass stopped asking me to play and Dad stopped trying to force it.

It never occurred to me until now, as she's turning around to face him, that she probably knows him better than even I do. I wonder how she sees him—a family friend? An uncle?

I can tell she cares by the way his pleading—something he's never done with me—has her stopping in her tracks.

"Don't do that," she groans, and my dad gives her a small smile that has her rolling her eyes.

"I really need your help, kiddo," he says, and I feel like I'm in the twilight zone. *Kiddo?* I don't think I've heard my dad say that in his entire life.

"Fine," she grumbles. "For a trial period, but if she's dead weight, I'm cutting her loose, and she goes back to being your full-time problem. Deal?"

"Deal," he says, offering his hand for her to shake, as if I'm not even here.

"Excuse me, what is going on right now?" I snap, crossing my arms at my father and this interloper.

My father smiles at me as he skirts behind us and out the door. "I'll let Cassandra explain," he says. "I'm late for a meeting with John, but, Birdie, be nice. You two need to get reacquainted anyway."

"George!" Cass yells, seemingly annoyed for real. I can't believe she just called him by his first name, and he didn't even get mad. What world am I living in right now?

"It's all in the folder!" he yells, rushing out the front door. "Along with a prepayment for the first week! Have fun, you two!"

We stare at each other when the door clicks shut. His car starts a few seconds later, the sound of his tires crunching the gravel sealing our fates. If this was a movie, there would no doubt be a squealing tire sound effect added in post.

"I can't believe he really left," Cass says, heading over to the desk to pop open the folder. She pockets the envelope full of cash and skims the papers inside, smirking as she reads.

"What's that?" I ask, but she pulls it back as I go to grab it.

"Hold on, I'm not done reading."

"Cassandra," I say. "Please."

"Oh no. Only your dad can pull that off, and only because he's done enough favors for my family that I legitimately owe him one. You've done nothing. Ever," she says, closing the folder. "Don't call me Cassandra. It's *Cass*."

Resentment bubbles up inside me. "Fine, *Cass*," I say. "I'm going back to bed, then."

"Uh. No, you're not. I have things to do today."

"So?" I say, turning back around.

"So, you have to come with me."

"No."

"Yes," she says, smiling. "Look." She finally holds the folder out to me. I practically rip it out of her hands, flipping to the first page, which is titled SUMMER RULES FOR BIRDIE.

I skim the list, paling as I go. No car, no social media. Fine, I already knew those two. But no leaving the island? No parties? A job? A freaking summer job? When all my friends are off living their best lives before leaving for college? Who is he even kidding?

If he wants to play the doting, involved father so bad, then he should take that up with Cass and leave me out of it. I've been just fine on my own, while he's been hanging out with the Adlers or whatever the hell he does out here. He missed out on the father of the year award a lifetime ago.

"I'm absolutely not spending my summer like this," I say, my eyes flashing.

"Looks like you are, if you want your trust."

"What?"

"Look at the back page." She grins and drops down into my father's chair, spinning it around as the expensive leather creaks beneath her. She's enjoying this. My life is crumbling in front of her, and she *likes* it. I want to smack that smug look right off her stupid perfect lips.

I flip to the final page, where he explains what happens if I don't willingly comply. "He's withholding my trust to be reevaluated when I'm twenty-one if I don't do this?"

"Apparently your dad got sick of bankrolling your car crash of a life. Can you blame him? He doesn't want you to end up like your mom, I guess. You should be glad about that. It's a kindness he's doing this to you," she says. "Even if it does kind of mess up my summer."

"Do *not* talk about my mom!" I snap, bristling at her words, even though I've thought the same thing myself. It's one thing for me to complain about my mom, but it's another for this fake daughter to do it while spinning in my father's office chair like *she's* the heir to the throne.

She holds up both her hands in an exaggerated surrender. "Hey, don't shoot the messenger."

I roll my eyes and go back to studying the pages. "This can't be real. Mom would never agree. Taking away my trust would ruin her season too."

Cass smiles. "I'm thinking she would since she sent you

here, right? That's what he said before you walked in. Well, technically he said she 'dumped' you on him, but same thing."

I take a deep breath and try not to scream. Cass is trying to get under my skin, but I won't let her.

"I'm not doing this. I'm not some spoiled brat who can't control themselves. I don't need a *summer job*. There has to be a loophole here. He can't have total control of my trust, right?"

"No idea." She shrugs. "Do what you want. I'll just text your dad that you're not feeling it and you're refusing to cooperate. I'm sure that will definitely make you look very mature and unspoiled. Good plan." She opens the envelope, counting the hundred-dollar bills inside as she stands up.

I grit my teeth. As much as I hate it, she has a point.

"Wait," I say as she starts walking to the door. "I'll . . . I'll do it."

"Do what?" She laughs, incredulous.

"I'll go with you. I'll do the things on the list. You're a lifeguard, right? I'll be one too or something. A job's a job."

"Can you even swim, Birdie? Outside of, like, a glimmering infinity pool, I mean."

"Does it matter?" I say, lifting my chin. "I'll figure it out."

"Right, let's just let everyone drown so you can play at being employed." She rolls her eyes. "Don't worry about it. I'm sure there *is* a loophole or else George will just get over it. If he doesn't, I bet your mom will make him. That's what always happens, right? Especially when it comes to filming things?"

I narrow my eyes; I hate how much she knows about my family. I hate how comfortable she is here. Above all, I hate the stupid dimples that pop out with her little sarcastic sneer . . . but I can't worry about that right now. I need to keep my eye on the prize.

"If my dad needs this to prove to him that I'm as responsible and worthy as he seems to think you are, then I'll do it. And fuck you very much for doubting me. You're not the only one on this island who can work hard."

"Okay, princess," she says, twirling her keys. "Your chariot awaits."

4

Cass

I'M SCREWED . . . AND not in the fun way.

As Birdie climbs into my Honda Civic, her nose scrunching up at the crumbs caught in my seat fabric, I can already tell that this is going to be a disaster.

One, she's looking at my car like she's going to catch a disease from it, and two, George's instructions say that I'm not supposed to let her out of my sight this week, except when he's home, if I can help it. I really am babysitting, even if he wants to call it something else.

I wait for Birdie to buckle up, trying not to roll my eyes at how stiffly she's sitting and how careful she is not to touch anything. She folds her hands neatly in her lap, like she's afraid she'll catch "the poor" if she does. I twist the key in the ignition and wince at the little clicking sounds the engine makes before it catches.

It's not the nicest car, but it gets the job done and I'm

grateful for it. Dad got it for me for $1,500 from a neighbor, and yeah, it has over 200,000 miles on it, but it runs mostly okay. I consider myself lucky to have it to haul my surfboards and lifeguard crap to and from the beach every day. I know the roof rack looks a little silly on top of such a small car, and yes, the rack—on loan from a friend who crashed his car and couldn't replace it—cost more than the vehicle itself, but still, overall, it's great. Or at least I thought it was.

"Are you sure this is safe?" Birdie asks, studying the cigarette burns in the half-detached fabric that lines the roof.

"I didn't put those there," I say, even though that's not what she asked. "I don't smoke."

She seems satisfied with that answer, or at least she's too horrified to ask anything else. Either way, I try to ignore her, pulling out of her pea stone driveway and focusing on surviving these super narrow old roads that should honestly be one-way. It always cracks me up when the tourists come in and cry about it, like it's not just an everyday way of life around here.

The roads here were made a billion years ago, more for walking and carriages, and then small cars, but the tourists try to cram their massive pickup trucks full of dude bros and drunk women onto the streets, or equally bad SUVs with third-row seating full of bratty kids and enough cargo space to house a small city. Then they rear-end and sideswipe each other for two months while taking over downtown and the mansions like they own the place. I hate summer people. I hate their disrespect, their rudeness, their sense of entitlement. Just all of it.

I glance at Birdie, feeling none too charitable. She's the epitome of summer girl, excelling with pride at the three R's—rude, rich, and reckless. The trifecta of horribleness, if you ask my best friend, Bentley, and the reason we imposed Rule Number One of Surviving Summer in a Tourist Trap: Absolutely *no* dating summer girls. Ever.

Except, as I look at her now, she doesn't quite fit the rude, reckless part. She looks . . . nervous?

"Of course it's safe," I say, trying to be nice, even though technically, I'm not really sure that's true. It did break down the other day, and Bentley had to come and tinker with it for a bit to get it going again. He's another local like me, although he's a full year older and already commuting to the local state college.

He's also my lifeguarding partner. We share a station—Tower Five to be exact, although we just call it Chair Five—which is pretty ideal. I get to listen to his horrible dad jokes all day and remind him to reapply sunscreen, and he gets to split his sandwiches with me and complain about his parents, while we *both* daydream about hot people, since we're both bi and have the same type almost exactly—which only caused a problem once, when we both inadvertently dated the same summer girl before we made the rule.

Like I said, summer girls suck.

As if on cue, the summer girl in my car huffs and crosses her arms. "This is supposed to be a vacation, and I'm stuck in

43

a questionable Honda from the nineteen hundreds. Perfect. Love this for me."

"It's a 2005, actually." I snort. "And I didn't get the impression that your dad considers this a summer vacation."

"True, more like prison with work release," she grumbles, putting her window down because yeah, the AC barely works in this heap.

"Look, this isn't how I want to spend my day off either, ya know?" I say, beyond sick of her shit. "Babysitting a spoiled summer girl who can't get out of her own way isn't exactly what I had planned when I got out of bed this morning."

"You're obnoxious," Birdie snaps, her lips pinching into a thin line as she goes back to looking out the window.

"I call it like I see it," I say, coming to a stop at a crosswalk teeming with people. They cross in a huge, writhing group, practically tripping over one another like they think I'm going to gun it instead of waiting here patiently for them to cross. I must be getting sun sick or something because even the rhythm of their walking makes me think of the ocean.

God, I wish I was out surfing like I was supposed to be. Why did I ever agree to go over to George's house today?

"Don't act like you know me. You don't," she says, yanking my attention back to her. "You can quit acting all smug. It's been a long time since we hung out. You don't know anything about me."

"You're the one who stopped coming," I point out. "And I do know you, actually. I think the whole world knows a little too much about you, thanks to your mom. I mean, didn't your potty-training video go viral—"

"I hate you," she says, and I can't tell if she means it. I hope she does. The feeling is mutual.

"Were you seriously live streaming your crash the other day?" I ask, deciding to poke the bear a little more. "Typical Birdie," I add with a laugh.

"It's not like I crashed on purpose," she says. I think she's trying to sound angry and indignant, but I pick up on the hurt under it and decide to move on. It's the right thing to do, probably.

Besides, this situation already sucks for both of us, especially me. Picking at her barely scabbed wounds is likely to just make my job harder.

She picks up her phone and starts texting and I keep driving. The wind from the open window is flapping her hair around, and for some reason, it keeps catching my attention. I narrow my eyes, sneaking glances at her in between checking the road, trying to see if I can still make out the girl she used to be—the girl she was before her mom started this streaming nonsense and her dad decided my family was the better option for him to be around.

I can almost see her in there, as she's squinting in the sunlight with her hair going wild, her glossed lips slightly parted—that same little girl who used to meet me on the beach and build horrible renditions of The Breakers out of sand. I wonder how much is left of her, though. Not much, I'm guessing. She's probably as much of a lost cause as her mother by now.

Birdie turns toward me quickly, scowling when she catches me looking. "What?" she sneers.

"Nothing," I say, sounding more defensive than I would have liked. I go back to watching the road and hope she drops it.

"You were staring at me."

"Don't flatter yourself," I say. "I wasn't."

She lets out a big, exaggerated sigh. "Sure, you weren't," she says, and then stretches her arms over her head. Her fingers knock on the ceiling, and she frowns.

I resist the urge to reiterate that the burn marks are from cigarettes that were probably smoked before I was even born. They've never bothered me before—I considered them part of history—but now she has me all twisted up about them. Screw that and screw her. I don't care what she thinks. *I don't.*

"God, you're so full of yourself," I grumble.

She studies me for a second before responding. "Pull over here," she says finally, gesturing toward the pier.

"What? No. Your dad said—"

"I don't care what he said right now. I'm not wasting my day with you. This is stupid."

"This is my job," I say. "So you will."

"Or what?"

"I'll tell your dad."

"And what's he going to do about it? Like really? He's never disciplined me a day in his life, and now he's going to start? When I'm nearly eighteen and already graduated? Give me a break."

"What about your trust?"

"I'd rather wait three more years for it than spend another second in this car," she says. "Now pull over."

"No," I growl, accelerating a little to get my point across.

"Fine, have it your way."

She pops open the passenger door, reaching for her seat belt buckle, and I slam on the brakes. "What the hell are you doing?"

She grins at me, hopping out of the car. "Getting you to stop." Before I can even react, she's slamming the door shut behind her and disappearing into the crowd.

I know by the time I find parking—if I can even find parking downtown during peak season—she'll be long gone. I groan in frustration when the car behind me lays on the horn.

We're not normally like this around here, especially not in the offseason. It's all these summer people and their fast-walking, short-tempered way of life ruining everything. Ruining me.

I take a deep breath and put my car back into drive, watching in my rearview mirror as Birdie's long brown hair fades into the crowd. Well, this is certainly a great first day on the job.

~~~

"She jumped from a moving car?" Bentley yelps. We're splitting a burger at the snack bar after his shift. Our days off don't always line up, so we have to take what we can get when one of us actually has something to say. Plus, our friend Laney is a line cook here and always hooks us up with free fries at the end of her workday.

"Technically, she scared me into stopping, but . . . I really think she would have."

"Wow, you certainly have a way with the ladies, Cass. Who would have ever thought you were single?"

I fling a fry at him, laughing as he wipes the ketchup off his cheek and smears it up the back of my hand. "I'm single because I hate summer girls and there aren't enough queer girls who live here in the offseason anymore." I roll my eyes. "Not because I make them jump out of moving cars."

"Sure, sure," he says, stretching out his long, muscular arms, which catches the attention of the gaggle of girls at the table next to us.

He laughs, not exactly unused to this. Bentley is the stereotypical lifeguard, after all: tall and cut, with shaggy brown hair, ruggedly handsome features, and a grin that has separated many a person from their bathing suit once he was off duty.

Adding insult to injury, especially when compared to my perpetually pink sunburned ass, his tan skin turns almost golden under the summer sun. He alternates crediting his Italian mother or his Iranian father for it . . . though, I once noticed a suspicious amount of bronzer under his passenger seat, which he naturally pled the Fifth on.

I snap my fingers, drawing his attention away from the girls and back to the drama at hand. "If I can't even keep track of her on day one, how am I supposed to do the rest of the things on the list?"

He shrugs. "I mean, it's not really your problem, right? Maybe you just step aside?"

I pull the envelope of cash out of my purse and slide it to him. He opens it, his eyes going wide. "Holy shit, he's giving you all this just to keep an eye on her?"

"A week."

"What?"

"He's giving me that *a week*."

"Okay, scratch that, she is very much your problem. Between this and the lifeguarding, that's gonna keep you flush all the way until you come home next summer, isn't it?"

"Yeah," I say, nodding with big eyes. "That's why I want to kill her right now. I had to pay thirty dollars to park downtown just to rush back to where she ditched me, but of course she was long gone. I walked up and down the main drag going into every stupid preppy store looking for her. It was like she vanished."

"Did you try Lululemon?"

"Yes, Bentley, obviously I tried Lululemon."

"Sephora?"

"Thank you so much for your help," I say, flicking another fry at him. "But yes, anything that looked remotely like someplace she would shop, I checked. It was like she disappeared right into the ether."

"Or she was just avoiding you. She probably saw you coming and just dipped or hid in the changing rooms. I bet she'll be calling you in a panic any minute to pick her up. It's been how long?"

"Like, six hours."

"How much shopping can one girl really do?"

"Have you ever seen the haul videos she does with her mom after one of their shopping trips? I'm guessing the limit does not exist."

"Must be nice," he says around a mouthful of burger.

"Okay, but say you do find her—are you really going to get her a job here?"

I sigh. "Yeah, I already texted Vince about it. He said he could use her as a lot attendant."

Bentley practically shoots his drink out his nose. "Oh my god, can you imagine that rich bitch stuck being a gate girl? Ooooh, what if he makes her walk around with the stick and pick up trash? I would live! I would die! You have to find her, Cass, please? The world needs to watch Birdie Gordon *cleaning* garbage instead of *being* garbage for once in her life."

I laugh. I can't help it. He's being super mean, and I should probably tell him to chill, but it's nice to have him on my side. It's rare to find someone else who's not swept up in all the pomp and circumstance that comes along with being a part of the Gordon family. How George manages to be a semi-regular person, I'll never understand. Maybe he can thank my dad for that?

Bentley opens his mouth to say something else—and judging by the smirk on his face, it's not going to be any nicer— just as my phone vibrates to life on the table in front of me.

"See?" he says. "I told you she'd call when she got desperate."

I check the caller ID and my heart sinks. "It's George, not Birdie. She probably told him what happened and he's calling to fire me since I couldn't handle her for even one single day."

"Damn," Bentley says as I answer.

"Hi, George," I say as sweetly as I can.

"Hey, Cass. I just wanted to check in after today."

"Yeah, sorry. I didn't mean to—"

"I don't know how you did it, but good job."

"What?" I ask, scrunching my eyebrows together.

Beside me, Bentley mouths, "Are you fired?" and I shrug, confused, as I listen to George rambling on about what great work I did today as Birdie's companion.

". . . and she said you guys had a great lunch together at Pier Seven. I love the clam chowder there. Please tell me you tried it."

"Uh . . . y-yeah," I stammer out, the lie catching for a moment behind my teeth. "It was great."

"Let me know if you need to be reimbursed for that. I know it's really pricey there."

"I don't," I say, trying to puzzle out what exactly is going on.

"Oh? Did Birdie cover it? That's great! Given how mad she was when I left, I wasn't sure how it would go. Thanks for keeping an eye out for her today. I really think I can get her back on track if I can just keep her away from those vultures for the summer."

"Yeah," I agree, even though I have literally no idea what he's talking about.

"Sorry to hear about the flat. Did you get that all sorted? If not, I can send over one of my guys."

"Hmm?"

"Birdie told me all about it. I'm surprised there was a nail in the street downtown, but it was a good call to send her home in the Uber. She probably would have been a nightmare waiting for roadside assistance."

"Right, of course," I say, shaking my head hard at Bentley

as he starts to laugh. "Well, it's all straightened out now, don't worry. My tire's all patched up."

"Perfect," George says, and I can hear the pride in his voice. "I'll see you tomorrow, then?"

"Y-yes," I say. "Have a good night, George."

"You too," he says before clicking off. I set my phone down and stare at Bentley with eyes so wide it almost hurts.

"What flat?" he asks.

I scrunch up my face. "I think Birdie covered for me with her dad."

"Why would she do that?" Bentley asks, looking extremely skeptical.

"I don't know," I say. "But I'm definitely going to find out."

5

Birdie

"GET UP."

Cass's voice rips me from sleep and startles me into almost falling out of my bed. "Oh my god, why are you in my room?" I cry, wrapping my comforter around myself. "What if I slept naked?"

"Fat chance. Your dad always keeps this house subarctic. You'd be slicing your sheets with your nipples if you tried."

My face flushes hot as I pull the comforter even tighter around me, crossing my arms over my chest. She raises an eyebrow and keeps leaning against my doorframe, her eyes sweeping down my blankets like she can see right through them. It shouldn't make my belly flip, but it does.

I'd be lying if I said I had *never* thought of Cass during some of my more . . . curious . . . moments, but it's not something I'm going to feed into.

About two years ago, I tried to tell a few people that I thought I was bi, and let's just say it didn't go well.

"That means you like boys too, right?" my mom said, when I stood in front of her nervously after my admission. "Focus on that. It will be easier for all of us." Then she left the room like it was that simple.

When I tried to tell Ada, she awkwardly said that was "so cool," and changed the subject. It's not that she's homophobic or anything—we have queer friends at school! So it must have been something about *me* that made it so weird for her.

Whatever, I could take a hint. After that, I stopped telling people and started focusing on making things "easier," which up until a few days ago meant Mitchell Riley.

Which means that now, here, with Cass standing in my room and talking about my nipples while I'm half-dressed like a fantasy come to life, I can't help but feel like I'm letting my mom down. I force a scowl on my face to try to cover up everything else I'm feeling, but Cass looks unimpressed.

"Get. Dressed," she says, knocking twice on my doorframe before disappearing downstairs. The second she's out of sight, I can breathe again, the warm weight that had been crushing my chest fading as soon as her eyes are off me. I need to get a grip. Pronto.

This is just a tiny little glitch in the system—no doubt caused by the fact that I'm clearly disoriented from sleep and not because I've just discovered that I might still be nursing the first crush I ever had on a girl. (A girl who definitely hates me now, and who I'm supposed to hate back. No, who I *do* hate back.)

I fling my comforter off the bed and stomp to my dresser, pulling out a tank top and shorts to replace my thin cotton sleep set. I take a brief detour to the bathroom to brush my teeth and finish getting ready.

I debate taking a shower, just to take longer and annoy her—she does owe me for covering for her yesterday—but then change my mind. I throw on a little mascara and gloss and head downstairs, steeling my nerves and squashing down the last of the residual butterflies. It was a momentary slip, hardly my fault. After all, startling awake to find Cass in my bedroom was the beginning of one too many of my early adolescent daydreams even *after* I stopped coming here.

I stuff those thoughts into the back of my head as I step into the living room. Cass is sitting in one of the overstuffed chairs, her legs slung over one arm, her head resting on the other, like she's done it a million times. There is a high probability she has, I realize, which sends a fresh tinge of jealousy prickling up my spine.

Good, focus on that.

"You're welcome for yesterday, by the way," I say, dropping onto the plush love seat across from her and doing my best impression of someone with their head in the game.

Cass sighs and looks over at me. "I was wondering when you were going to bring that up." She looks at her phone, making a big show of checking the time. "Wow! Five seconds into coming downstairs. That's gotta be a world record for passive-aggressively holding a favor over someone's head. Congrats! I'm sure you make your parents very proud. Well, your mother at least."

I cross my arms, annoyed that she somehow got the upper hand already, even though I carefully crafted my opening shot while brushing my teeth. She laughs, like she can tell what I'm thinking. This time my scowl is real.

"Do you need breakfast?" she asks, kicking her legs down. "Or can we go?"

"Go where?" I snap, trying to ignore the rumble in my torso that suggests yes, yes, I am starving.

"To work?" Cass says, scrunching up her forehead. "A summer job was on the list of things your dad told me to figure out for you, so I did. Just new-hire paperwork today, though. You don't start yet. Think you can handle that?"

"What *exactly* do you believe I'm going to be doing for this summer job?"

"Working at the beach," she says, like it should be obvious.

"No offense," I say, stretching my arms up over my head casually like this conversation isn't annoying me as much as it really is, "but I thought about it last night. If I'm *really* going to be working this summer, it's going to be assisting my dad or one of his friends, probably playing secretary somewhere air-conditioned."

"Mmm," she says. "Don't you think your dad would have already set that up if that were the case? Pretty sure he brought me on for exactly this."

Did I say *butterflies* earlier? Because what Cass really gives me is maggots. Writhing, miserable, can't-wait-to-smack-the-smirk-off-her-face maggots. "Clearly, that was an epic miscalculation on his part," I snark. "You couldn't even keep an eye on me for an hour yesterday."

She rolls her eyes, the smirk falling away as her eyes dart to the window, no doubt double-checking to make sure my dad isn't home. I assume he isn't or he would have been the one to wake me up when Cass got here instead of sending her into my room.

She crosses her arms, one finger tapping away on her arm. "Why *did* you cover for me yesterday?"

I consider lying, telling her that I wanted to make her owe me. My mom is the queen of doing favors for people just to get something in return, and I know Cass would believe it. She clearly thinks the worst of me anyway. But something makes me tell the truth instead. "I don't know. I thought when I walked in, he would be furious at me for ditching you. When I realized you never told him, I figured I'd return the favor."

"Oh, got it. You just didn't want your dad to be pissed at *you*," she says, confirming my theory that she thinks I'm a monster. "And here I thought you were actually being nice."

"No, you didn't." I laugh.

"No, I didn't," she says, standing up. "So grab a banana or whatever and meet me in the car. Vince is expecting us soon."

"I don't have to listen to you, you know!" I call after her as she heads to the front door.

"Then don't." She shrugs. "I'll be in the car. Come out if you want. I'm not coddling you. It's time everybody stopped."

"Oh, screw you, Cass. Just because you hang out with my dad while he's pretending to be 'a man of the people' doesn't mean you actually get it."

"I know you're a spoiled little clone of your mom. What

else is there?" she says, before slamming the door shut behind her.

I stand there stunned for a minute. She is *sort of* right, I begrudgingly admit to myself. Not about the whole spoiled-clone-of-my-mom thing. That is decidedly *not* true—ask Ada. But about people coddling me and me not being used to having someone around who doesn't.

Thanks, I hate it.

I stand there a moment longer and debate just ditching her completely, but that feels too much like letting her win. Plus, there is still the matter of my trust fund. If I can avoid Dad holding it over my head by looking cute in a lifeguard chair, what's the harm? I linger in the foyer, debating with myself, until I see her start to back out of the driveway. Without thinking, I yank open the door and rush out, chasing after her until she stops the car.

Cass's laughing "Thought so" grates on my nerves as I get in, but this just became war, and I'm not about to let her win.

～～～

The drive to the beach is tense and silent. As in, she doesn't even have the radio on.

If I thought things would get better after we parked, I was sadly mistaken. Cass walks across the parking lot and up the beach with purpose, leaving me to trail after her like a little lost puppy dog. I'm even forced to stand there awkwardly while she greets seemingly every worker on earth and even some beachgoers. It's clear she's beloved here, which makes my resentment for her tick up another notch.

Of course, she would take every opportunity to show me how much better she is than me. How much more well-liked and appreciated she is. I don't know why I expected any different.

The sand is burning hot as it seeps into my sandals while I struggle to follow her up a little man-made dune toward the snack bar, slipping twice in a way that earns me a smirk. We finally make it to a little deck crowded with tables and umbrellas, and I brace myself for whatever fresh torture comes next, but she just gestures toward the nearest table.

"Wait here," she says, before heading behind the counter.

Gladly. I unbuckle my new Tory Burch sandals and try to shake the sand out but give up when I notice a smudge along the edge. *Ugh, did I step in gum somewhere? Gross!* I'm going to have to send them out for cleaning, *if* Dad even lets me. I shudder at the idea of him not, but it feels like a reasonable fear. He and Cass seem to agree that I'm an overcoddled fuckup. Forcing me to pry gum off my shoes with my own two hands is a demented punishment but totally within the realm of possibility.

Cass comes back a few minutes later, a tall older man in tow. He sticks his hand out and introduces himself as Vince Shanahan. Apparently, he acts as kind of a general manager for the beach, handling scheduling for the various jobs and overseeing all the new hires. He has a big stack of paperwork fixed on a clipboard, which he sets in front of me. The pen is tied to the little clippy thing on top, and I glance over at Cass like *Seriously? Does he think I'm going to steal the pen?*

She frowns and jerks her head toward Vince, an unmistakable gesture meaning *Freaking pay attention already.*

"Cass already gave me your social security card and working papers, so I just need your license and I can go make copies."

"She did?" I ask, fishing my license out of my Gucci mini bag and passing it over.

"Your dad left it out for me this morning." She shrugs, like that's normal at all. "I texted him you had new-hire paperwork today."

I want to scream. Of course my dad knew before me that I had to do this, and of course Cass laughed when I said I would probably just work as someone's assistant. She already knew that was off the table and that Dad agreed with her idea . . . but Vince is watching me, and if this is my only chance to prove my dad—and Cass—wrong, then I guess I'm going to take it.

"Right, yeah," I say, forcing a smile in Cass's direction. "Thank you."

Her raised eyebrow tells me she's not buying it at all, and I turn back to the papers in front of me, feeling more exposed than I want to.

"Alright, I'm gonna go make copies of this," Vince says. "Cass, come on back with me. I want to figure out some schedule stuff."

"You good?" Cass asks, like she's nervous to leave me or something. I nod and wave her off. Seemingly satisfied, she follows Vince behind the counter, leaving me to it.

I take a deep breath and start to tackle the stack of forms. The first one is easy enough—just a basic application asking where I went to high school and if I'm over eighteen or have working papers, simple stuff like that. The second one is an emergency contact form. I pointedly don't put my father. Yes, it's true I probably should—he's the one here, after all—but I'm annoyed enough at him that I'd rather not. Plus, I get a sick sense of satisfaction from knowing that if something did go wrong, he would have to hear it from my very angry mother instead of from a nice calm doctor or my boss.

The third page, though, is really tripping me up. It's some tax form asking about deductions or exemptions or withholdings or something. I've never had to fill out anything like this in my life. Money just magically appears in my bank account, or I use my Amex, which also gets paid in full every month by someone who is not me. I've never had to worry about a deduction of anything ever. I don't even know if we pay taxes, let alone what I might have to withhold for them.

"Birdie? Is that you?"

I snap my head up to find Carly Whitmore—the very frenemy who snapped a picture of Mitchell cheating on me—standing on the sand directly below this little deck.

"Carly, hi!" I say, quickly flipping the clipboard over like she's going to somehow see what's on it from all the way over there. "What are you doing here?"

"I could ask you the same thing! Hang on, I'm coming up!"

No. No, no, no, no, no. I can't risk her figuring out what I'm really doing. She'll tell everyone back home and I'll be the laughingstock. We don't do summer jobs in our circle unless it's just for show. Fetching coffee for overworked interns at *Vogue* because your mother is a star designer, like Carly did last year? Very cool. Working at a public beach for minimum wage or whatever they offer me? Humiliating. Horrible. Mortifying.

"Don't bother," I call to her. "I'll meet you down there." I glance behind the counter, hoping I can let Cass know I'll be back, but the office door is still firmly shut. There's no way to tell her what's going on, and she probably won't care what excuse I have anyway. I leave everything on the table face down and run to meet Carly, pulling her farther down the beach and even ducking behind a lifeguard chair for good measure.

There are so many people crowding the beach already, even this early in the morning, that I think there's a good chance I won't be spotted if Cass does get back before I beat her there. I hope that doesn't happen, though. I'm so tired of her having things to hold over my head.

"Whoa, slow down," Carly says, rubbing her wrist. "Who are we hiding from?" She smirks, seemingly pleased to have sniffed out some gossip to glut herself on.

"I didn't know you were in town," I say, hoping to change the subject.

"Only for the week. My mom thought it would be good to spend a few days with Nana and Papa before I leave for school. The beach at the club was a serious downer, though. Like the median age was probably forty. So gross. Anyway, some of the girls and I snuck down here."

"Who else is here?" I ask, a little too quickly.

"Hmm, Blake, Tashi, Fatima, Jesse . . . just the usual Rhode Island summer crew. I would have invited you if I knew you were in town. I know you've been lying low since you embarrassed yourself at your dad's gala and everything, but . . ."

I know she's trying to piss me off with that little dig, but I don't take the bait, focusing instead on getting her to leave before she realizes I'm not just here for a visit. "I've been doing my own thing this last week," I say. "Relaxing and all."

"You haven't been streaming at all either. People are talking."

I scramble to come up with an excuse to cover for that part but come up short. Luckily, if there's one thing I know Carly can't stand, it's parents. I decide to play the sympathy card. "Yeah, my dad is being a total nightmare about it. He doesn't want me going live at all. No socials for me for a minute. He's being the worst."

"Ewww, gross," she says, an exaggerated fake frown on her face. "Does your mom know?"

"She's on a business trip," I lie, because letting her know that my mom was the one who sent me out here would be too embarrassing. "She's definitely going to murder him when she finds out. Like, total bloodbath."

Carly laughs. "At least he lets you go to the beach, right? Even if it is the public one. What were you doing up at the snack bar anyway? Please tell me you aren't eating that fried food. Our kitchen girl made me a basket this morning. Wine, cheese, hummus, grapes—anything you could want. Do you want to go back to the cabana we set up? Everyone would be so happy to know you're alive. Fatima was just saying she thought they, like, locked you in a dungeon or something, but I reminded her that your dad has more money than god, so I doubt he was that upset about Mitchell's McLaren anyway."

"Thanks, but I can't," I say, watching her eyebrows rise in disbelief. No one turns down a Carly Whitmore invite, or at least they hadn't until now. "I would love to, but I just . . . I was filling out some . . . fundraising papers up there. If you saw me with a clipboard, that's why. People are so excited I'm here, naturally, they want me to make appearances and stuff."

I am lying through my teeth, and I have no idea if it's working. The face Carly is making right now—which looks somehow like a mix of confusion and . . . horror?—isn't helping either.

"Summer's not for working, silly," she says, firmly linking her arm with mine. "Come on, everyone's going to die when they see who I found."

"Great," I say, realizing this isn't so much an invitation as a demand. We barely take two steps when my phone starts buzzing in my pocket. I ignore it, positive it's Cass, but it starts up again. And again. And why do I suddenly feel like, no matter which direction I go on this beach, I'm marching toward my death?

"Do you need to get that?" Carly asks, and I sigh.

"Probably. Look, the truth is . . ." I start, almost ready to be honest just to get out of having to face the mean girls from back home, but I then quickly change my mind. "The truth is my dad's assistant is an absolute monster and basically thinks it's their duty to know where I am at all times. Just kill me, right?"

"Give me the phone. I'll answer. That's fucked," Carly says. "You ruined your dad's party. So what? He and his assistant need to get over it. That was *so* last week."

"No, my dad will flip if he knows I ditched out. I really should head back. I'll catch up with you later," I say. "Tell everybody I said hi and I'm so sorry. I'm just on really thin ice right now." I lean in conspiratorially and whisper something that I know will really get her on my side. "He keeps holding my trust over my head too. If I don't do what he says, he might withhold it until I'm twenty-one."

"He what?!" she practically shrieks. "You earned that money! Our trusts are set aside for *us*, not for them to use as a bargaining chip." Looks like I hit just the nerve I was going for. Carly's dad recently pushed hers back a year too, and she hasn't spoken to him since.

"I knew you'd understand."

"Oh my god, go," she says, practically shoving me back the way I came. "Do your little fundraiser stuff, but text me, seriously. We need to hang."

"Will do!" I smile, even though I have no intention of texting her. I head back toward the snack bar and this time answer my phone when it rings. "I'll be there in one second," I say, before Cass can even say anything, and then I hang up again.

At least the phone stops ringing after that.

Unfortunately, I can tell she's fuming as I trudge up the

stairs to the snack bar, even though I try not to meet her eyes. It's just her waiting there—no sign of Vince, which is probably for the best.

"What. The. Hell?" she grits out between clenched teeth as I sit back down and flip over the clipboard.

"Do you know what an exemption is?" I ask, ignoring her. "I'm stuck on this form."

"Where did you go?" she grumbles, pulling the clipboard in front of her and scribbling down some answers on the form for me. "There. It's not rocket science."

"Thank you. I . . . ran into someone. What's the big deal? Where's Vince? I'm done. That was all I had left to do anyway."

"In his office, because we came out and you were gone!" she shouts. "I told him you must have run to the bathroom, but then you didn't come back, so he went back to work while I tried to find you. Because, I know this will be shocking for you, but some of us have work to do, Birdie. Some of us need to earn money to live. We can't just mooch off our mommies and daddies like you do."

I roll my eyes. "I was gone for, like, ten minutes. Chill."

"It looked like you ditched out again, and not for nothing, but I work here too!" she says. "Are you intentionally trying to make me look bad?" The emotion in her voice has my eyes snapping to hers.

"What? No. I just—"

"If you screw up, it looks bad on me. And I need this job!"

"I'm sure my dad is paying you more than whatever you're making here."

"Right, like you're not going to tap out in another week or two or get your dad to change his mind again. I'm sure it won't be long before your mom is back to screaming at him that actually you *should* be continuing on your path to becoming just another vapid influencer. That is your only real use in life, isn't it?" She sneers. "And when any of that happens, that pay is going to go poof. I need to make sure I still have a good reputation here when it does."

"You're such an asshole," I whisper under my breath.

"Guess what? I don't care what you think of me. All I'm asking is that before you do your little crybaby ride off into the sunset, you don't ruin this for me."

"I'm not a crybaby, Cass," I say, standing up. "I need you to stop talking to me like this. Don't forget that I did you a favor by not telling my dad. You owe me."

"You know what?" She shakes her head, taking a deep breath before meeting my eyes again. "This was a bad idea. Let's just forget it. I'm going to go tell your father the truth about yesterday before it comes back to bite me. I obviously can't work with you, and I can't unleash you on any of my friends here either."

"No," I say, offended that she thinks it will be that easy to get rid of me.

"You don't get to tell me no," she says, walking away. "I quit. That's what you wanted, isn't it?"

I rush after her and pull on her arm before I even realize what I'm doing. "Wait."

She shakes me off and keeps going. A tendril of anxiety

sneaks up my spine at the thought of really having scared her off for good.

"Cass, wait," I say again, still chasing after her, but she keeps ignoring me. I *hate* being ignored. "Please!" That at least earns me a look.

She raises her arms and drops them to her sides as she keeps walking away.

"Don't you give up on me too," I quietly beg, the truth coming out even though I tried to choke it down. "I'm sorry I didn't take this seriously. I . . . I can do better."

She doesn't turn around, but at least she stops walking away so I can catch up. I march over and come around to face her, expecting her to say something else rude and hurtful out of anger or frustration . . . but her face looks neutral, impassive. I suppose that's better than before.

"I know what you think of me, and I know why," I say, because I don't know how long this moment will last, and there's no use trying to lie anymore after what I just blurted out. "I can't stand here and say you don't have a good reason for it. Especially after I ditched you yesterday, but . . . just, come on. I know I fucked up. Again. It's all I seem to do lately." I roll the tears back in my eyes and try to blink them away. I don't know why this is getting to me so bad, or why I care so much what she thinks, but I do. I can't help it. "For what it's worth, I mean it. I'm sorry." And I am. I am. Because this was my chance to prove not just to her, but to my father and myself, that I'm capable of rising to the occasion—and I've already messed it up.

Cass winces and pinches the bridge of her nose. "Go turn in the paperwork. I'll meet you in the car."

"Yes!" I squeal, breaking out into a smile. I'm so relieved for a second that I forget I'm supposed to hate her. "Thank you, seriously, thank you."

She sighs. "Don't make me regret this, Birdie."

6

Cass

I'M WAITING IN the driveway this time.

Before I dropped her off last night, I told her to set her own damn alarm and meet me in front of her house by 8:00 a.m. The fact that I can see her running around the house in a panic through all those glass windows should not be surprising, but it is. I guess part of me thought this new leaf she was trying to turn over would mean I'd pull up to find her already sitting pretty on the porch waiting for me—trying to prove herself or whatever. But this is Birdie Gordon after all, and as my dad always says, "That girl will be late to her own funeral."

I tap my steering wheel, watching the clock on my stereo tick over to 8:11 a.m. At some point, I need to just back out—fire off a text telling her that she's already blown her fresh start and then head on my merry way, forgetting all this ever happened. Forgetting all about yesterday and the way she sounded like her heart was breaking when she asked me not to give up on her.

I really shouldn't care. I don't care, actually.

I'm just . . . curious. About what exactly, I'm not sure. Everything? Maybe? But especially the way she's going to look sitting in that little rusty lawn chair in the parking lot taking twenty-dollar bills from sweaty tourists like her life depends on it.

Plus, there's also the fact that I want to keep all the money in the envelope, which means I have to at least survive this first week with her.

So, I continue to wait.

I turn off my car around 8:15, right as she flings open the front door long enough to hold up one finger and shout, "Just a sec, I swear!" before disappearing back inside.

I try to stay annoyed, but she looks so ridiculous with her hair half curled and the frantic look on her face, and I'm smiling before I can catch myself. Besides, she's not technically late, even though *she* doesn't know that.

We don't actually have to be on the road for another fifteen minutes. My shift doesn't even start until nine anyway. Sure, her dad's house is less than five minutes from the beach, but with summer traffic, everything is a half hour or more—which is why I lied to her about what time she needed to be ready . . . just a little extra insurance in case she was late to her fresh start.

Still, when she plops into the passenger seat smelling like summer flowers, in a bathing suit and cute denim shorts, breathlessly apologizing as she checks her lip gloss in the car mirror, I decide to run with it.

"You're late," I say, as gruffly as I can manage, because I should be annoyed. I am annoyed. I want to be annoyed, anyway.

"Sorry, I couldn't decide on a suit, and I wasn't sure if they issued me one. Honestly, the idea of wearing someone else's bathing suit kind of squicked me out anyway. Hopefully this is okay?"

"I don't think they really care what you wear," I say, backing out of her driveway and pointing my car to the beach.

"Okay, good," she says, and then we both settle into silence as I drive.

I unroll my window a little while later—once I've survived the worst of the summer traffic and the beach finally comes into view—taking several deep inhales of the salty air. It settles my soul in a way that makes me almost forget the *annoying* passenger beside me. I just need to survive until we get to the sand. Everything will be fine once I can hear the waves. Just a few more minutes to go . . .

The beach has always been my happy place. My dad likes to tease me that I turned my obsessive beach people-watching into a lifeguarding career, because even as a kid I used to spend long days sitting under an umbrella being baked alive while keeping an eye on everyone around me. Sure, there was way more sandcastle building involved then than there is now, but still, same basic premise—except now I watch people to keep them alive, rather than just because people are inherently interesting. Well, when they aren't talking to me anyway.

"You're *sure* they won't care about my bathing suit?" Birdie asks, fidgeting in her seat.

Of course the silence was too good to last.

I shake my head. "I know your mom made you think that you're the center of the universe, but trust me, no one cares what you wear to work at the beach."

"Okay, I didn't know," she says, "because it looked like you guys all wear red usually."

"Huh? Who does?" I ask.

"The lifeguards," she says, like I'm the one not making sense.

"Why does it matter what *we* wear?" I ask, baffled. And then it hits me—she was serious the other day when she asked me about lifeguarding. "Oh my god. Wait," I say. We come around a sharp corner, the ocean finally opening up around us as we crest a small hill, and I can't help but smile. "I'm sorry, did you seriously think *you* were going to be a lifeguard too? Birdie, no. There are, like . . . tests you have to take and . . . I mean, you have to actually be able to swim. I thought you were kidding when you brought that up."

"I can swim," she huffs.

"In the ocean? For long distances?"

"I can work up to it," she says, because of course she thinks that drowning victims would be super happy for her to "work up to it" while they're choking on seawater.

"You're a parking lot attendant," I say, giggling hard enough I start to lose my breath. This whole situation is ridiculous. My god. This girl really has no clue. I try not to be infuriated she thought my job was so easy that she could just hop right into it without any training or prep at all. What a joke.

"A what?" she asks, clearly on the verge of freaking out.

"Did you honestly think . . ." My laughter dies when I see how red she's gotten. I want to mess with her a little bit, not all the way down to humiliation street. She probably gets enough of that from her mother's live streams. "Sorry," I say, holding up a hand and catching my breath. "I shouldn't have laughed. It's just . . . lifeguards are kind of important."

She crosses her arms tighter. "Then how come you're one?"

And okay, that gets my hackles up. *What does that mean anyway?* Just more classic rich-girl bullshit, thinking that some townie like me can't do anything important.

"Because I'm good at it," I say, raising my voice a little. "Plus, I have extensive training, regular workouts, and I'm constantly having to recertify! People can count on me, unlike you!"

"People can count on me!"

"For what? Ads for personal juicers and vitamin gummies?"

She smiles at that as I pull into the lot—waved on by Kiera, the other lot attendant working today—and that somehow pisses me off even more.

"What are you so happy about now?" I snap, keeping my eyes set in front of me on all the parents dragging their children across the parking area. One kid carries a giant inflatable chicken twice his size that we'll definitely be confiscating later. Stuff like that blocks our view of people in the water. They must be tourists; no townie would pull crap like that.

"Nothing," she says. I flick my eyes over to hers, and she *still* looks like the cat that got the cream.

"What?" I ask. "Whatever you're thinking right now, say it."

"It's just nice to know you've been checking my Insta, since you clearly know my sponsorship deals. Thanks for the add, *kiddo.*"

"Oh, Jesus Christ." I sigh. "I don't follow you. I looked at your page once, after your dad hired me, just to see what I was up against. Trust me, I couldn't care less about your little deals."

"My vitamin ad was three months ago. Must have really been doing a very deep dive."

Dammit, I think, feeling my cheeks heat. I did do a deep dive, but I didn't exactly want her to know that.

"What can I say?" I grin, putting up as much false bravado as I can manage. "I'm very, very thorough. Most people like that about me."

She swallows thickly and looks away, the blush back on her cheeks and neck instead of mine. My eyes fan down to the flush blooming on her chest, watching it disappear beneath her bathing suit. Now it's my turn to swallow hard.

Screw this.

I pop my car door open, grateful that she's looking out the window, properly mortified. "Come on," I say, "let's get you to work."

A few short minutes later, I'm handing Birdie off to Kiera and telling them to have a good day in a tone just patronizing enough to earn an eye roll from my charge and a laugh from Kiera before I head out to my locker. Five minutes and a quick change into my lifeguarding suit later, I'm climbing up the large wooden ladder that leads to the stand for Lifeguard Tower Five, aka Chair Five, where Bentley is waiting for me.

He breaks into a smile. "Hey, you survived the drive in today! I was worried about you. Has the summer girl been delivered to the parking lot gods?"

"Yes, much to her dismay. She honestly thought for a minute she was going to be a lifeguard." I giggle, grabbing the sunscreen and applying it liberally before taking my place beside him.

"Wild," he says, never taking his eyes off the water. "Did she think we don't train for this?"

"I don't know what she thought, honestly."

"Well, we do," he deadpans. "Speaking of, I'm taking my run in a minute, now that you're here. Chair Six is coming to get me."

Chair Six. Bentley's crush. The one that gets him so flustered every time he says his name that we've just taken to referring to him as Six instead. Six is cool and all, and a great lifeguard, but unfortunately technically summer boy adjacent—he used to only come for the summer to visit his grandma. Bentley believes this classifies him as off-limits under rule number one. I disagree—especially since Six stays here full-time on college breaks now—and have been trying to hook them up for two summers. I think I'm getting close.

I shove Bentley's arm a little, raising my eyebrow, and he shakes his head. "Don't start, Cassandra."

"Don't call me Cassandra or I'll embarrass you in front of Six."

"Don't threaten me or I'll tell everyone you've been ditching us for a summer girl *by choice.*"

"No one would believe that," I say.

He sighs. "You're right. No one *would* believe that."

"Believe what?" a voice calls up at us, and I glance at Bentley, who is shoving the binoculars into my hands with a rapidness I've never seen before.

"Nothing," he says, already down the steps. His suitor has arrived.

ᵕᵕᵕ

Bentley drags himself back up the ladder about forty minutes later looking significantly sweatier than when he left. Anticipating this, I've already propped up an umbrella to give us some shade from this nasty beating sun and made sure his favorite brand of water is on top of the cooler. I pass him a bottle as he drops into the chair, still slightly out of breath but clearly elated.

"We're getting coffee," he practically chirps.

"Who?" I say, feigning indifference, which earns me a stiff punch in the arm.

"Me and Six, obviously!"

"Are you still going to call him Six when you're on your date?"

"It's not a date; it's coffee . . . And maybe," he adds with a laugh. "He seemed to like it when I called him that to his face by accident on our run. Oh, by the way, Courtney wanted me to let you know there's a girls' run starting in, like—" he checks his Garmin watch—"well, *now*, if you want to get it done early."

"Are you sure you're rested up enough to take over? It's been pretty quiet on the water, but still."

"Yeah, I'm good! Go for it. Maybe you'll get a coffee date of your own. You know Court has a thing for you."

"Not interested," I say, heading over to the ladder to climb down. "Rule number one! But thanks."

"If you expect me to make an exception for Six, you can make one for Court."

"Hardly the same thing. If we both start messing with the constitution, it'll fall apart. Pretty soon we'll be breaking rule number two too!"

Bentley shudders. "I will never break that one, don't worry."

I grin. The rules need to be respected, especially the first two. Rule number one: Absolutely *no* dating summer girls. Ever. Rule number two (nearly as important): Never order the fish from the snack bar because it's always mystery meat no matter what they label it.

"Okay," he calls down to me. "But does Court really fall under rule number one? She's not rich-rich, and she *works* here!"

"Yes." I laugh, feeling my feet sink into the already too hot sand. "Anyone whose family rents a house just for the tourist season counts. Now shut it before someone hears you. They're coming."

His eyes dart down the beach to the splashes of red racing toward us. Just about every girl and woman on shift right now seems to have joined Court for this jog. I fall into formation as they pass by, earning me a big smile and a "Glad you could make it" from Courtney.

Before I know it, the pounding of feet on sand, the sound of waves splashing, and the low murmur of all the beachgoers have turned into white noise around me. All that exists is me and the ocean and the sand beneath my feet during moments like this. It's one of my favorite parts of the day, and I've been known to meet them for a run even on my days off.

Physical fitness drills, like these runs, are mandatory. We do them several times a day, only being excused if we participated in a rescue, understandably. Bentley and I are lucky— our section of the beach is pretty chill. Sure, we have to call in people who wander too far out all the time, but as for rescues or assistance calls? Probably only a couple times a week. And life-or-death ones have been pretty rare since I started. I'm happy to never have had one of those yet, although Bentley did once last year. Drunk frat boy who panicked when he got caught in a pop-up rip current—it didn't end well. Last we heard he was still in a rehabilitation center.

I watch the ocean waves roll in and out as I run. I love these runs and getting to see parts of the beach I don't spend a lot of time in. Each chair is responsible for their own section, although we all pitch in as needed. Bentley and I cover the space in front of the snack bar; everything between towers four and six belongs to us. I know every rock and sandbar as well as I know my own skin. Occasionally, the weather changes things, currents shift just enough to keep us on our toes, riptides can pop up, but largely we know the dangerous areas and how to keep people safe.

Every chair also does things their own way during their work period. There's no direct supervision really; once we get up onto the tower, it's up to us to make our own decisions and pray we're making the right ones. It's a huge responsibility. Bentley and I worked it out so we take turns, each being "on" officially for fifteen-to-thirty-minute chunks—except for when we're covering for fitness breaks, but even those we try to keep as close to a half hour as possible. Whoever isn't on is still scanning the beach and keeping an eye on things, but they're not fully "locked in"—instead they're doing tasks like reloading the cooler, adjusting the umbrellas, or just generally getting the fidgets out and relaxing their mind for a sec. We figured out pretty quick that anything much longer than thirty minutes, and your mind starts to wander. You can't have that when you're responsible for people's safety.

Sure, we chat and laugh a little on the job. But our priority is standing guard, and we take our job seriously. I think that's why I like these runs so much. I can just turn my brain off and be part of the background. It's a great way to reset after staring at the ocean under the hot sun all day.

"Hi," Court says, dropping back in the formation to jog beside me as we near the end of the run.

There goes my blissful mindlessness, but I can't really blame her. She set this run up, after all. Plus she's super nice . . . for a summer girl. Still, I'm glad I can see my tower up ahead.

"You going to the bonfire tonight?" she asks, probably trying to sound casual, but I don't miss the hope in her voice.

"Not sure," I answer.

The truth is, there's a bonfire somewhere on the beach, like, every night . . . It gets to be tedious, so I try to space them out.

"I hope you do," she says, being a little more forward.

"Usually, I only go when Bentley makes me," I blurt out. *Smooth, Cass, real nice.*

"Got it," she says with a frown, officially letting me know how awkward I've made it.

"Maybe, though?" I say to her back as she picks up her pace. I don't want to be rude.

"Maybe," she says, not looking back. Thank god we're almost back at my chair. Otherwise I might consider just running into the ocean and never looking back.

I hop out of the group as we run past my chair, and I wave up at Bentley. He gives me a thumbs-up and goes back to scanning the water. He knows my routine by now. A post-run smoothie is on the books to recharge me for the rest of the afternoon. If he's nice, which he always is, I'll even bring him one too. Then I'm on duty, and he gets to chill for a few.

"You good?" I call up, because sometimes I need to take over a shift before getting my smoothie.

"Yep," he says, kicking down my flops, knowing it's the next thing I'll ask. I don't mind running barefoot—in fact, I prefer it on the beach—but I draw the line at my naked feet touching the deck of the snack bar, or god forbid, the nasty, nasty bathrooms.

"Thanks. I'll be back in ten," I say, which earns me another thumbs-up.

I shove my feet in my shoes and start hobbling my way to the snack bar, realizing too late that I must have left my wallet in the car when I rushed to the locker room this morning. Dammit, Birdie.

I glance up to see who's working the counter today. Lindy will for sure spot me; they know I'm good for it and that I'll pay up before the end of the shift today . . . But unfortunately, it's Dolly behind the counter, which means I'm out of luck.

Dolly is a nearly eighty-year-old retiree, sharp as a tack and fit as hell, especially for someone her age . . . but also a stickler for the rules. Vince usually schedules her for days that he himself can't be on-site because he knows what a tight ship Dolly runs.

Looks like I'm definitely not getting out of running back to my car for money. I sigh and head around the corner of the building, dodging harried tourists and grumpy moms dragging wagons full of toys behind them. I finally make it to my car, frowning at the rush of heat that hits me when I open the door. I grab my wallet as fast as I can before I melt. I'm just about to head back up to the smoothie station when I hear it.

"Oh my god!" a voice shrieks from the SUV that just pulled up to the entrance. "You do NOT work here. Tell me you don't."

I make my way over, recognizing the voice as belonging to one of the more notorious summer girls of the island, one I had the displeasure of seeing just the other day: Carly freaking Whitmore. Ugh. I liked it better when she stuck to the club. I don't know why she keeps nosing around here. I follow her gaze to see who she's shouting at and find Birdie, flushed scarlet again as embarrassment stains her cheeks and chest.

My smoothie can wait, I decide, picking up speed.

"You said you were doing fundraising, you little liar! This is too much, Birdie. Is this your *punishment*? Oh my god, as your friend, I promise I'm going to rally everyone to save you."

"Please don't," Birdie practically begs. "Don't tell anyone. Seriously!"

"You're holding up the line," I say, gesturing to the long string of cars currently trapped behind this banshee of a "friend" Birdie seems to have.

"Do you even know who I am?" she asks, looking me up and down, before turning back to Birdie. "Do you know this woman? If you do, maybe you should tell her how things work around here."

Birdie looks at me in a panic, her mouth opening and closing like she doesn't know what to say.

"Birdie?" Carly asks, glancing back and forth between us. "Oh my god, are you friends with the locals now? This is wild. I was just about to text you to see if you wanted to come to my mom's white party next week . . . but it looks like you might be busy. This is ridiculous. I feel so bad for you."

"Move your car," I say, knocking on her hood.

"Do not touch my car again, or I'll own you."

"Now," I add, glaring at her and refusing to break eye contact.

She scowls but finally pulls out of the way, heading off to find a spot and hopefully leaving Birdie alone for the rest of the shift. I turn toward Birdie, expecting her to look relieved, but she just looks pissed.

"What is wrong with you?" she shouts, catching me completely off guard, as she stomps over to the next car in line.

"Wrong with me? I just saved your ass!" I yell back, following after her.

"From who? My friend?"

"If that's someone you call your friend, I'd hate to meet your enemy."

"It's . . . complicated," she says, in between collecting twenty-dollar bills from cars and shoving them into the bag strapped to her waist.

"I guess so," I say, waiting for some gratitude or maybe even an apology, but none comes. After a minute or two of me standing there uselessly, she turns back to me.

"Did you need something else?"

"A thank-you would be nice!" I snap.

"For what? Making my life harder? Now they think I'm friends with a townie!"

Hot anger flares through me at her words. I always knew, on some level, that she would never see me as more than that . . . but the way she says it? Like the worst thing that could possibly happen to her is people thinking she's my friend? It hurts—a lot, if I'm being honest. But I'm not, or I don't want to be, so I let the anger and resentment bubble to the surface instead.

"Suit yourself," I say, turning to leave before I say something I'll regret.

"I will." She grabs the money from the next car without even looking at me—meanwhile the driver's head is swiveling around like a bobblehead, soaking up the drama from every angle.

"You know what? Fuck off, Birdie," I add, stomping off in search of my smoothie.

I don't have time for this, and even if I did, she's not worth it.

7

Birdie

DON'T CRY, DON'T cry, *don't cry.*

I repeat those words in my head like a mantra the entire drive home, because the one thing I hate more than anything is people seeing me cry. I'll be damned if I add Cass to the list.

It was bad enough that Carly saw me today—no doubt she's already texted the entire school out of fake concern over me working as a parking lot attendant while they're all out on their summer yachts and European vacations—but I hate the fact that I was such an asshole to Cass that she was mad enough to swear. Which is something I don't think I've heard her do since I got here. The proverbial cherry on top of my misery sundae.

I think I'm even more sick of letting people down than I am of crying in front of them.

I glance at Cass once more before going back to looking out my window—just in case she seems to have gotten over things. But no, her jaw is tight, lips set in a thin, straight line instead of her usual pout, just like the last time I looked at her.

The sun has turned her skin even more bronze than it was this morning, but I can't even appreciate it with the absolute rage radiating off her. I don't know why I was so nasty to her. Well, no, I do. I was embarrassed twice over. Carly finding out where I worked sucked enough, but for Cass to see me being made fun of on top of that? The girl who everyone—even my father—thinks is so much better than me? Naturally, I lashed out, like I always do, instead of appreciating the kindness that was offered to me. And she was being kind—I see that now, thanks in part to Kiera calling me out on it after Cass left. Who knows how long Carly would have sat there in her car making a spectacle of me if Cass hadn't stood up to her.

My head knocks against the window as Cass pulls into my driveway a little hard, banking left severely and coming to an abrupt stop. "I'll see you tomorrow," I mumble, at a loss for how to fix any of this.

"Yep," she says, not meeting my eyes. I've barely shut the car door before she's squealing out of the driveway.

My dad's not home yet—no surprise there—so I let myself in and head up to my bathroom to shower. I peel off my bathing suit, which has been stuck to me in uncomfortable, chafing ways since this morning, and let it drop to the floor. What a colossal mistake that was to wear. How ridiculous to think that I would be the one in the water in the first place. I'm such a joke, from top to bottom. I have no idea what I'm even doing anymore, and for the first time, I wonder if I ever even did. Streaming—alone and with my mom—seemed to make so much sense; everything was blocked out and preplanned. (Until it wasn't.) The camera was suffocating, yes, but it's not like I knew life without it.

Now that it's gone, I just feel lost. Like the world has somehow gotten a thousand times bigger, while I've shrunk into an echo of who I used to be. It's fine. It's whatever, right?

I flick the water on in the shower and kick the bathing suit away, glancing at myself in the mirror. I look like a disaster: sweaty and a little pink from sunburn because I didn't bring any sunblock. Kiera offered me hers in the morning, but I was too shy to ask to reapply.

I step under the spray of the water, wishing I could wash away the day's embarrassments as easily as I can my sweat. Working as a parking lot attendant is . . . less great than it sounds. Which is an impressive feat since it doesn't sound great at all.

I spent the entire day watching people pull in, with the hot exhaust from their cars blowing up in my face and their sticky, sweaty twenty-dollar bills beneath my fingertips . . . Because we're apparently in the Stone Age here, so they take cash or checks only. No credit cards, no Venmo, no nothing. I mean *checks*?! Who even takes checks anymore? Who even carries them? I'll tell you who: three senior citizens who came in today and held up the line even longer than Carly did. They were arguing over how to split the twenty-dollar admission evenly between them, each one carefully writing out their check after a rousing game of rock paper scissors to determine who would pay $6.66 and who would pay $6.67, along with some friendly teasing over who was the "most devilish."

It probably would have been cute if it weren't for all the angry drivers honking behind them, or the fact that I was working alone covering for my partner's lunch. Kiera came back from break horrified and explained that next time I should have the car pull forward so I can keep collecting money from the beachgoers behind it while the people writing checks figure stuff out.

I didn't tell her that I hoped that it would never happen again.

I finish up in the shower, getting dressed and then peeking out the window. The driveway is still empty; Dad must be working late. Deciding that I don't want to be alone with my thoughts, I figure the best thing would be to FaceTime Ada and hope that she has some words of wisdom for me.

"Birdie!" she says, the second we connect. "Oh my god, I've missed you so much!"

She's all done up to go out, her hair in an edgy updo that she definitely didn't do herself and her makeup more perfect and steadily applied than she can pull off alone. Either she paid for it or one of our friends has taken my place helping her to get ready. Adding insult to injury, I can't even tell where she is, but I can tell it's not her own bedroom. She must be at someone else's house.

"Hi! Missed you too," I say, blowing her a kiss. "Where are you?"

"My stepmonster is renovating our whole condo, and my

mom is in Greece on a girls' trip, so they put me up in a hotel for the rest of the summer to keep me out of their hair. I'm so bored. I don't know why I can't just go to the summer house. I'd rather be in the Hamptons than here, even if they do have a great salon and spa. But apparently I have to look at swatches in person because 'text and email won't do them justice.'" She rolls her eyes in frustration. "Hey, at least there's a killer walk-in closet in the penthouse," she says, spinning her phone around so fast to show me that I feel a little dizzy.

The jealousy that was creeping up inside me quickly dies as I take in what she said. I know she hates when her parents ping-pong her around like this. "I wish I could be there with you."

"I know. This sucks."

"Well, if it helps, you're probably still having a better time than me," I say.

"Yikes," she says, nibbling on a chocolate-covered cherry and then flopping onto her bed. "That reminds me. Carly texted me this afternoon. She said your dad's assistant was some kind of monster forcing you to do manual beach labor. I told her there was no way, but . . . she insisted. Are you okay out there?"

I fight the urge to cry again. Of course, Carly has already told everyone. She probably even posted pics of me melting in my bathing suit in that horrible lawn chair they give us to sit on between rushes.

"Yeah, it's messed up. Dad wants me to work, and I—"

"Is he cute at least?"

"Who?" I ask, utterly confused. "My dad?"

"Eww, no!" She laughs, licking the last bit of chocolate off her lips. "I mean the monster. Your dad's PA. Is he at least cute?"

"Oh, it's not a—" I cut myself off before I can correct her.

Because maybe this will be the first time I can actually talk to my best friend about my complicated feelings for someone who's *not* a boy without having to make things weird again. Things were so awkward the last time I mentioned even a hint of bisexuality. And besides, is it really lying? Or is it just not being fully forthcoming? The person is the person, regardless of gender, right?

"Yes," I say. "Unfortunately, they are distractingly cute."

This is the first time I've admitted out loud that I'm attracted to Cass, and it sends a little thrill coursing through my veins.

"Okay, well, that we can work with." She winks. "Tell me about him."

"Well, he's—" I pause, the pronoun feeling like acid on my tongue, and try to shake it off. "They're adorable," I admit, hoping she doesn't realize I've switched to a more neutral pronoun. "I knew them when we were little, but it's been a long time. Our dads kind of work together too, which is complicated. I hate how my dad favors them, and I hate how they act better than me half the time . . . but there's just something about them that I can't shake."

"Boinking daddy's assistant," she says excitedly. "Scandalous."

"No one is boinking anyone," I say. "They absolutely hate me, and my opinion of them changes every five seconds."

"Where is he from? Do I know him?"

"No!" I say a little too fast. "They're not from Boston."

"Oooh, fresh meat?" she squeals. "You are a dirty Birdie."

I roll my eyes. "It's not that big of a deal. They're probably going to go further in my family business than I ever will," I say, admitting the truth that's been bothering me so much.

"It will be if your mom finds out," she says. "If they aren't Mitchell Riley level, you probably won't have to worry about your dad cutting you off, because your mom will first."

My stomach sinks, because I have no idea if Ada's right or not, and that terrifies me. All the more reason to keep my terrifying, complicated, fucked-up feelings under wraps.

"She won't, because there's nothing going on. Like I said, they hate me, and half the time, I hate them. Besides, I don't think Mom's even coming out here this year. Dad mentioned something about her opting to get a house in Martha's Vineyard. She said it would be good for networking, apparently."

Ada sighs, but then shifts closer to the phone. "Okay, fine. There's nothing going on. I don't care. Tell me more about this *adorable assistant* that you're hopefully going to get all enemies-to-lovers with by the end of the summer. How can he be both adorable *and* a monster? I feel like your dad wouldn't pick a PA that was truly horrible. He's kind of chill, isn't he?"

"I'm sure my dad thinks they're great. It's me getting tortured."

"But the fact that he's nice to look at makes up for it?"

"Kinda, but they're also . . . I don't know. They're infuriating but mostly fair. Usually, when we get into it, it's my fault."

"I doubt that." Ada frowns. "You're the sweetest person in our entire friend circle."

"That's not a very high bar," I say, and she smirks back at me.

"True."

"Did I mention they're also a lifeguard when they aren't working for my dad?"

"Holy shit, Birdie, you did not bag a lifeguard your first week in town! Iconic."

I laugh and shake my head. "Nobody has bagged anybody, and they definitely aren't interested," I say. "Again, they hate me."

"I don't see how! You're probably just in your head. I bet he's crushing on you as much as you are on him."

"No, I've been pretty horrible to them so far. I kind of . . . ditched them, twice? And made their job way harder than it needed to be. Plus, today we got into a fight, and they basically told me to fuck off."

"Birdie Gordon!" she shrieks. "Are you trying to have a summer fling or make a mortal enemy?"

"Neither," I say, which earns me a harrumph from my best friend. "Look, I told you it was complicated."

"Did he at least deserve it today?"

I wince, dreading answering, because the truth is, no, Cass didn't deserve it. Even I could tell she was trying to be nice today. And it isn't really her fault that I'm maybe, sort of, a little jealous of how much my dad seems to respect her while shitting all over me. Maybe I'm the one who's a monster.

"Birdie, tell me he deserved it," she says.

"No, not really," I say eventually, with a sigh. "I was being humiliated by Carly and was already about to lose it. I knew Carly was going to tell everyone about it. I felt like my life was about to blow up anyway, so I decided to just light the fuse myself."

"Right, right," Ada says, waving her hand at the screen as if to say *Get to the good stuff.*

"So, I basically told her—them, the PA—off," I say, adding, "Sorry, I'm so tired, I don't even know what I'm saying," to play off my misspeak. "But yeah, I insulted the hell out of them, and then they still had to drive me home from work. It was such a nightmare. I don't think they said one word the whole time."

Ada is frowning at me. I can tell she feels bad, but there's a hint of something else there. Resignation, maybe, that her best friend is, and probably always will be, a colossal screwup.

"Well, the good news," Ada says—because she's a glass-half-full kind of girl even if it kills her—"is that you'll be with him every day for the rest of the summer. Plenty of time to apologize or decide to hate him back?"

"That's if this parking lot job doesn't kill me." I groan. "Look at me. I'm completely sunburned, and I'm so tired I feel like I've just finished, like, five hours of hot yoga and then had my personal trainer show up. I'm not cut out for this kind of stuff. Maybe I should just quit and let my dad hold my trust a little longer. I don't know if I can do this again tomorrow."

"Look at me, Birdie," Ada says, her words dragging my watery gaze back to her. "This summer could be the best thing that ever happened to you. Don't blow it. Give yourself a real chance."

"How do you figure?" I snort, utterly unconvinced.

"Forget about the hot monster. I was just having fun with you. The last thing you need is another complicated relationship. You should take this time to figure yourself out—away from the cameras and the outline your mother has for your life. For the first time, you don't even have to worry about what people are saying about you on social media!"

I gulp. "Is it that bad?"

"No, they love you, as they should," she says. "Team Birdie in the breakup all the way. But even though they're being nice, you don't need all the noise right now. Just . . . consider what I'm saying."

"I don't even know who I am without all that stuff. I don't even know what I like to eat anymore, because I was so caught up in what plating would look the prettiest to post, or who was sponsoring an ad, or what was the best place to be seen. How am I just supposed to decide all of that by myself?"

"You just do, Birdie. Eat the pizza! Wear the sweats that aren't trending but *are* comfortable! Stop plucking your eyebrows! Okay, maybe not that last one. I remember you having a little unibrow problem in first grade before your mom took them over."

I laugh; I can't help it. "What does that even mean?"

"It means I'm rooting for you. I always will be, even if you come home and put everything right back the way it was." She gives me a reassuring look. "But let's find out who the girl is under the streamer, okay? You can do this."

"Yeah?" I smile, feeling a thousand times lighter just talking this through. Maybe Ada is actually onto something.

"Promise," she says, and I can tell she wishes she could give me a supportive hug right now. I wish she could too.

"Okay," I say.

I got this, I tell myself as we say our goodbyes so Ada can go grab some non-camera-worthy dinner from the bistro downstairs. *I got this.*

8

Cass

"I JUST DON'T know why George had to pin this on me," I say, shoveling some of my mom's French toast into my mouth over breakfast the next morning.

"Mr. Gordon," my mom corrects me. She never really trusted the man, and I think it grates on her how casual we are about him, like he's a long-lost uncle instead of someone who controls the majority of my family's income at any given moment. My dad sighs and goes back to reading the local news on his iPad, deciding not to get involved. Luckily, I don't push the issue. I'm not looking to cause any problems during our sacred summer breakfasts.

Family breakfast is a routine around here we can usually only indulge in during the summers, when I don't have school and Dad goes in later, since daylight lasts longer. My mom relishes in cooking for us, spoiling us near daily with French toast, omelets, and casseroles, not to mention her famous made-from-scratch home fries.

It's basically the only time we all have at home together, except for when we're sleeping, that is. Dad's now helping manage *all* of George's properties on the island—acting as both manager and general contractor. My mom keeps her usual noon-to-midnight nurse's aide shift at the local low-income retirement home, and I spend all day babysitting tourists who swim too far out in the ocean . . . and *Mr. Gordon's* daughter.

"He trusts you, Cass. Take it as the compliment it is," Dad says, digging into his overstuffed veggie omelet. "I'm sure he's paying you very well for the trouble."

"I don't know if there's enough money in the world to make me want to spend extra time with Birdie Gordon after what she said to me yesterday," I say, which makes my mom laugh in a sort of *See, I told you so* way. She was against this from the very first night.

"You two used to be so cute together when you were little. She can't be that bad," Dad tries again, obviously hoping to smooth things over.

"Yeah, but that was before she turned into another stuck-up summer girl looking down her nose at me. We're not building sandcastles anymore, Dad. Did you know she didn't even *apply* to any college that she could have gotten into? George—Mr. Gordon," I say, glancing at my mom as I make the correction, "said she didn't even send in any essays to the ones she did apply to and wasted everybody's time filling apps with nonsense. She just expected him to hand over her trust and send her on her merry way. The entitlement is unreal!"

"That sounds like the Gordons," my mom says, smiling as she takes a bite of her potatoes.

"She gets that from her mother, not her father," my dad says, picking up his coffee. "You should be glad you didn't have to grow up in that house."

"Yeah, having my every whim catered to while I lie around and go live on Instagram talking about lip gloss and vitamins seems like *such* a hard life."

"Cass," my dad says, his tone a warning, "be nice."

"Why? She's not nice to me."

"Your daughter has a point, John."

"It's ridiculous!" I say, glad that at least my mother is on my side. "She's irresponsible, immature, entitled, spoiled, and—"

"Cassandra!" my father says, his voice louder than I'm used to. "We raised you better than this. Have some empathy for the girl!"

"What does that even mean? I'm not allowed to be annoyed when someone treats me like crap?"

"You *are* allowed to be annoyed," Mom says, squeezing my wrist gently. "Of course. But I *think* what your father is getting at is that we can't really know what anyone else is going through, even if they stream it." She winks, letting me know I haven't totally lost her. "Plus, you could have chosen to turn the job down when it was presented to you, like I suggested. Since you didn't, I expect you to show a little compassion and patience with this girl. You were very young when she was around all the time, so you may not remember, but she didn't have the easiest time with her mother then, and I'd imagine it hasn't gotten any better over the years."

"I definitely remember." I huff. "I remember that she wouldn't play in the sand. I remember she never wanted to swim. I remember that she was so worried about getting dirty or messing up her hair even then." I roll my eyes. "And then she just stopped coming at all, until now. I think she was just born this useless, Mom! I swear to god. What five-year-old is too worried about getting sand under her nails to build a castle?"

My mom sighs and looks at my father, years of marriage allowing them to communicate without words. My dad nods at her and then turns to me. "Cass, she stopped coming because of me."

"Because of you?"

My dad frowns. "I convinced George to confront his wife about how they were treating Birdie, and it backfired spectacularly. Instead of saving Birdie, we accidentally threw her to the wolves."

"Confront her mom about what? Buying too much Dior for Baby Birdie to run around in back then?"

"About treating that child like a little doll on a shelf until Verity was ready to film," my dad says, his voice uncharacteristically harsh. "But then Verity started threatening divorce and a custody battle and lawsuits, and George . . . dropped the rope. He had to essentially take up residence in the summer house because Verity made his life as miserable as she could."

"Sorry, I guess I didn't realize," I say, wanting to get back to enjoying my breakfast before spending another frustrating day around Birdie.

"Your memories are your own, Cass. Of course I can understand why it was upsetting when Birdie never wanted to play," Dad says. "I'm just asking you, with the benefit of age and hindsight, if you can consider that maybe there was something more to that. Because as I recall, she did want to play with you, very much. It wasn't that she didn't want to get dirty, as much as she was scared of the consequences if she did."

I narrow my eyes, trying to make my memories line up with this new information. Sure, I guess it makes sense, but what does that have to do with *now*? "Okay, but if she didn't want to be like that anymore, she wouldn't have to be. I mean, she's gotta be eighteen or close to it, right? You can't honestly expect me to give her a pass on her behavior just because her mom sucks."

My mom scoops another spoonful of food onto my plate. "Eat your potatoes, dear, before they get cold," she says, glancing at my father and then getting up. It's clear I've disappointed them.

"Fine." I sigh. "I'll try to be nicer to her. As long as she stops trying to ruin my life."

"That's all we're asking, honey," Dad says, going back to his iPad.

~~~

I'm still thinking about the conversation I had with my parents when I pull up to Birdie's house, fully expecting a repeat of yesterday. I'm shocked to find her already waiting on the front porch, ready to go. She smiles and does a little wave as she trots down the steps and to the car. I notice today she's in a much more comfortable tank-and-shorts set, with her hair pulled back in a completely normal and plain pony instead of whatever that weird updo was yesterday. I fight back the little whirl of pride that wells up inside me. But seriously, ready *and* appropriately dressed? The girl is learning.

"Hey," she says, hopping into the car and buckling up.

"Hi," I say, wanting to be nice like I promised my parents, but also still more than a little annoyed about yesterday.

We barely make it to the corner before she angles toward me in her seat.

"About yesterday," she says, and I raise my eyebrows, flicking my eyes to hers only for a second. She sighs and then sits a little straighter. "I know you were trying to help . . . in your own way," she starts, and my lips turn into a scowl all on their own.

In my own way? In my own way?! Is she serious right now?

"Forget it," I say. "Won't happen again."

"That's not what I meant." She flops back into her seat. "You're just like—"

"I'm like what?" I ask. I can't wait to hear this one.

"Impossible," she mutters, and I grin.

Impossible. I kind of like that. A girl like Birdie should find me impossible. We are opposites in every way that matters, a fact that I'm quite fond of.

"Thank you," I say, surprising myself when I realize I kind of mean it, although probably not in the way she hoped.

Nobody says anything for a little while, and I almost start to feel bad for her as she shifts in her seat. Her energy has taken a nosedive from the annoying Labrador vibes she had when she bounded down the front porch steps, to something much more subdued. Every few minutes she opens and closes her mouth like she's trying to find the right words.

Thinking of my mom's disappointed face, I decide to extend the tiniest olive branch. "Got any big plans for this weekend?" I ask, knowing that we're both off. "Going to any yacht parties?"

"No, no yacht parties," she says, sounding offended, like she thinks I'm making fun of her. It was a genuine question. I mean, her friend drove a G-Wagon to a beach parking lot yesterday, where it was all but guaranteed to get scratched by some toddler with a shovel. A yacht doesn't seem like a stretch here.

"Something better going on, then?" I try again.

"I don't know. What even is there to do around here? What are *you* doing?" she asks, in a way that makes me think she doesn't believe I could possibly have any plans.

"I'm working at the Coalition with my dad for a while Saturday," I answer honestly. "Not sure what I'm doing after that. It's kind of hard this time of year. The place is overrun with tourists staying at all the little short-term rentals."

"The Coalition?"

"Yeah, my dad started the Affordable Housing Coalition about a year and a half ago to combat all the landlords who were buying up run-down houses and flipping them into Airbnbs and stuff. They're *ruining* the neighborhood, and we're trying to fight that and keep people in their homes and apartments."

Birdie shrugs. "From what I've seen of this place lately, it kind of looks like they cleaned it up."

"Of course you would think that," I say, my hands tightening on the steering wheel. "Since your dad is one of the worst offenders."

She looks confused. "My dad buys half of the condemned buildings around here and fixes them up. If anything, he's saved your neighborhood, not hurt it."

"Yeah, exactly. He buys them from people who are desperate and then outprices everyone who used to live here. And to make matters worse, instead of at least turning them into condos or apartments for people to live in, adding to the community, he turns them into short-term vacation rentals!" I shake my head. "There's a massive shortage of affordable housing around here. A lot of my friends' families have already had to move. I know you obviously can't relate to that, but trust me, it sucks. The neighborhoods don't even have any personality anymore, just the same stupid fake shiplap tossed on hastily done remodels. It's all cookie-cutter. It makes me want to throw up."

"If you and your family are so against it, why do you work for my dad? Why do you act like you're all friends?" She shifts in her seat again, looking genuinely curious, no judgment in her tone or face at all. I decide to match her openness and be real with her.

"Honestly? Your dad gave mine a job when we were in a tough spot. I think at first Dad felt like he owed him for that, but over the years they genuinely became pretty close. My mom has always been on the fence about him, but she's kind enough when he's around that he still feels welcome even though he knows where she stands. Normally, when he's in town, he's eating at my house more than he is at yours."

"Really?"

"Yeah, I'm assuming he just wants to be home for you at night now, though. We've hardly seen him since you got here."

She looks puzzled by this, but I decide not to press. What happens behind their closed doors is none of my business, and I need to stop getting caught up in it. Still, I decide to throw her a bone.

"Anyway, my dad says yours is one of the good ones. Well, as good as someone hoarding wealth and making a living as a landlord can possibly be anyway."

She half rolls her eyes but lets my comment go. It's unsettling how gentle she's being today. Abrasive Birdie was so much easier to hate.

She surprises me again by asking, "So what does your coalition do?"

"A lot of things. We help people find housing whenever we can. We teach people about available grants and file requests to help them keep their own homes, and we raise money to help people pay off their liens when loans or grants aren't an option. We even lobby the city and state to put protections in place so people like your dad can't just come in and turn everything into short-term rentals. We've actually made some headway with that one," I say proudly. "It's a lot harder to put in a new short-term rental than it used to be. You have to jump through some serious legal hoops now, thanks to my dad and the rest of the board. Of course, people with enough money, like George, or some of the other investors around here, can still make it happen, but at least it's a start."

"So . . . you're basically my dad's worst enemy." She laughs.

"Kind of," I agree. "But somehow also his best friends."

"I don't get it." She shakes her head.

"I don't either," I say. "But George has never missed a birthday party or family event at our place since we've known him. And he at least listens to my dad. I think he *tries* to make better decisions, even if his investors don't always let him."

"Yeah, I know what that's like."

"Oh?" I snort. "Beholden to many investors, are you?"

"You could say that." She frowns, that familiar blush rising up her neck.

I immediately go back to staring at the road and clear my throat. *Did it just get even hotter in here?*

"Hey," she says, her hand covering mine on the gearshift.

I almost pull away in surprise, but her warm skin sends a jolt of . . . something not altogether unpleasant coursing through my veins. My brain momentarily short-circuits, and I snap my eyes to hers, grateful that we're at a red light.

"I think it's pretty cool what you guys are doing. It sounds really, really important," she says earnestly, and then takes her hand away.

I try to ignore the sinking feeling in my chest, that tiny voice whispering, *Wait, do I want her to touch me again?* But the longer I'm in this car with her, the harder it's getting.

I nod, my voice frozen inside me. When the light turns green, I shoot forward and speed the whole rest of the way to work. I'm desperate to get her out of my car now, not because

I can't stand her, but because I'm realizing that maybe a part of me *can*. A big part. The part that's taken by the smell of her perfume and the way her eyes crinkled when she said I was *important*, or at least my work was. I try to tell myself I'm just mixed-up and spiraling from my parents suggesting that there might be more to Birdie, and I could be, but it feels like more than that.

It feels like my olive branch is trying to stretch itself into a tree . . . but if there's one thing I know, it's that I absolutely can't latch my roots on to this girl.

Birdie smiles as I stop in front of the parking lot entrance to let her out. She gives me a little wave, and I jerk my car forward, hitting the gas a little too hard. This earns me a weird look from Kiera, but I quickly pull away. I make it to my usual spot behind the snack bar—the one I picked because the Honda will be at least partially in the shade during the day—and then lean back in my seat, rubbing my hand where she touched me.

Because what is going on with me today?

No, I think, trying to forget how nice it felt to have her skin on mine. *No. Nope. Not going there. Absolutely not. Rule number one. Remember rule number one.*

9

Birdie

IT'S SWELTERING OUT, and sitting in a gross, old lawn chair—or more accurately, sticking to it—isn't helping. Neither is the asphalt radiating heat in my face from every direction.

This job sucks.

Not in a spoiled *Oh, I'd rather be doing an internship in air-conditioning* type of way, but in an actually, truly, *Hard to imagine a worse or more boring job* kind of way. Even if I do love working with Kiera, who is hilarious and sweet . . . and nose deep in her social media accounts on her phone. At least she has *something* to do during the downtime. Meanwhile, all I can do is stare straight ahead, trying to zone out until the next car comes.

They're few and far between now as we head into the early afternoon hours. The morning people aren't quite ready to leave yet, and I assume the afternoon people are still nestled in their hotels and Airbnbs, just waking up.

Boring.

I wipe the sweat out of my eyes and lean back in the chair, trying to refocus my attention on fun, more important things, like what I want to sample next from the snack bar—I'm taking Ada's advice and trying all the things—and also not dying of heatstroke.

"Your phone's buzzing," Kiera says, nudging my foot as she stands up to stretch and take a swig of water. She just got back from lunch a few minutes ago, but she's definitely feeling the same sweaty boredom I am as she cycles through phone-stretch-drink-repeat.

I blink hard, shaking off the haze in my head as best as I can and sending droplets of sweat cascading down from my hairline. Gross.

"Thanks," I say as she plops back into the chair next to me.

"Do you want to take a fifteen?" she asks. I check the time—it's barely one, but maybe a break wouldn't be so bad. I wasn't planning to take my full lunch break until closer to two, but a few minutes away from the lot sounds like heaven.

"Yeah, okay," I say, "that works. I might grab a slushie from the snack bar or something. Do you want anything?"

"Nah, I'm good," she says, already going back to scrolling on her phone.

I pull my own out and head to the little shaded spot behind the main building. In another hour or so, it will be completely swallowed up by the sun, but for now, it's my little desert oasis.

I rub the sweat off my face and lean against the wall. I have two missed calls from Ada, so I FaceTime her back, putting it on speaker—muscle memory from my streaming days. Old habits die hard.

"Birdie, hi, where are you? I've been calling!"

"At . . . work?"

"Again?!"

I blow out a breath, amused. "That's usually how it works, yes."

Ada rolls her eyes. "Fine, can you talk?"

"For a minute. I'm on break. What's up?" I ask.

"You sound tired. Are you tired?" she asks, slipping into typical worried-Ada mode. "How hot is it even over there? I hope you're at least getting a good breeze from the beach and soaking up those views."

"Ha." I snort. "No, there's a massive dune separating the parking lot from the water, probably so all these cars don't 'ruin the ambiance.' I would kill for a breeze. It's, like, ninety-two out today, even without the asphalt baking me alive," I say. "Did you really call to ask about the weather?"

"Birdie," she says slowly, sounding like her heart is legitimately breaking for me. It probably is. Even my dad calls her one of my "better" friends. A classification reserved only for Ada and . . . well, pretty much only Ada. Although maybe someday Cass would fit under that heading too, if we ever figure out how to stop making each other mad.

"Ada," I say, imitating her tone. "I'm fine, I promise. This blows, but if this is what my dad needs to see in order to give me the seed money, then this is what it takes."

"How is the whole purse thing going, anyway? Are you working on any new designs?"

"I'm too sunburned to move," I admit. It's true. All I could do last night was slather myself in aloe and flop on my bed, waiting for the air-conditioning to lure me to unconsciousness until I had to get up and do it all over again. "Once I'm out of here, though, it's on again," I say, thinking about the dozens of ideas I have pinned up on the wall in my bedroom back home.

"Your father is being such a monster . . . or I guess his assistant is."

I laugh; I can't help it. "I don't know. They were nicer today on the drive in," I say, thinking back to this morning when I accidentally touched Cass's hand. The fact that she didn't yank it back seemed like a good sign. Although, I wish I'd caught myself before doing it so I didn't make things awkward. Cass looked like I had burned her when I finally pulled away. I kind of liked it, but she *clearly* did not.

"I don't care how nice he's supposedly being. Anyone who makes my best friend bake under the sun during a ninety-plus-degree day is a monster!"

"They're an ogre at best," I say. "And technically, they're baking under the sun too."

It's nice being able to talk to Ada about Cass like this. Really nice.

Mitchell never made me feel that butterflies-in-your-belly way—and while I had plenty of crushes before him, it was rare that I actually *wanted* to talk to my friends about them. But Ada calling Cass a "he" because she assumed the assistant had to be a boy for me to like them, and me continuing to not correct her, feels . . . icky. Even if I try to tell myself it doesn't really matter.

Cass can't stand me, after all. It doesn't matter how nice her hand felt in mine on the ride in today.

"He's practically trying to murder you by keeping your pale ass out there in the sun, but sure, downgrade him to an ogre," she says, clearly exasperated. "Just because you think he's *so cute*. You have got to ask your therapist why you keep falling for people who treat you like shit."

And wait, that's not what I'm doing, is it? Suddenly it feels much hotter here than it did even a minute ago. "I mean . . . they're not *that* cute," I stammer out.

"Okay, Birdie, is this where we pretend that I don't know you like the back of my hand? Come on, you get crushes the way other people change their underwear, whether you admit it or not . . . which is kind of what I wanted to talk to you about," she says, her tone getting serious as she switches gears.

"My . . . underwear?" I ask, completely baffled.

"No, your . . . crushes, for lack of a better term. Ogre aside, did you see what Mitchell posted on his socials?"

My heart sinks, and I brace myself for whatever meanness comes next. "No, you know I'm still banned! What did he say?"

"I didn't save it, but he basically tried to imply that the breakup was your fault."

"What?" I yelp. "He cheated on me! Like, I found out on camera! How could it possibly be my fault?"

"Yeah, I was there," she says, sounding just as disgusted as

I am. "I think he was trying to do an apology for his fans who saw your stream, but somehow it turned into this half-assed rant about how it was wrong to cheat but you weren't there for him enough, blah, blah, blah. I don't know. He had all these bullshit reasons. He's such a garbage person."

"I wasn't there for him? I was late to our own party because I was getting his shitty-ass car! Oh my god." I groan. "Are people buying it? I guarantee you that Carly or someone told him that I can't go online right now. He knows I can't make a statement!"

"No!" Ada's quick to say. "No, his socials are blowing up with Team Birdie hashtags and stuff. No one is buying what he's selling. If I had to guess, I'd say he just ruined his rep even more. I'm sure his mom is flipping. But even though everyone is fully Team Birdie, I wanted you to hear it from me instead of Carly or someone worse."

"I appreciate that, seriously, even if it sucked to hear," I say. "Can you, like, make a post refuting it or something?"

"I don't think that's a good idea," she says. "I mean, if you really want me to kick the hornets' nest with a post of my own, I will, but that's not the point."

"Then what is? I can't have him trashing me online! Even if people don't believe him, this isn't what I want to pop up when they google me! If I'm seriously going to start my own business, my reputation matters."

"Maybe I shouldn't have told you about all this." She sighs. "Especially when you're stuck out there until god knows when."

"No, you definitely should have."

"But you're getting all stressed out and focusing on the wrong thing!" she practically shouts.

"What am I supposed to be focusing on?" I ask, utterly incredulous. "My ex is telling the whole world that I'm to blame for *his* actions! What the hell do I do with that?"

"No one's believing it," she reminds me. "I just wanted you to know what he was saying, in case he does ever try to pop back up in your life. You need to remember how awful he is, okay? Just keep using this time for you. Don't get distracted by Mitchell's drama or the ogre being one percent nicer to you on the ride to work today. Raise the bar a little, okay?"

My heartbeat pounds in my ears as I take in her words. I'd be lying if I said I wasn't at least a little bit happy about the suggestion that Mitchell might try to win me back—even if he is being horrible to me right now.

Not because I want him to—the thought of him ever touching me again makes my skin crawl—but mainly because I want him to feel bad. I want him to admit he blew a good thing and mean it. I want him to be the sorriest man on the East Coast, because I deserve that. I deserve for someone to care when they hurt me. Mitchell clearly hasn't gotten there yet, but if he's posting about me—even horrible lies like this— then I'm definitely still under his skin.

"Birdie, I'm serious," she says.

I wipe the sweat from my forehead with the back of my arm, letting her words settle into my brain. "Yeah, I know. You're right; you usually are about these things."

"Exactly. No Mitchell and no cute ogre either. Just be Birdie, for a little while."

"You don't have to worry about the cute ogre," I say. "Even if I wanted to make something happen there, I'm pretty sure it's a no go on their end."

"Good," she says, and I frown. Is it, though? *Probably.*

"Look, I have to get back. My break's almost over," I say. It's not—there are ten minutes left—but I want to be off the phone. This whole conversation has my head spinning.

"Okay, love you," she says, sounding like she means it. "And you got this."

"Yeah, hope so." I sigh. "Love you too."

I click my phone off and slide it into my pocket, letting my eyes slip shut for a second. I'm trying to stave off the oncoming headache as my thoughts continue to swirl around in my head.

My eyes jolt back open when something freezing cold touches my arm.

"What the hell?!" I screech. Fight-or-flight is in full effect, sending adrenaline coursing through my veins, and suddenly I'm not so tired after all. But instead of some tentacled sea monster or a very cold mugger or anything else my brain dreamed up all in the span of a second, I'm met with the sight of a very amused Cass.

She struggles not to laugh as she holds out a large water bottle, the same brand they sell at the snack bar. I raise my eyebrows, but she just smiles and waves it closer to me.

"You going to take it? Or do I have to pin you down and pour it in your mouth too? It's boiling out here. You need to hydrate."

Okay, her . . . aggressive concern? rudely approached

kindness? lack of total assholery? . . . should not make my belly do the little swoop thing, but it does. Damn, I must truly be starved for affection if my little Cass maggot-butterflies are perking back up over the fact that she told me to drink water on a hot day. Ada is right; I need to raise the bar.

I rip the bottle out of her hand and do my best to look grumpy about it, pretending I'm not oddly touched *because I shouldn't be.*

"Thanks," I grumble out, "but you shouldn't sneak up on people."

"And you shouldn't be sleeping on the job, but here we are."

"I wasn't sleeping on the job. I'm on break. Same as you, I'd imagine."

"Yes, except I actually use my break to do the sensible thing, like drinking water, instead of napping against a too-hot building and being even further baked alive." Looking especially frustrated, she reaches over and twists the cap off the bottle, the crinkle as the seal gives way echoing in my ears. "Drink," she says, pushing my arm up to bring the bottle closer to my mouth.

"I'm not that thirsty," I say, just to be annoying. *Raising the bar and all that.*

"That's probably because the heat exhaustion is already setting in. Seriously, Birdie. You have to drink if you're going to be sitting out in the sun all day. I know you aren't used to this, but just . . . just trust me on this, okay?" she says, a hint of desperation in her voice. "I don't want anything to happen to you."

"Aww, you do like me." I grin before chugging some water. "Thanks. That was very nice of you."

"I like you conscious and not dying of heatstroke," she huffs, with a smirk that's there and gone in the blink of an eye. Still, I caught it, and I *liked* it. I want to make her do it again.

"You know, you could have just taken the compliment," I tease as she turns to head back up the beach the way she came.

"Oh, come on, Birdie," she says, turning toward me with a mischievous look in her eye. "What kind of an ogre would I be if I did that?"

My mouth falls open, but she's jogged around to the front of the building before my brain even has a chance to reboot. And oh. Oh no. How much of that call did she hear?

10

Cass

BIRDIE TEXTS ME a little while later that her dad is picking her up from work today.

A part of me wonders if it's because I went too far with my little ogre joke, but I just couldn't resist. When I overheard the tail end of her conversation with her friend—the part where the friend said to raise the bar higher than an ogre being 1 percent nicer to Birdie on the ride to work, and realized I was the ogre in the scenario?????—I knew I wanted to mess with her about it. Naturally, I had to focus on the calling-me-an-ogre part, not the Birdie-is-obviously-talking-about-me-to-her-friends-in-the-context-of-raising-the-bar-for-romantic-partners-and-apparently-thinks-I'm-cute????!!!! part that had my thoughts racing to some unacceptable places.

It was bad enough that I couldn't stop thinking about her touching my hand that morning—and why did she have to act so interested in the affordable housing thing?—to the point where I got an extra water bottle just to have an excuse to see her early. But to overhear the call on top of it? It was too much for one person to take.

I didn't think throwing it in her face like that was going to make her actually freak out and avoid me. I'm sure she didn't *really* mean I was cute or whatever, and she probably wasn't *actually* talking about me in the context of, like . . . bars being raised romantically or not.

Plus, it's not like I care if she didn't mean it.

And it's definitely, *definitely* not like I want her to actually mean it, or even better, see me as an *already-raised bar*. I mean, I did get her water, though. Compared to her ex, how am I not an already-raised bar?!

It's fine, though. This is silly—a total nothing burger. I don't care what she thinks about me or what she tells her friends about me. At all. *Period.*

So I don't know why I'm so frustrated when she gets a ride to work the next day too.

I tell myself it's just because now George is basically paying me for nothing, but I know that's not really it. In fact, I'm so antsy all morning at work that Bentley sends me out for not just one, but two group runs.

I just . . . I hate being avoided. That's all it is. The rest is just a technicality.

Halfway through Bentley's latest turn scanning the water, I'm stretching over the back of the chair and notice Birdie coming around the edge of the main building. She climbs up the steps to the snack bar, pointedly not looking in the direction of my tower. I guess she's not even going to wave hi to me. I check my watch—it's 2:00 p.m. She must be on lunch break.

Bentley catches me frowning, darting his eyes to where I'm looking before quickly going back to scanning the water. There are only a few minutes left before it's my turn again, and I hope he just lets it go. Of course, I've never been lucky.

"That summer girl's really got you turned around," he says, casually sharp, like a shark scenting blood in the water. Except, unlike the aquatic murder machines, Bentley has the good sense to check for danger before committing any further to the bit, immediately going back to scanning instead of saying anything else.

"No," I say, crossing my arms and turning to face forward in the chair. I reach over and angle the umbrella so that it's covering me a little more than it is him, in gentle retaliation.

Bentley shakes his head, but never takes his eyes off the water. I sigh and stand up, joining him even though it's a little early to be switching. I just . . . I need something to do. Something to make me forget about how mortifying it is that I actually watched *Shrek* last night just to remind myself that there are much, much worse things than ogres.

Maybe Bentley's right. Maybe Birdie does have me turned around.

"Fine, yes." I sigh, glancing at Bentley just in time to see his lips twist into a concerned expression.

"I figured, when you were acting so off all day," he says, and I resist the urge to smack him in the arm. Being professional and all that. "You know this is one of the worst ideas you've ever had, right?"

"What idea? I don't have any ideas," I say, watching a child who looks a little too young to be off on his own playing in the shallow water. My brow furrows, but I relax when a man walks over and picks up the child, who squeals in delight as they both wade deeper into the water.

"Yeah, I clocked that kid too," Bentley says. "I was giving his parents another minute before I climbed down and walked him up to the snack bar to have them call for help."

I nod, knowing we're both thinking about a few summers ago when a ten-year-old wandered too far out and drowned. Neither of us were working as lifeguards yet, but the people on duty were really shaken up by it. A bunch of them quit. It really puts into perspective how dangerous the ocean can be—it's easy to lose sight of that. I love being on the water so much—all of it, lifeguarding, surfing, kayaking, swimming out in open water—it's easy to forget that at any moment, it can turn on you.

"What are you doing, Cass?" he asks quietly, passing me the binoculars before going to grab a protein bar.

"Nothing, literally nothing," I say, surprised that I sound almost disappointed by the truth. "I just think that she shouldn't go around calling me a cute ogre and obviously talking to her friends about me and then avoid me forever! Like, am I a cute ogre or not, ya know?"

"Pardon?" He laughs. "Do you . . . want to be a cute ogre?"

"I don't want to be a cute ogre. I just want . . . Wait." I zero in on the people from earlier. "Come here. Do you think that dad and his kid are okay?"

"They're pretty far out, yeah, but it's low tide. He can still touch, but it's questionable."

"It's a lot farther than I'd recommend with an armful of toddler. I'm bringing them in." I blow three sharp whistles and gesture for him to move back to shore. Bentley stands up beside me, matching my gestures and urgency.

"You good over there, Five?" The walkie-talkie comes to life, Chair Six checking up on us. Bentley grabs it while I keep my eyes pinned on the dad and kid.

"Think so," he says. "You guys got eyes on the dad and his toddler in the back? He seems to be drifting your way as he comes in. Guy went way too far out."

"Yeah, I see him," Six says. "Looks like he's coming in steady."

"Yeah, you can thank Cass for that. She clocked him."

"That's why we have partners," Six says.

"True, and mine's the best. She—"

"Shit," I say, throwing Bentley the binoculars and rushing down the ladder. "Huge wave. He dropped the kid."

I grab my rescue float and am running down the beach before I can say any more. I know that behind me, Bentley will be radioing for help, watching me through the binoculars as he does.

I'm sure one lifeguard each from Towers Six and Four will be right behind me in the water, but I can't wait for them. I keep my eyes on the dad screaming for help and frantically diving over and under the waves. I can see him coughing each time he surfaces, no doubt choking on sea-water in his panic.

The kid isn't back up. I start swimming as soon as I'm deep enough—it's much faster than wading through the water. Best-case scenario, this is going to become a two-person res-cue. I don't want to think about the worst case.

"Everyone to shore!" I hear Bentley bellow behind me through his megaphone. "Everyone out of the water! Now!" A second later, the other towers and the snack bar sound system begin repeating the message.

We need to clear the water, fast, especially if the kid is drifting. It'll be easier for the spotters on the beach to scan the water with everyone ashore, and the last thing we need is even more swimmers trying to be heroes and having to be rescued.

I make it to the dad as fast as I can and grab him before he can go under again, sliding my rescue float under his arms. "Stay here!" I yell, already knowing he's going to fight me on this. He moves to ignore me, but I pinch his arm, forcing him to meet my eyes. "If you want me to help your kid, stay put until the next lifeguard gets here. Otherwise, I'm gonna swim you out myself first, and that won't be good for your son. Understand? We don't have much time."

He nods, crying, and as disgusted as I am that he would bring a small child out this far, I can tell it was just a simple mistake. A bad judgment that I hope won't cost his son his life. Nobody deserves that when they're just trying to have a nice day on the beach.

Satisfied that he believes me and will stay on the float, I dive under the waves to scan underwater as best as I can without my goggles. There are no rocks in this area that the boy could snag on, which feels like a lucky break. As long as he didn't get pulled too far out, there's a chance he could pop back up. He's been under for so long, though, I know it's unlikely he'll be breathing when he does.

I surface and shake my head at Six, who's already tending to the dad. The dad lets out the type of wail I hope to never hear again, as a lifeguard from Tower Four, Maisy, comes up beside me.

"What do you think? He get pulled out? We've got guys from Eight and Nine paddling the boat out now."

"I don't know," I say, spinning slowly to look in all directions. "I would think the initial wave would have pushed him forward, but who knows, with the push and pull of the others. We can't wait for the boat."

"It's already been over two minutes," Maisy says, looking at her watch.

"I know. I know," I say, when I see a flash of red in the water. "Look! There!"

"Where?" Maisy asks, putting her hand up to shield her eyes from the glare of the sun, but I'm already swimming toward it. I can see even more as I get closer, the paleness of his skin in sharp contrast to the red of his little swim shoes and the bright green dinosaurs on his trunks. I dive down, rushing to his side.

"Got him," I yell, waving my arm up as soon as we surface. I start rescue swimming with him back to shore. *He's not breathing. Damn, he's not breathing.* I swim as hard as I can.

If Maisy already clocked two minutes, that means, at most, I have two minutes more to get air into him before we risk serious brain damage.

I want to scream. This isn't fair. *It isn't fair!* And finally, I'm close to the shore, and Bentley is there lifting the kid out of my arms and starting CPR in the cold, hard sand on the edge of the water. Six's partner grabs my elbow to steady me as I take the last few shaky steps onto land.

"The EMTs are only a minute out. You did good, Cass," the other lifeguard says, patting me on the back before heading over to help count compressions for Bentley.

I just stand there, watching, completely numb. *Did I do good? Did I do enough? Should I have called them back to shore sooner, even if they could still touch? Should I have waited to see where the waves took him before charging off into the water? Is this somehow all my fault?* Maybe I am an ogre. Or worse.

"Hey," I hear, as someone wraps a towel around me. "You're shaking."

I look up to see Birdie standing there, her big brown eyes looking into mine with such concern I could cry.

"Here, come sit," she says, trying to pull me away, but I shake my head.

"I have to help."

"You did help," she says, and then I hear it. The best sound I've ever heard.

Coughing.

The kid is coughing.

Bentley rushes to tip him on his side as seawater pours out of his mouth and nose, and he starts to cry.

"I'm here, Carden! I'm here!" the dad cries, flinging himself toward the child.

Six holds him back with a curt "Give them room to work" as Bentley continues his rhythmic slapping of the kid's back to help him clear the rest of the water.

The sight of the EMTs running toward us has me so relieved my legs almost give out, but Birdie's there, catching me, walking me over to a beach chair someone has dragged over for me to sit in.

I plop down, crouching over and taking big heaving breaths between my knees as Birdie kneels in the sand in front of me, rubbing soothing circles into the back of my neck.

I turn my head to look over at her, to tell her that she shouldn't be nice to me, that this is all my fault, that I was thinking of her right before it happened, that she's too much of a distraction . . . and then she smiles at me.

"You saved his life," she says, tucking some hair back behind my ear and wiping away my tears. "You're incredible." She leans closer, resting her forehead against my shoulder in an awkward hug.

"Birdie?" I whisper her name softly, hoping she can hear my questions. There are so many. I want to ask her a million things right now, like why is she being so nice to me when I've been such a dick? And doesn't she know that if I was better, faster, stronger, maybe the boy wouldn't have stopped breathing in the first place?

"Shh," she says, like she can somehow hear my thoughts. "Don't ruin it."

I lean into her, grateful for her warm, solid body and the hug I so desperately need.

And I won't ruin it. I won't.

11

Birdie

DAD AND I are sitting on the third floor of The Landing, an upscale restaurant owned by one of my dad's oldest business associates, Pedro Casada. The two of them have invested in the flipping, or Airbnb-ification, of dozens of buildings here—both commercial and residential. But this place? This place is all Pedro.

Dad calls it Pedro's "baby," and in a childless, never-been-married, confirmed-bachelor kind of way, I believe it.

Pedro designed it with the usual upscale nautical vibe you find around here—rich woods, gleaming cutlery, lots of navy and white, the whole thing. That part's typical. The clever part is the design. The restaurant itself boasts a unique floor plan, situated in a way to accommodate nearly every type of guest that might stroll down the street during peak tourist season. The first floor is for casual dining, the second floor is for more formal dining—jacket required and all that, but you can still order off the menu—and the third floor is a world all its own. It has its own tasting menu and requires full black-tie dress . . . unless you're my father or one of his guests.

I did put a dress on for the occasion; I'm not an animal. But instead of an uncomfortable evening gown, I went with a Stella McCartney summer collection number that makes me look like I just stepped off one of the yachts docked outside. Dad, however, is in khakis and one of his casual sport coats.

We'd probably both be better suited a floor down, if the strange looks we're getting from the other patrons are any indication, but I don't care. I love this table, "Dad's table" as I've come to think of it, even though it's been a very long time since we both sat at it.

It's a gorgeous, long mahogany affair, in the most ideal spot to overlook the ocean. Tonight, Pedro has even dropped the glass walls. A gentle breeze flutters through my hair, as if the dozen sailboats dotting the waterline have sent it my way personally. It's the epitome of "the best seat in the house."

The faint smell of fresh fish and salt wafts through the air—you'd think I'd be sick of it after working at the beach all day, but I'm anything but. I don't know how you could be. I breathe deeply, soaking it in. I wish I'd never stopped coming here to visit. Why did I, again?

"Your mother called. She says you aren't answering her texts," my dad says, reaching for his gin and tonic. "She was afraid I had taken away your phone completely."

Oh, right. That's why. Mom.

"Sorry," I say, but before I can elaborate that I just needed a little break from her, a little break from *my old self* really, Pedro appears at the top of the stairs.

He's carrying out an order of calamari himself. This is one of Dad's and my favorite foods and something that's definitely not on the tasting menu. (Believe me, it was the first thing I checked.) I'm delighted by the surprise.

Pedro sets the plate down and winks when he looks at me. "You still love the calamari?" he asks, his accent still thick despite the fact he moved to New England not long after I was born. I'm about to reply, but he's already turned toward my father with a grin. "She's getting so big! You must love having her all to yourself for the summer, Georgie."

My dad smiles, clearly sharing the sentiment. "It's a wonder to have her here," he says. "I wish it didn't cost me one hundred and fifty-eight thousand dollars to do it, though, but I'll take what I can get."

I slump in my seat, but Pedro flashes me a conspiratorial look. "What's a little car accident between friends, no?" he asks. "It's not like Georgie doesn't have the money."

Before I can reply, or address the frown on my father's face, Pedro deftly moves the conversation on to a piece of property he has his eye on—some bodega with an apartment on top—which instantly lights up my father's face like it's the best news he's heard all day. I zone out a little, wondering if maybe it is. It occurs to me now that I have no idea what he does all day besides hanging out with Cass's dad. If that's even what he does.

I check my phone quickly while they talk, hoping for a text from Cass. Her dad came and picked her up after the ambulance left and things had settled down. I told her to text me to let me know she got home safe, but I guess she decided not to. I tried not to let it get to me—she's probably fine, right?—but I still sent a just checking that you're okay text on my way over here anyway. She hasn't responded yet, but hopefully she will.

Pedro squeezes my shoulder as he leaves, no doubt heading off to schmooze someone else, and I glance up at my father, who is tapping away at his phone—most likely already trying to look into the property Pedro mentioned.

"How was work?" I ask, trying to get my mind off Cass.

"Frustrating," he says. "That's why I wanted to come here. Thought it might be nice to relax a little, and you've hardly been out since you got here. Although I guess you *are* still working off quite the tab."

"You must really be overestimating what they pay me at the parking lot if you think I can afford to pay off a McLaren . . . unless you're willing to release the trust, now that I've proven what a responsible, trustworthy young woman I am," I tease.

Dad waves me off. "It was a joke, Birdie," he says, not unkindly. "A poor one I should probably stop making since you *are* rising to the occasion. Credit where credit is due." He shakes his head, chuckling to himself. "Did it really have to be a brand-new McLaren, though?"

"You know why it happened, right?" I ask as he places some calamari on a small plate and passes it to me. We never really talked about it, and it occurs to me for the first time he might not have the full story.

"I do." He frowns. "Just because I don't like filming and

haven't been in the Boston house much these last few years, it doesn't mean I don't keep up with you."

"Then you know I wasn't just being flighty or not paying attention?"

He tips his head toward me. "I think a case could be made that streaming while driving is pretty flighty, don't you? That was dangerous, Birdie, and extremely irresponsible. You could have killed someone."

"I get it. Believe me, I learned my lesson. I won't *ever* do that again, but . . . you do know what happened with Mitchell at the party, don't you? You never brought it up, so—"

"Yes," he says, patting my hand. "Although your mother did an impeccable job of editing around things to make you look whimsical and him look like he wasn't, in fact, hoping to fuck a cater waiter in my walk-in pantry." Dad's other hand tightens on his napkin, a blink-and-you'll-miss-it motion that betrays his calm exterior. Is Dad . . . mad?

I don't think I've ever seen him mad in his life. He always comes off relaxed and confident. He's firm but never emotional, the exact opposite of the hurricane of demands and feelings that is my mom.

Maybe he's different out here, though. Maybe he lets himself off the leash, just a little. I've heard him laugh on the phone with Cass's dad more than I think I ever have in Boston. Come to think of it, he's bigger here. Takes up more space than he does in the Boston house, where he's too busy avoiding my mother to have a real presence.

"Enough about that unpleasantness. How was *your* day at

work today, Birdie?" he asks. "Cass isn't being too hard on you, is she?"

"Cass was incredible today," I say, before I can catch myself. I instantly feel my ears heat, and no doubt a flush is creeping up my neck.

"Incredible?" he asks, arching an eyebrow. "That's quite a one-eighty, though I'm glad to hear it. She's good people, and I think one day she'll be an asset to the company."

The familiar pang of jealousy ripples through me—I want him to see *me* as an asset too—but it fades just as quickly when I remember the weight of her body as it trembled against mine this afternoon, and the coolness of her wet, sand-dappled skin. I hope she's warmed up now. I hope Bentley is off shift and keeping her company.

"Birdie?" Dad says, probably waiting for me to say something.

"She saved a kid today, Dad. It was—"

"She what? Is she okay?" He cuts me off, already pulling out his phone. "John said he had to take off early for an emergency, but he didn't say *that*. I'm going to text him."

"Yeah, she's good, Dad. I was there. I . . . took care of her after." I can't even feel jealous over his concern for her; I'm just happy to know that she has people who worry. People who will care about her, even after I leave.

He sets his phone down on the table, glancing at it again before looking back to me. "What happened?"

I take a deep breath and tell him the whole story of the rescue: how I noticed her running out to the water while I was at the snack bar, the way she handled things, the way the rest of the team helped. I mention that I got her a towel, but I definitely leave out that once I wrapped her in it, I didn't take my arms away, and that I wish I was with her still.

Dad listens with rapt attention to my whole story, grinning when I finish. "Man, that girl has an iron will and a heart of gold, doesn't she?"

I nod, but a part of me can't help but wonder if he ever talks about me like that. *Doubtful.* But then again, I don't know that I've ever given him reason to. I expect that realization to stir up the all-too-familiar "I'm not good enough" feelings that I'm so used to back home, but for some reason, it doesn't. I'm just . . . proud of her. Sure, Cass has set the bar pretty high as far as fake daughters go, but maybe there are worse people to be compared to.

Dad's phone buzzes on the table, and he picks it up, frowning as he reads the text.

"Everything okay?" I ask.

"It's your mother again. You really should call her tonight."

I groan, but he pushes more calamari toward me.

"After dinner, of course." He smiles, a little peace offering.

"After dinner," I say, content to soak up a little more time with my dad. Who knows, maybe by the time I have to leave, I'll have given him things to be proud of too.

~~~

I don't know what I expected my first call with my mom since she sent me away to be like, but I definitely didn't expect her to open with "I need you back here."

"What? Why?" I ask, dropping down on my bed, not even caring that I'm probably going to wrinkle my dress.

"It was clearly a mistake to send you there, darling," Mom says, doing her best to sound motherly and apologetic, even though neither of those things are her strong suit. "Madelyn Whitmore called me the other day. Do you know what she said?" My mother doesn't wait for me to answer, even though I could probably guess. "She said that George has you working as some kind of parking lot girl!" She sounds disgusted when she says it, which shouldn't make my skin prickle—I mean, I felt the same way just a few days ago—but it does.

"Mom, it's fine. I'm used to it now. I'm getting pretty good at it."

She sighs. "Getting pretty good at being a parking lot girl? Birdie, come on."

"It's fine, Mom, really. If it's what I need to do to prove to you and Dad that I'm responsible enough for the trust, I don't mind. It's kind of fun, if I'm being honest. I like the people I work with," I say, carefully sidestepping the fact that I seem to like one person in particular a little bit more than I probably should.

"I understand how manual labor can be good for the soul," my mom says. I can practically hear her pinching her nose from here. "That's why I went along with your father's little plan at first. Although, you have more suitable talents than working at a parking lot, and frankly, your father should never have allowed you to do that. He shouldn't be holding that trust over your head either. If the terms didn't specify that your father alone could dictate its disbursement, you know I would have given it to you."

"I know, Mom," I say. "But it's okay. Seriously. Everyone's great here. You don't need to worry."

"People are talking, Birdie. The Whitmores are talking." Ah yes, there it is: the truth of the situation. Mom doesn't really care if I hate the lot attendant job or not; she just cares that the Whitmores—one of the oldest, richest families back home—witnessed her daughter doing something she feels is beneath me.

"Let them talk," I say, even though the shame is already rising up in the pit of my belly. I never felt like I fit in with the young and rich crowd I ran around with back home. Besides Ada, I don't know if anybody there really has my back. They're probably all laughing at me. They're probably all—

"Birdie!" Mom says, interrupting my thoughts. "You have to remember that these are the people you will be dealing with for the rest of your life. Do you want them looking down their noses at you because you spent the summer roughing it with the locals?"

This is quite possibly the worst pep talk I've ever had, and that's saying something. I start spiraling all over again until I catch her last sentence.

"You remember that you're not one of those people, right?"

"What people?" I ask.

"People like your dad's handyman or his little daughter, trying to ride your father's coattails. They are not like us, no matter how much your father tries to pretend they are."

"She's not like that. She would never ride anyone's coat-tails," I say, bristling. "And John Adler's not Dad's 'handyman'; they're practically partners and definitely friends."

"Partners," my mom scoffs. "If you really believe any of that, Birdie, you're even more naïve than I thought."

"What does that mean?"

"It means, yes, your father entertains the girl. He's taken her on as some kind of charity project because he feels sorry for her. He pities her out of some sense of guilt over being born rich. I swear he thinks if he can keep her out of that poverty mindset she was born into, it will absolve him of all of his sins or something. As for the rest of the Adlers, keep your friends close and your enemies closer."

"What does *that* mean?"

"You're aware John Adler has actively campaigned to change the housing regulations in Newport, correct? The same housing regulations that currently benefit your father, and us, immensely?"

"Sure. Cass told me about it. The Affordable Housing Coalition thing, right? It sounds good for the area. She was telling me how some of her friends have even had to move—"

"She's brainwashed you!" my mom yelps. "That's it. You're coming home."

"I'm not brainwashed, Mom," I say. There's no reasoning with her once she gets too worked up. "I promise, I'm fine, and Dad is too. He seems to believe in the stuff that the Adlers are doing." I feel a tinge of warmth at the idea that at least one of my parents has good intentions. "They try to work together on things."

"No, the only reason your father pretends to go along with John's bullshit is because it makes him keep giving up information on what he's up to. That way, Dad and his legal team can stay a step ahead while searching for loopholes. That's it."

"That's disgusting. It's not true," I say, scrunching up my face. "Dad's not like that! He's not like—" I catch myself before I can finish that sentence. *You. He's not like you,* I think. She's projecting. She has to be.

"Ask him," she says. Her assistant calls to her in the background, happily announcing she needs to move on to the next thing. Apparently "talk to my daughter" was just another item to cross off the list.

"Bye, Mom," I say, barely waiting for her to reply in kind before I hit end on the call.

Part of me is tempted to go downstairs, where I know Dad's sitting in his office, and ask him if Mom was telling the truth. Another part of me doesn't really want to know.

It was nice being here this past week, pretending I had a normal family and a regular life and that nothing that happened back home really mattered anyway.

I'm not eager for that particular bubble to burst, especially not now.

My phone buzzes in my hand, and I look down reluctantly, worried that it's my mom again—one last thing to ruin my night for good—but it's not. It's Cass, finally replying. I flick open the message, my mood ticking up a few notches at the words on my screen.

Cass: Hey, sorry. I fell asleep when
I got home. Probably the adrenaline
crash. Thanks for checking up on me
though and . . . Just thanks, Birdie.

I smile down at my phone, the maggots turned butterflies flapping wildly again.

Me: Anytime. You were incredible today.

Take care of yourself tonight. I'm
here if you need anything.

She sends me a thumbs-up reaction, but it's enough. It's a start.

12

Cass

YOU WERE INCREDIBLE . . . *I'm here if you need anything.*

Birdie's texts from last night keep rattling around my skull, sending my head spinning in a thousand not altogether unpleasant directions—like what it would be like for her to hold me again. Or if we talked, really talked. Or if maybe next time we were both in my car, I leaned across and kissed her. Or if— I take a deep breath. I need to focus.

It's Saturday, my day off, which means I'm helping out at the Affordable Housing Coalition with my parents. I love everything about this place—the smell of warm ink as people print and photocopy flyers and petition sheets, the low hum of multiple conversations happening at once, the fact that someone has always made cookies or brownies or something else to share and left it on the back counter for us to nibble while we do good, important work. Important work like what I'm doing now, which is taking everyone's coffee orders and not at all desperately trying to avoid thinking about Birdie and her particular brand of complications. Or the fact that falling for a summer girl would potentially be the worst thing to ever happen to me, even if this particular summer girl *is* starting to feel different from all the rest.

Focus, Cass.

I glance around the bustling office, taking it all in. The fact that we set up shop in an abandoned storefront, one that we rent out for a steal from a landlord who was facing foreclosure before we came along, is pretty cool, if you ask me. Even if it does still have big tubs lining the wall from its old pet groomer days—which my mom covered with nice wood slabs in an attempt to make them look a little more like standing desks.

Most of the interns have set up shop over in the "standing desk" area, leaving the actual desktops to the volunteers, while the board spends its time huddled around a large round table discussing strategy and next moves. The table was Dad's idea, once he expanded the organization from a one-man show to hosting a full board. Mom and I may have called him King Arthur for a while after it was delivered, but even I have to admit, it's worked out better than we could have imagined.

The interns come from all over—my dad has built a pretty great reputation and gotten some media attention, especially once he started helping other tourist traps set up organizations of their own—but most of the volunteers are local. I even roped Bentley into helping here in his downtime. It somehow still kind of feels like a family affair, even though it's grown to include so many more people.

The best part of having so many people involved is that my parents don't have to be here every waking second anymore. I don't miss those long hours they used to put in getting it off the ground, but it's kind of amazing how far they've brought it, and how much "sweat equity," as my dad calls it, my family has put into this organization.

It started off small, truly a grassroots campaign. We collected signatures from residents, talked to the town board and planners, and even held town hall–style meetings to get everyone's input on what was needed the most. In the beginning, we did lots of fundraising, trying to help people pay off tax liens or catch up on rent, but it wasn't long before Dad started approaching local politicians to make changes on a larger scale.

He worked with such passion and fervor back then, it was like he was possessed. Once, I asked my mom if she thought he was working so hard out of some sense of obligation, like he had to spend all night making up for being part of Mr. Gordon's evil empire all day, but she just told me to hush.

I still think that had something to do with it, but I had no choice but to file it under Adult Things My Mom Doesn't Want to Talk About.

She's always been big on keeping me as sheltered as possible—"Let kids be kids" is a motto she lives by. It's why I didn't always realize when money was so tight, or at least I acted like I didn't. I would pretend not to see her stressed out and taking extra shifts at work, pretend none of it bothered me. Because the one time I didn't—a night Mom spent crying over an unexpected hospital bill from me breaking my elbow and I brought out my old piggy bank and all the money I had saved from birthdays—it just made her feel a hundred times worse.

She wanted to protect me, always, and I had to let her. Which meant I was afraid that if I even asked for poster board from the dollar store for a school project, I would somehow upset the apple cart and send our finances cascading down like a house of cards. I had no idea how tight things were or weren't at any given moment.

Honestly, it almost would have been better if they had just been upfront with me about what was going on. It was probably less precarious than I thought at times, especially as Dad moved up the ranks with George, going from essentially a caretaker to call as needed to his right-hand man.

That's why my feelings about the Gordons are so damn complicated.

George saved our family—no two ways about it, he did. And he doesn't hold it over our heads or take advantage of my dad or act like we owe him. He's kind, much kinder than most of the summer people are, but still . . . he's not one of us, and some of his decisions have really messed up the community. He's priced people out of their own neighborhoods, and yes, I get on some level that if it wasn't him, it would just be someone else. But it wasn't someone else; it was my dad's best friend.

Dad has invited him here, more than once, to see the impact firsthand. George never took him up on it, though. Sure, he nods politely whenever me and Dad discuss it with him, but then he usually steps away to make a phone call or reply to an email.

I think it makes him uncomfortable, even though it shouldn't.

If he got on board, like, fully on board instead of just sort of looking the other way, we could collectively make a serious difference around here. People would listen to him; people *do* listen to him! His economic privilege and connections give him a degree of power that we could only dream of . . . But instead, he just kind of doesn't get in our way, even though he knows on some level that we're trying to get in his.

I thought starting this organization would be a nail in the coffin of their friendship, and maybe even their working relationship, but it wasn't. George still comes over for dinner about once a week, still laughs and shares beers with my dad on the back porch, looking just as comfortable as he does inside his giant McMansion on the coast.

It almost feels like George is two people sometimes. I don't know how he lives like that. I wonder if Birdie lives like that too. God knows the girl I see in her old streams and the girl who held me on the beach yesterday don't seem anything alike.

It all feels like one of those horribly complicated situations the "adults" have been trying to shield me from for way too long.

Like Birdie herself, who by the way absolutely should not be standing on the other side of the door when I pull it open to go get coffee for the board as they prepare for a meeting with the mayor in a few days.

I stand there, stunned at the sight of her, mesmerized by the way the sun is hitting her just right, dragging out a hint of red in her hair and turning her irises into deep chocolate pools. I blink hard, ignoring the way the air suddenly feels different, more charged around us.

I'm embarrassed, standing here in front of her now, after everything that happened yesterday. Like vulnerability is a weakness I should have never let her see.

"What are you doing here?" My voice comes out a little sharper than I mean it to, not because I'm not happy to see her, but because . . . well, it's complicated.

She steps back a little bit, my tone probably catching her off guard. I want to apologize to her, but also I *do* want to know what she's doing here, and I have coffee to get, and if I don't leave soon, the board is going to get gently annoyed about it.

"Sorry, that was rude. You just surprised me," I say, hoping that makes up for things.

"Good surprise or bad?" she asks.

"I guess that depends on why you're here," I say, not wanting to admit the truth, which is that lately she's been the good kind and I don't know what to do with that. "I was volunteered to get coffee for the board, and if I don't hurry up, they might get cranky. Walk with me?"

"Okay," she says, smiling, and I look away, biting the side of my lip. A simple smile should not make me feel as giddy as hers does.

"How did you get down here anyway?" I ask, trying to ground myself. "Is your dad letting you drive again?"

"No, I took his electric scooter. Mortifying."

"It's an eight-hundred-dollar scooter, Birdie. I doubt it's that mortifying," I tease.

"And I drive a Maybach at home, so yes, it is." She snorts, and suddenly I remember exactly why this is so complicated. Birdie's laugh makes my stomach twist in a good way, a great way, even, but the way she casually talks about the things she has—well, *had*, I guess, since her dad took her car away . . . It's like she's from another planet and doesn't even realize it.

The coffee shop is barely two blocks away, and we make it all the way there—and even get my order in—before my tolerance for idle chitchat runs out and I have to ask, "Are you going to explain why you're here?"

"Well, for one, I wanted to check up on you in person. Yesterday was a lot."

"Thanks," I say awkwardly, not sure what to do with this sudden rush of feelings I'm having for the girl I thought I hated. "I . . . appreciate that. I'm surprisingly okay, I guess. I talked to my parents a lot last night, and then Bentley slept over. The boy's mom called this morning to thank us, and Vince let us know. I guess he's going to be fine."

"Because of you." Birdie beams at me, bumping her shoulder into mine. "I'm glad you're okay."

I smile at her. This is *nice*. Unexpected, but *nice*. "Well, now that you've got proof of life, what else are you up to today?"

"That's the second reason I came down. I want to help," she says, like it's the most logical thing in the world, like it should be obvious. Of course she would complain about not having her Maybach one second and then be volunteering for the Affordable Housing Coalition the next.

"What do you mean by *help*?" I ask, suddenly feeling a little protective of our organization, a little confused. Her designer

shirt alone probably cost as much as some of the relief applications we've gotten in this week, and she doesn't even know
it. She might not even care if she did . . . No, I'm being unfair.
Or maybe I'm not. It's so hard to think when the sun is shining on her through the windows the way it is—lighting her
up like the universe wants to make sure I don't miss a thing.
Message received.

"I don't know. I figured you guys needed someone like me,"
she says, her words tugging me back into the moment.

Someone like her? What does that mean? The less generous
side of me wonders if this is more of the inadvertently classist
crap she doesn't always catch herself saying. Like when her
dad starts making himself out to be the savior who keeps this
town running instead of the interloper ruining it.

"Cass?" the barista calls from behind the counter. She must
be new; I don't recognize her.

"Right here," I say, grateful for the interruption.

There are eight coffees waiting for me on two trays. I go to
take them both, but Birdie grabs one, grinning at me like she's
really doing something, like I didn't have it handled already.

"Ready to head back?" she asks.

"I can take it," I say, reaching for the other one, but she
shakes her head.

"I got it. Relax, I won't spill," she says, like that's what I'm
worried about. The smile has slipped off her face, like maybe
I don't trust her not to screw this up, but it's not that. It's not.
It's just now I'm spiraling and . . .

Like I said, it's complicated.

"Okay." I sigh, heading out the door.

"Are you . . . annoyed with me all of a sudden?" Birdie asks, and I don't know what to say. Yes, no, a little?

"I just don't know what you're doing," I say, walking a little faster.

"I told you in the car that day that it sounds like you have something really cool going on here. I just want to help out. Is that a problem?"

"How could you help out?" I blurt. I don't mean to be so blunt, but I can't stop myself. I can't help but try to find her angle here, because there must be one. Even her father doesn't come here, and he has way more reason to.

"I can carry coffee." She snorts. "Same as you. Plus, I know about branding and influencing and stuff. Your website looks like it's from the early 2000s. I know people who could fix that up for you, dirt cheap. I might even be able to do it myself. Maybe I could make some videos or—"

"Is that what this is about?" I ask, my hackles rising.

"What?"

"I know you're not allowed to live stream anything right now, but this would be a loophole, right? Because you'd be helping us poor people to do it?"

"No, that's not— What are you *talking* about, Cass?"

But now that I've let loose, I can't seem to stop, all my worst fears about her coming out, even though my brain is screaming at me to stop, to shut up, to swallow the venom instead of spit it. "Not to mention all the goodwill you would regain from your followers who currently think you're just a selfish, spoiled—"

"What the fuck, Cass?! Is that honestly what you think of

me? You honestly think I'm just looking for an excuse to get online again?"

And I hate that I'm doing this. I hate the way her eyes start to water, knowing it's all my fault. I try to tell myself it's better this way. It's better we're not friends. It's better I don't spend another second wondering what it would be like to kiss those perfect, pouty lips, because then . . . then we don't have to break each other's hearts the way I know she'll gladly break mine if I give her the chance.

"You don't get it, Birdie," I say. "Not really. You were just talking about how embarrassing it is to have to ride a scooter that's as *expensive as some people's rent.*"

"There's no rent that cheap around here." She laughs. Part of me knows she's probably just trying to defuse the tension, but also, that's the exact wrong thing to say.

"Yeah, exactly, because of people like you!" I'm being unfair. I'm being awful, but there's no backing down now. If I let her keep texting me, if I let her hug me again or touch my hand or—

"People like me?" she says, coming to a stop just in front of the Coalition door. "What do you mean, people like me?"

"Like your dad. I mean, he's the reason for all of this, you know. Him and people like him, people like *you*. You want to come here on vacation—or as 'punishment' in your case, because, god, going to your beach mansion is only torture for the truly clueless elite—"

"Where is this coming from?" she asks, her chin wobbling as I look away. "I thought . . . I thought we were becoming friends after . . . everything. After yesterday."

149

"I was hired to babysit you, summer girl," I say, because it's easier than saying the truth, which is that it scares me how much I like her, even though I know she's going to run right back to her old life the first chance she gets. She can't leave me if I chase her away first.

I refuse to be the lovesick local that she will eventually pretend not to know. I've seen it happen too many times, to too many people. Us both being in Boston this fall—her back to her glamorous life with her rich bitch friends, and me, the scholarship kid desperate to fit in at a new college—makes it even more likely to happen sooner rather than later.

I have to respect rule number one. We both do.

Why doesn't she see that I'm just trying to save us both the heartache?

"You're really not even going to give me a chance? We can't be friends because of some preconceived notions you have about me?" she asks, shoving the other coffee tray into my hand and almost making me spill them both in the process. "News flash, Cass, you're no different from all those rich assholes you claim to hate."

I look at her, trying to hide my real feelings behind a glare and failing miserably. I can feel the heat stinging my own eyes too now, the tears that are threatening to fall.

"You're just as close-minded and ignorant as anyone else," she says. "You talk about me supposedly looking down on 'townies,' but it's you looking down your nose at me, like both our lives weren't just the luck of the draw.

"You act like I'm a user with an ulterior motive, but you don't seem to have any problem using my allegedly horrible father for a recommendation letter or an internship or those envelopes full of cash he leaves you every week. Maybe you need to take a good long look in the mirror before you start judging me."

"Birdie," I say as she grabs her helmet and unhooks her scooter from the rack.

She glares at me. "You know, my friend Ada told me to raise the bar. I can't believe I thought I actually had."

Her words hit me like arrows, and I want to run away, desperate to go lick my wounds in private. Except I run into my father instead. He pulls the coffee trays from my hands just in time, and I grab the door before it smacks into us both. I turn my head, watching Birdie leave, cursing myself for still somehow finding it cute the way she's angrily scootering away. There is something seriously wrong with me.

"I heard shouting," Dad says, sounding concerned. "What was that all about?"

"Birdie showed up and wanted to help." I shrug, trying to play it off like I'm not just as upset as she seems to be right now. Like I didn't just hurt my own feelings as much as I hurt hers.

"So you yelled at her until she left? Great strategy, Cass. I can see why your petition numbers are so high with that bedside manner."

"She just . . . I can't have her here," I say, like that makes any sense.

"Why?"

"Because she's . . . she's everywhere. All the time! Just always there!"

"I see," he says, fighting a smirk. "And that's very bad, right?"

"I'm getting paid to supervise her, not be her friend."

"Right, right," Dad says, "and that's why you smiled so big last night when she made your phone ping?"

I shake my head. "I can't, Dad. I have to have boundaries with her, even if I wish I didn't. This is better—this has to be better. Can we just drop it?" I ask, walking away from him.

He sets the coffees down on the table, leading to a chorus of "Thanks, Cass" from the board—who all have their faces buried in the papers in front of them—and then follows me over to the photocopy machine. I aggressively press buttons to make more petition signature sheets. If he wants to see good numbers, I'll show him good numbers. I'll have these all filled up in no time.

"Cassie," he says gently, using his nickname for me from when I was little, as he settles his hand over mine to get me to stop jabbing at the machine. "Why don't you take a break?"

"I don't need a break. I need to work! Most importantly, I need to not be distracted by stupid rich girls and their stupid rich-girl problems acting like they care when they don't."

My dad pinches his lips together, and I know that look. He's disappointed. I've disappointed him, again, which I hate doing more than anything. I look away, feeling entirely too close to the verge of tears.

"Sorry, I'm just venting," I say, hoping we can sidestep the issue entirely.

"Take the afternoon off. Go surf or something. Blow off

some steam. We'll still be here fighting the good fight next weekend, Cass."

"Fine," I say, knowing this isn't a winnable argument. When he decides someone needs time off, he'll make sure they get it.

"But, Cass," he says, and I hesitate to turn around, but do anyway. "I think you might owe her an apology."

"Noted," I say, giving him a little wave before heading out the door and walking to my car. Because he doesn't know the half of it.

13

Birdie

I'M HUDDLED IN the lifeguard chair under a scratchy blanket that someone left draped over one of the picnic tables behind me. It's gross and sandy, but the air whipping off the inky black water of the ocean is a little less breeze and a little more wind underneath this moonlit sky tonight, and I'm still in my shorts and tank top from earlier. Desperate times and all.

I might be sad and upset right now, but I'm not about to freeze to death on top of it.

Honestly, I don't know why I came here. I didn't mean to. I didn't mean to go anywhere really, after my fight with Cass. I just . . . did. Dad had already told me that morning that he had to go back to Boston for a little while for some business meetings with a new investor, and I didn't want to go sit home alone and mope. I certainly wasn't going to call Carly to see if she was still out here, even though I was sure she would invite me over, if only for gossip.

The only other place that remotely felt like home was here at the beach, but still I avoided it until the battery was nearly dead on my scooter. I don't know. I just wanted to keep moving, I guess, and probably a part of me wanted to wait for everything to close down for the evening. Even the parking lot is blocked off this time of night.

The beach seems lonely and desolate, just a few stray people sneaking in here and there, like me, enjoying the moonlight reflecting off the ocean. I tuck myself deeper into the blanket, trying not to feel pathetic that I picked Tower Five to sit in. My skin crawls with the memory of how Cass looked at me today, how she talked to me.

I thought we were getting closer. I thought something had changed between us. I felt like I was finally seeing her, and I hoped she was finally seeing me. Everything she said today proves that's not true, though. I'll never be anything but a summer girl to her, the lowest of the low in her eyes.

It was my dad's idea for me to come here, even if he doesn't know it. He could tell I was upset after my phone call with Mom last night. He asked if I wanted to go watch the waves together for a bit before bed. He said watching them at night always makes him feel better when things are hard or sad. I declined, too afraid I wouldn't be able to hold back from asking him about what Mom said about him and Mr. Adler and would ruin both our nights. Maybe it doesn't even really matter—their friendship seems to work for them, so what business is it of mine? Or maybe the truth is I don't want to know. I guess I just thought, if they could make their friendship work, then maybe Cass and I could too. I didn't realize that how much she hates tourists would outweigh how much she might like me.

I lean back against the seat, watching the waves and trying to imagine what my dad sees when he's sitting on the beach. I can see for miles up here, which I guess is kind of the point, but right now, it's just suffocating darkness. I stand up, walking straight to the edge of the chair, the way I've seen Cass do a dozen times before. My stomach does a little swoop, and I tell myself it's from the height and not from the thrill of standing somewhere she always stands without anybody knowing about it.

It's stupid really, me thinking I could understand her better by sitting up here. I shouldn't even want to, not after how she treated me today. But . . . I don't know. I can't help it.

"Scanning the water's supposed to be my job."

I jump back, startled, and trip back against the seat. Cass scrambles up the ladder, quickly checking me over—ready to save lives even on her day off. I pull away, even though I don't want to, even though I wish she would keep letting the warmth of her skin seep into my bones whether she hates me or not. This is so embarrassing.

"What are you doing here?" I ask, wedging myself into the corner to create as much space between us as I can. She hurt my feelings today, badly, and I know she doesn't deserve my forgiveness, even if I want to give it. (I do want to give it, unfortunately.)

"I saw your scooter and wanted to see what you were doing."

She's lying. I stashed my scooter in front of the snack bar. There's no way she saw it while driving by, and it's not like she could even get her car in the lot after hours. "You saw my scooter? You're going to have to come up with a better lie than that."

She sighs, clearly wrestling with herself over how honest she wants to be. "Your dad texted me your location. He checked on your phone and got worried that you hadn't come home. He asked me to check on you, so I did."

My stomach sinks. She's not even here of her own volition. She's just here as my *babysitter*. This is somehow even more mortifying than her yelling at me in front of the Coalition today.

"Yeah, guess you need to check up on the spoiled fuckup, right? God forbid she gets into any more trouble or sets any more of Daddy's money on fire." I stand up, fully intending to climb down the ladder and take off, but suddenly Cass's hand is back on my wrist, more tentatively this time, but just as warm.

"I was already looking for you, Birdie. He just pointed me in the right direction."

I turn to look at her, expecting it to be another lie, but she looks open and honest instead.

"Why?" I ask, poised on the edge of the ladder, still ready to climb down.

"I thought you would ignore me if I texted, so I wanted to find you and talk in person." She drops her hand and looks away. "I think I owe you an apology."

"You think?" I mutter, raising my eyebrows.

"Will you sit down with me?" she asks, meeting my eyes. When I don't move, she adds a quiet "Please?"

It's the please that does it, or maybe it's the way that desperately sad yet somehow hopeful look on her face sends a wave of warmth crashing over my body, like the water dancing across the sand below us.

Maybe the truth is that Cassandra Adler has always felt inevitable to me, from my very first crush on her as a little kid. Maybe I always knew she would find me here, and that's why I came.

I'm moving to sit down beside her before I even realize it.

"Here," she says, tugging off her hoodie and passing it to me. "You're cold." She gestures to the little goose bumps dotting my arms.

I suppress a shiver, not quite wanting to give her the satisfaction. Not yet. Not until I hear what she has to say. "If I take it, you'll be cold."

"Doesn't matter."

"I have a blanket," I say, tugging it over my legs.

She shrugs and sets the hoodie between us—a silent peace offering that's mine to leave or take. I leave it, for now, wishing I wasn't so stubborn but also knowing that she doesn't deserve for this to be easy, not after how she talked to me.

"I'm sorry," she says. "I was way out of line earlier. You just wanted to help and—"

"And you accused me of trying to find a loophole to stream and then berated me for being a summer girl."

"Not my proudest moment, yeah," she says, and then looks out to the ocean. I think she's done then, the world's worst apology. I don't know what I was expecting or why I got my hopes up that maybe her showing up here meant more than it clearly does . . . But then she sighs and quietly adds, "You terrify me, Birdie."

"I do?" I laugh. "I don't know. You don't seem all that scared with the way you treat me."

She frowns, still scanning the water while I watch her. The way the moonlight shines across her skin makes her look eerie and pale, like a ghost come to haunt me instead of a girl choking on an apology.

"It's fine," I say, after she doesn't say anything for a while. I know it's not very "raising the bar" of me, but Ada isn't here anyway.

"It isn't," she says, finally looking back at me. "I shouldn't have called you a summer girl. It was messed up."

"As far as insults go, I've been called worse, by much meaner people than you," I say, trying to lighten the mood, which has gone heavy and sour around us.

"I hope not," she says earnestly. "People shouldn't . . . You shouldn't let people treat you the way you do."

I shake my head. "Seriously, 'summer girl' is cute. I don't mind—"

"Summer girls are what we call the insipid pieces of trash that come in for peak season, ruin the island, mess with our hearts, and screw everything up for everyone."

"Well, that's . . . less cute," I say, nudging her, trying to get the pained expression off her face.

She was looking for me, and as terrible as she is at it, she's apologizing. That counts for something. That *raises the bar.* I reach forward and pick up her hoodie, leaving an empty space between us as I tug it over my head. I'm instantly enveloped in the smell of her—coconut sunblock, sporty deodorant, a hint of dryer sheets. It's so perfectly Cass, so sunny and bright, even in the cold darkness of her crude apology. I can't help but burrow inside, tucking my hands up over my nose to discreetly inhale, wanting her inside and out.

I glance at her just in time to see her shoulders drop, the tension bleeding out of her as I've accepted the olive branch, and it is one—I'm sure of it now.

"Thank you," I say.

"For what?" She sounds surprised.

"For looking for me? For apologizing. It matters."

"You matter," she says. "I feel like you forget that sometimes, the way you let people treat you. The way you let me treat you. You shouldn't forgive me this easily."

"Why not?"

"Because you deserve better. You deserve someone who doesn't panic and try to scare you off."

"That's why you were such an asshole to me today? You wanted to scare me off?"

"It's better if we keep hating each other, Birdie. It really is."

"I don't hate you."

She shakes her head. "You really should."

"No, I'm good on that," I say with a small smile.

Cass looks down at her hands, picking at her nails. "I can't . . . like you. I'm not supposed to like you. We're not the same. You should be out there, on the yachts and at the fancy parties, with someone who can—"

"Is that what this is really about, Cass? You think I deserve 'better'? You think we can't have feelings for each other, because what? Because my dad's rich and owns a fancy scooter?"

She looks away. "Not just that."

"Then what?"

"I'm not nice. I haven't been to you."

"If you really believe that, I have bad news for you. When you're not being a total asshole, you are literally the nicest person I've ever met. You spend your Saturdays volunteering. You save people for a job! You didn't give up on me when I gave you every reason to. You're weirdly obsessed with keeping me hydrated." She huffs out a breathy laugh, and I smile. "You're nice, Cass, but most importantly . . . you're enough. More than enough, and that has nothing to do with your bank account or what you mistakenly think I need or deserve."

She looks away, fighting a smirk as she shakes her head, and then turns back at me, her expression more serious than I've ever seen it. "I'm sorry about today. I'm ashamed of myself. You didn't deserve that. I was obnoxious and scared, and I just—"

"Why are you so scared of me?" I ask, pressing my knee against hers, warmth blossoming between us as we both stare down at the point where we meet.

"Because you were supposed to be a job. You were supposed to be horrible, and stuck-up, and all the things that I've built up in my head about you ever since you stopped coming here to play when we were kids. You're *supposed* to be a summer girl. I needed you to be a summer girl."

"Why?"

"Because I have a rule about them, and it would be so much easier if I followed it. It would be so much easier, Birdie. Why can't you just be easier? Why do you have to turn everything on its head all the time? Why is everything about you such a fucking surprise to me? Why can't you just be horrible?"

I would laugh at her compliments being thrown like insults if she didn't look so torn up right now. "I don't want to be horrible to you."

"I wish you would."

"Why?!" I groan, getting frustrated.

"Because then I wouldn't keep thinking about kissing you!" she yells, like it pains her to say it.

"You—"

"All the time, Birdie. All the time. You're all I've been thinking about lately! And I keep saying to myself, 'She's a true summer girl. You have a rule about summer girls. Don't let her get in your head.' We've seen them destroy so many of our friends. We've seen them act like it was love and then go back to their regular mansions in god knows where, only to come back the next year and treat my friends like they're the help. Like we're so far beneath you guys, and I . . . I can't do that. I can't! Because I know, *I know* that if I kiss you, I'm not going to want to stop."

"Cass—"

"Even if we *did* somehow make it work all the way till we're both in Boston, I'm going to be so busy with school and you're

162

going to be back to your big life where we don't fit together anymore, and it'll . . . it'll really fucking hurt when we fall apart, Birdie. It's better if we just hate—"

I rush forward, cutting her words off with a press of my lips, because she just said she wants to kiss me forever, and right now that sounds very perfect. None of that other stuff matters, none of it, not really, not when Cassandra Adler wants to kiss me and never stop.

Cass freezes at first, and I worry that I've done something wrong, but then she's there matching my energy. I part my lips and swallow her whimpers as her hand finds the bit of skin between my shirt and shorts. Her thumb is hot and rough from working, and it drags across my tender skin, sending shivers down my back.

She chases my tongue with her own, and I smile into her eagerness, because this? This! This is incredible! We could have been together this whole time if we weren't so caught up in our heads!

I pull back for air, smiling, and she looks at me with a heated gaze.

"You really shouldn't have done that," she says, her voice low.

"Yes, I should have." I laugh when she slides me closer, tucking me against her. I burrow into her neck even though I'm the taller one of us, soaking in the scent of her skin.

"What are we doing?" she asks, and I can practically hear the gears turning in her head as her panic kicks back up.

"We're watching the waves," I say, "and keeping warm."

"That's one way to put it, I guess." She sighs.

"Stop overthinking." I tap her forehead gently, shifting up to kiss the very same spot. "I like you, Cass, and judging by how you kissed me, you like me too. That's what matters. Forget your rules, and forget your preconceived notions of summer girls, and forget trying to figure out where I fit on that scale and what you think that means for the future. Just be here. With me. *See* me, see the real me."

"I do see you, Birdie," she says, so quietly I nearly miss it over the sound of crashing waves. "I promise I do."

14

Cass

I PICK UP Birdie for work the next day, worried that things will be awkward or strained, but they're not. They're perfect.

She's all blushing and sweetness, stolen glances as we drive, her pinkie linking with mine as we dangle our hands off the armrest, warm elbows pressed tightly against each other, skin to skin.

I really, really want to kiss her. In fact, it's all I can think about the entire drive, but I don't, not even when I drop her off and she hesitates just long enough to make me wonder if she's thinking the same thing I am. But even still, I'm not sure what this is, especially in the light of day.

And while the pinkie link is certainly reassuring, I'm still scared the bubble will burst as soon as we're around all our coworkers. A lot of things melt under this scorching sun; it's possible her feelings for me might as well.

I sit there for a second, getting my bearings before I get out of my car, and then sprint through the hot sand to my chair. Bentley is already waiting for me, even though I'm over fifteen minutes early. I climb up the tower, trying to play it cool.

It doesn't work.

"Why are you smiling like that?" he asks as I shimmy out of my shorts and stretch, enjoying the feel of the sunlight hitting my tight back muscles.

"Like what?" I ask, dropping onto the bench beside him and trying not to think about last night, when it was someone else here beside me. Someone much prettier, much softer.

He narrows his eyes. "Like you made out with somebody and are dying to tell me about it."

"I am not!"

"Interesting choice of words," he says, adjusting the umbrella and organizing his supplies for the day.

"How so?"

"Because you said 'I am not' as in 'not dying to tell me,' instead of 'no, I didn't' as in 'no, I didn't make out with anybody.'" He smirks in a "gotcha" sort of way that makes me roll my eyes.

"That proves nothing," I say, looking away with a pout that's fighting for its life to not turn into a full-on grin.

"Let me guess, she works here?"

I bite my lip and nod, feeling torn. On one hand, I might combust if I try to keep this inside much longer. On the other, there's that whole bubble conundrum, and I don't know if telling Bentley is going to burst it.

"It's probably not Court, is it?" he says, like he dreads my answer. "You wouldn't be so cagey about it if it was."

I shake my head, and he sighs, dropping his head all the way back. He stares up at the clouds for a minute before tipping his head toward me with a pained expression.

"The summer girl?"

"She has a name."

"She's terrible," he whines, shutting his eyes dramatically.

"She's really not," I say, flicking his hip to make him look at me. "Hey."

"Hey yourself." He pouts. "You're the one suddenly breaking all the rules!"

"Sometimes rules are meant to be broken?" I wince. "Maybe."

"I just don't want you to get hurt."

"I don't want to get hurt either," I say. "But she's . . . she's not like we thought."

"I hope you know what you're doing," he says, nudging my arm. "But I'm here for you either way. She *is* pretty cute."

"She definitely is." I smile.

"Did you actually make out with her?" My eyes flick to where he's sitting automatically, and he makes a horrified face. "Please tell me you did *not* defile our sacred lifeguarding station!" He mimes gagging, and I burst out laughing.

"You're just mad you didn't think of bringing someone here first." I pick up the binoculars when I hear the parking lot gate creak open, signaling the start of the workday. "I'll take first shift."

"Wait, wait, wait—do you mean to tell me I could have been making out with Six here this whole time?!" He tugs on his hair. "What a waste!"

"You're the one who got freaked out and kept your coffee date platonic! I told you to go for it," I say, and start scanning the beach. It will be at least a few minutes before any of the morning crowd makes their way out onto the sand, longer still till there are actually people in the water. "I was very clear I didn't think he even counted as a summer person, so that's on you."

He seems to consider this for a moment, and then raises his eyebrows. "You're only telling me because you're gonna bring her to the bonfire tonight, aren't you?"

"I'm definitely going to bring her to the bonfire tonight," I say, even though I haven't even asked her yet and am only hoping she will say yes.

"You're the worst," he says, stretching his arms up high over his head and running his hands through his hair. I don't miss the fact that he's perfectly timed this for when Six is jogging by with the first runners of the day.

Six waves, and I watch Bentley practically go heart-eyes in real life.

"You bringing Six, then?" I ask.

"Can it, Cassandra," he says with a smirk . . . but we both know that means yes.

～～～

Birdie's dad is still back home in Boston, and while he asked me to check in on her tonight, I'm not exactly sure if taking her to an illegal bonfire on the beach is exactly what he meant. It's possible. I mean, he wasn't specific. Besides, I didn't take the new envelope of cash he left on his desk for me anyway. It felt too weird to keep taking it, given that Birdie and I are . . . well, whatever we are.

Not that I'm in a rush to put a label on anything, or even want a label, or know what that label would be if it did ever exist. I'd be lying if I said that I didn't want to know if *she* wanted a label, though. If she does, she's being awfully tight-lipped about it.

Birdie seems uncharacteristically shy as we approach the party—it's only about a dozen people, most of them our coworkers she already knows, plus a few kids from town. Lana Del Rey is blaring from a big speaker somebody must have brought. Her music pairs perfectly with the crackle of the fire and the spray of the ocean waves as they lap at the sand, so it's only natural she makes several appearances on the official bonfire playlist we all made together at the start of the summer.

This is kind of a routine event around here. Townie kids have been taking back the beach at night since the dawn of time, doing their best to erase the daily footprints of the interlopers and their CoolCabanas that stain this sand all day, every day, this time of year. But this is probably the first time a townie has ever brought someone like Birdie here. I try not to act nervous about it, though; I can tell Birdie is nervous enough.

Ahead of us, a group of kids jumps into the waves. Laughter cuts through the thick night air as one of the boys tosses a girl over his shoulder—Betty Heiner, I think—and trudges out deeper into the water, pretending to throw her. I watch her squirm against him, playfully smacking at him until he finally sets her down and she dashes back to the safety of the beach.

Birdie nudges me, and I realize I've stopped walking.

"Sorry," I say, a little bashfully. "I can't always turn off the lifeguard in me at these things. Especially once people start drinking."

"It's sweet," she says, and I feel my cheeks go hot. I'm still not used to this casual compliment thing, especially not from her, so I start scanning the beach in search of anyone who might want to hang out and save me from the awkwardness.

Bentley sees me and waves us over to a giant rock that he's set out some blankets on, along with a couple of bags of Doritos, ever the consummate host. I should have thought ahead and brought stuff too, considering this is basically Birdie's and my first date. Or at least I hope it is.

It feels like it to me.

"Summer Girl," Bentley says, nodding toward Birdie, and I wish that I had been a little bit vaguer with her about what that phrase means to people like me and Bentley.

She seems to take it in stride, though, hopping up onto the rock and settling onto a corner of the blanket with a smile and a quick "Lifeguard Boy," which makes Bentley laugh, seemingly delighted.

"Where's Six?" I ask, searching the party for his face and coming up empty.

"Late." Bentley frowns. "He better come."

"He will," I say, finding a spot between him and Birdie and pulling off my slides. "He definitely will."

"Six?" Birdie asks.

"His crush," I helpfully supply.

"Shhhhh," Bentley practically hisses. "What if he walks up?!"

"Hold on, do you honestly think he doesn't already know?" I shake my head. "You guys are both so obviously into each other it hurts to watch. That's how I know he'll be here."

"Do you all just have nicknames for everyone, then? Summer Girl? Six?"

"Pretty much," I say, and Bentley just shrugs.

"Just the ones we aren't sure are gonna stick around long-term," he adds, studying her reaction. "No use learning your name if you're only here for a couple weeks, right, *Birdie*?"

Birdie's smile falters at the warning in his tone. I whip my head toward Bentley and mouth, "Be nice." It's one thing to haze her a little bit, or tease me for that matter, but it's another to actually make her feel uncomfortable in pursuit of your very own overprotective bestie award.

As much as I appreciate him looking out for me, I want Birdie to feel good here. I want her to feel like she fits, and currently, Bentley isn't helping with that *at all*.

"C'mon, you wanna dance?" I ask.

"What?" Birdie cries. "No way!"

"No?" I whine, more than a little disappointed. I've been looking forward to it since this afternoon when she agreed to be my date.

She glances around. "I mean, no one else is dancing."

"They will when we start," I say, even though I have no idea if that's true. I just want to get a little space from Bentley, get back into our bubble, and the songs playing tonight have me feeling sappy in a way I'm not used to. I don't care if we just stand there and sway; I just want to hold her, want everyone to see she's mine.

She sucks on her bottom lip, thinking. "I don't know how."

"I'm not asking you to perform, Birdie. I just wanted to . . . Never mind, it's fine," I say, feeling suddenly self-conscious. Of course she wouldn't want to dance. It's embarrassing that I even asked her to.

"I changed my mind," she says, hopping down and reaching for my hand. "I want to."

"You do?"

"Limited-time offer, Cass. Either we do this before I lose my nerve or not at all."

I grin and hop down after her, glancing at Bentley just long enough to see that he's smiling too. "Let's go, then."

We go a little way away from the bonfire, where we can still hear the music well, but aren't right in everyone's faces while they're trying to roast marshmallows and talk. I pull her close to me and tug her arms around me when she stands there nervously for a beat too long. I rest my head on her shoulder, enjoying the height difference for once instead of feeling insecure about it, soaking in the scent of her lotion and suntanned skin, and feeling more settled than I have any right to be.

"Do we just . . . do this?" she asks, swaying to the music with me.

"Yeah," I say, pretending I know what I'm doing.

The truth is, I don't know how to dance either, and I don't think I've ever asked anyone. I just . . . wanted to, with her.

Naturally, I step on her foot by accident during the second song. Then again in the third. She ignores it at first, but when I mumble yet another apology during the next one, I'm not so lucky.

"You can't dance either," she says, her eyes shiny with amusement in the light of the fire.

"No, not really," I say, and she raises her eyebrows. "Okay, fine, not at all. Besides an obligatory dance at prom just to say I did, I'm practically a dance virgin."

"Why did you ask, then?"

"I wanted to get you all to myself for a minute."

"Then you shouldn't have invited me to a party." She laughs. "You could have just come over."

"Maybe there's a little more to it." I gesture to the other couples who, sure enough, have started dancing too, lost in their own little romances. "People always end up doing this at these things. I guess I wanted to see what all the hype was about. I wanted it to be my turn to have someone to dance with."

"Awww," she says, looking at me like I'm a little lost kitten or something, and I'm tempted to run into the sea just to escape the burning feeling that wells up in me.

I try to look away, but she gently guides my chin back until our eyes meet.

"Did it live up to what you imagined? Or did us tripping on each other ruin it for you?" She's teasing, but I still sigh, embarrassed.

"Sorry, I really wanted to do this right."

"Do what?"

"Take you out and—"

"Wait, are we on a date?" she asks, sounding surprised, and I step back, suddenly feeling even more mortified. *How have I misread things so badly?*

"Sorry, no," I say, scrambling to think of an excuse or an alternate explanation for what I just said. "I just—"

She cuts me off. "Because I would love it if we were. I *hoped* it was."

"Then it is. I mean I want it to be," I say, the words rushing out. And god, my eagerness is ridiculous, but I can't even care right now, because she's practically beaming at me.

"Good," she says, leaning forward to press a gentle kiss between the collar of my hoodie and my jaw that sends a shiver ghosting down my spine. "Good," she says again.

I turn my head, wanting to kiss her for real and feeling like I might die if I don't. I want this moment to last forever. I want her to feel—

"Have you seen Bentley?" Six's voice slices through the moment, slamming us back down to earth.

Birdie takes a quick step away from me, sending the cool night air rushing in to replace her warmth. I'm not a violent person, but if I was ever going to pick someone up and chuck them down the beach, it would be Six and it would be now. "Uh, hi," I say, clearly annoyed.

He looks from me to Birdie, and I realize he's waiting for an introduction. "This is my . . . Birdie," I say. *Smooth, Cass, real smooth.*

"Hello, *your* Birdie." Six grins. "I'm Marshawn, but most people call me Six, as in Chair Six."

174

"Oh, you're Bentley's Six!" She grins, and I can't tell if she's teasing him right back or is just genuinely pleased to have made the connection. "He's on the rock waiting for you," she adds.

Six seems to take the hint. "Awesome, I'll go find him. If I don't see you later, you girls have a good night," he says, before jogging away.

Birdie waits for him to get out of earshot before raising an eyebrow in my direction. "*Your* Birdie, huh?" I open my mouth to protest, or at least try to explain, but she presses her finger to my lips to stop me. "I like it," she says. "As long as that means you're also *my* Cass."

My mouth curves instantly into a smile at that thought, as she replaces her finger with her lips.

15

Birdie

I'M WALKING TO meet Cass for breakfast a few days later when my phone vibrates in my pocket—a FaceTime call from Ada.

I answer the phone, grinning in the sunshine as I walk. I could have scootered, especially since it's just under a mile to The Breakfast Spot, but I didn't want to have to lug it around in Cass's car after. Yes, she would have picked me up, but that's the problem: She's always picking me up. I hate that I have to rely on her and can't treat her the way I'd like to. I figure, since I can't actually pick her up until my dad lifts my driving embargo, meeting her there feels enough like returning the favor.

"Morning!" I say brightly.

Ada furrows her brow. "You're awfully chipper this morning."

"It's sunny. It's warm. I'm near the beach, and I don't have to work today. Why wouldn't I be chipper?"

"Are you walking somewhere right now? Wait, did my best friend run off to a seaside town and suddenly take up cardio? Have you finally been ripped from the jaws of Pilates?"

"Ha ha," I say, stepping around a crack in the sidewalk. "No, but I'm still not allowed to drive, and I'm meeting someone for breakfast."

Ada tilts her head. "Who?"

"Just a friend," I say, blushing.

"And how many times have you kissed this friend?" She snorts.

"What? None!" I lie, but I can tell right away that she's not convinced.

"Birdie, we've been friends long enough that I can tell when you're lying. Who is it?"

"I hate you," I say, laughing as I roll my eyes.

"You love me soooo much," she coos. "But seriously, who is it? Spill! I know Carly has a bunch of cousins out there on the boat. Is it one of them?"

"No, it's seriously no one you know," I say. "They aren't even someone-you-know-*adjacent*."

"Okay, if I don't know them, I at least want to know how *you* know them."

"It's someone I met here."

"Oh, another summer resident. Nice. Where's he from?"

"They have a house here," I say, trying not to give anything away.

"I figured, Birdie," she says, like I'm not understanding. "But where do they live when it's cold?"

"We didn't get that far," I lie, figuring it's better to make her think I'm a dumbass who kisses complete strangers than the alternative, which is that I've fallen for a townie.

She wouldn't understand. She thinks she would, but she wouldn't. For as down-to-earth as she believes herself to be, she's still rich in a way that a lot of people can only dream of, and that changes the way you think, which is something Cass has really been making me realize.

"Birdie!" she practically shrieks. "How can you make out with someone when you don't even know who they are?! You don't even know where he lives!" She drops her head back and spins in her chair, making an exaggerated groaning sound. "What happened to finding yourself?"

"I am finding myself," I argue, tipping my phone away so I can see the sidewalk better, giving Ada a nice view of my better side. "I'm finding out a lot about myself, to be honest, and this person is kind of helping me."

"You can't find yourself in another person, Birdie. That's what I've been trying to tell you. It's something you have to do yourself."

"No, I know." I sigh, jumping to the grass just a child comes barreling at me on a tricycle. Perhaps FaceTiming while walking isn't the best idea. I look both ways before stepping back onto the sidewalk. "Trust me, I know. That's not what I mean. I just meant, like . . . I'm learning things about myself. The more time we spend together, the more I—"

"What does the monster say about you dating anyway?

178

It sounds like this mystery person is taking up a lot of your time. I know you've barely even called *me* lately!"

"Ogre, remember?" I say. I don't know why it feels so much nicer than monster, but it does. "They're fine with it."

"He's fine with it? The evilness hired to keep you in line is fine with you making out with someone you barely know on his watch. Seriously?"

"Yeah, turns out, they're not as bad as I made them out to be. I was wrong about them."

"Oh. My. God!" Ada yelps, leaning forward so one of her eyes takes up the whole screen. "You're making out with the monster, aren't you?! Don't lie to me—I'll see it!"

"What? Why would you think that?"

She leans back, crossing her arms. "That's not a no, Birdie."

I hesitate, not sure if I should tell the truth or keep trying to hedge things, not even sure if I *can* hedge things anymore without outright lying to her. Something I really don't want to do to Ada. Lying by omission is one thing. Letting her think things—like that Cass is a *he*—and not correcting her is another, but outright lying to her face . . . that feels somehow worse.

"It's not a no," I settle on.

"You're dating your dad's assistant?" she asks, looking a little worried. "Is that who you're meeting for breakfast?"

I stop walking, looking away and then back to the phone. "It's complicated, but . . . yeah, I am."

"Birdie," she says.

"Ada," I answer.

"What do you think your dad is going to do when he finds

out you're hooking up with the guy he's paying to keep an eye on you?"

"I honestly don't think he'll care. He likes . . . his assistant, and they're not taking the money anymore."

"Does he like his assistant making out with his daughter, though? How old is this guy, anyway? I know you're almost eighteen, but this is seriously creeping me out now."

I can't correct her on the guy thing, or at least I'm not ready to, but I can at least make sure she's not thinking Cass is a huge perv. "We're the same age, basically. Cass is only a few months older than me."

"Okay, that's good at least. It's not a *total* trash fire, then. Ooooh, so Cass is his name? What's that short for? Casper? Cassian?"

"Mm-hmm," I say, hoping she assumes that means yes so I don't have to try to figure out what the boy version of Cassandra is. Cassander? Who knows?

"Okay, so age-appropriate Cass is treating you better now? I'm assuming?"

"Very much so," I say, relieved that we can finally talk about something honestly. "Cass sees me, Ada. Like really sees me. I've never had that with anyone."

"Birdie," she says gently, "you know this can only be a fling, right? I mean, it's your dad's assistant. You said it yourself—you don't even know where he's from. Don't go falling in love with him. I ran into your mom this morning, and she said not to worry about you because she's bringing you home really soon. She said two weeks!"

"Two weeks?"

"Yeah, she told my mom you were coming home right after the Founders' Day Gala. I can't believe you didn't tell me! That's, like, your birthday weekend! We'll get to celebrate together!"

"Oh," I say, trying to absorb what Ada is telling me. Of course I didn't let her know; I'm just finding this out now myself, as I'm standing outside The Breakfast Spot, a cute little SoHo-chic restaurant that caters to locals and only serves breakfast. Cass is inside by the window, happily studying the menu.

She has no idea that our week of bliss is about to end abruptly when I tell her I have to leave in fourteen days. I wish I didn't know either. I wonder if I can get my dad to let me stay longer. I have a job! I have friends here! A girl I really care about! I'm not ready to go. I thought I'd have at least until the end of the summer.

"Why don't you sound excited?" Ada frowns. "You're being paroled earlier than we thought. We'll still have time to hang before I have to leave for school! I can't believe you didn't call me to make plans when you found out."

"I . . . I didn't find out," I stammer. "This is the first I've heard of it."

"Shit. Well, act surprised when they tell you," she says, wincing. "And act happy now, will you?!"

"I'm happy, I am," I say, thinking about how nice it would be to have my best friend back. Just the idea of being able to pop over to her house—or her hotel penthouse, I guess— whenever I feel like it again feels great, not to mention getting back to city life, where there's always something to do. And back to focusing on my designs and finally getting my business off the ground full-time—that's important too. I love it here, I do, and I love spending time here with Cass, but I'd be lying if I said I didn't miss my old life sometimes too. "It'll be nice to be back home," I admit, even though it makes me feel guilty.

"Right," Ada says. "So, whatever you do, do *not* fall in love with that boy."

"I won't," I say, but as soon as the words leave my mouth, Cass looks up, her whole face breaking into a smile, and I know it's already too late.

I think I've been in love with Cassandra Adler since we were kids. There's no use trying to stop now.

16

Cass

I CAN'T STOP smiling.

It's silly—I know it is—but it just feels *good* to be around her. Like she and I are something that was always supposed to happen and we've just finally set it right, rather than it being a mistake.

It's been a week since the bonfire. A week of stolen kisses when George isn't home and holding hands while driving to work. A week of Bentley and me giggling about Six and Birdie high up on our chair, where it feels like nothing can hurt us. And if my binoculars occasionally drift over to the parking lot on my sweep . . . Okay, no, I'm not irresponsible enough to actually do that, but one time *after* the end of our shift, I did. Just to see if I could see her from my chair. Spoiler alert: I can't, not really.

I know somewhere in the back of my mind, the little rational part of me is still not fully trusting this. It's easy to ignore, though, on a day like today, when we're both off and she's looking at me the way I look at new surfboards that are way, way, *way* out of my price range.

Like I'm expensive and precious and deserve to be taken care of.

"Does it really count as a date if you're taking me to the place where we both work?" she asks, helping me carry a bodyboard to the back of the pickup truck I borrowed from my dad.

"We're not going to that beach, so yes, it does." I laugh, slotting the bodyboard in between the surfboards. "The whole ocean isn't our place of employment."

I want to teach her how to surf today, or at least I'm going to try. She's insisting she won't pull it off, even though I pointed out how nice dancing together was even though we both sucked at it. Still, we're bringing bodyboards as a backup. If she wants to just kick around in the water with me, that's fine. As long as we're together, I don't really care what we do. I know we only have a short time left here—five weeks until I leave for MIT at most—and I want to savor every second of it.

She hops into the truck beside me and wrinkles her nose. Dad uses this truck to work with George, so it smells a little like dirt and gasoline, like hard work and hot summer days and *life*. It can be a little much, but I can't help but smile at all the memories I have in this truck—Dad taking me to work with him when I was little; George asking me if I wanted to go with him to Home Depot and bribing me with a Happy Meal, even though we both knew if I stayed behind with my dad I'd just be in the way, covered in spackle or whatever the day's task entailed.

Having Birdie in here beside me—driving to my favorite surf spot as the sun just peeks up over the horizon—is really the icing on the cake of the whole situation.

"It's so early," she says, letting her eyes drift shut.

I drive even more carefully, trying to miss every crack and pothole in the road in case she drifts off. It's only a half hour's drive to my favorite spot, a little out-of-the-way surfer's cove surrounded by long, harsh rocks that jut out from the coast like a warning, coaxing all the waves to be just that much bigger as they fold into the little inlet.

As expected, Birdie is fully asleep by the time we get there, her chest rising and falling slow and steady, just like the waves I love so much. I open the door as quietly as I can. She shifts in her seat but doesn't open her eyes. I decide to leave the door open, rather than risk the noise of closing it, and get to work.

There are a few other surfers here I know, so we exchange waves and nods as I walk to the back of the truck and start pulling out the boards. I don't miss their grins as they notice the second board and bodyboards I pull out—the telltale sign of someone's first ride.

This is a secret spot, which means there's an unspoken agreement that if you bring someone here, they have to be important to you. It doesn't have to be romantic at all—it can be a friend, a family member—but to share something that feels like such a huge part of us, to share the sacredness of the water, you don't do that with just anyone. Especially not here.

Bentley even asked me if I was sure yesterday when I told him my plan for today. And when Birdie climbs out of my truck, her expression soft, her clothes a little rumpled from the awkward sleeping position, I know I could never be anything less than positive.

ᗢᗢᗢ

Birdie is not a natural at this. She is, in fact, whatever the opposite of a natural is. I don't know that I've ever seen someone struggle this hard to stay on the board, let alone actually try to get their feet under them.

For a second, I was worried maybe I was just a bad teacher—except I even taught my sixty-four-year-old great-aunt how to surf last summer, a self-proclaimed couch potato who calls anything athletic "sports ball," so I know it's not me. It's just Birdie . . . she's . . . well, she's goofy.

I don't know how else to explain it. Watching Birdie try to surf is like watching a baby giraffe trying to take its first steps . . . in the middle of a hurricane . . . that's happening at the same time as an earthquake. Well, okay, maybe it's not quite that catastrophic, but it's close. I knew she was tall and lean, but I didn't realize how absolutely uncoordinated she was.

It's beyond endearing, if I'm being honest, even if she is getting a little embarrassed about it.

She manages to get up exactly once, and then immediately tumbles off, her board hitting her head so hard when the wave crashes over her that I'm rescue swimming her to the beach before I realize she's hysterically laughing, not crying.

"Oh my god, I'm *bad*," she says, once we're safely to shore. I dig our boards into the ground and flop back in the warm sand, not even caring that it's all going to stick to me. I'm going to get back in the water, hopefully. If Birdie's up for it.

Propping her head up on her hand, elbow digging into the sand, Birdie stretches out long beside me and looks down at me. I pop open one eye and then shut it again, fighting a smirk on my face. "Are you pretending to have fainted because of my horrible surfing skills?" she asks.

"No." I smile, pushing up to my elbows so we can be face-to-face. "Just taking a break after saving your life."

"Hardly." She snorts, and I reach up to run my fingers over the red bump forming just beside her temple.

"Are you okay, really? Maybe we should stop by urgent care. I wanted you to have fun today, not risk your life."

"I'm good," she says, leaning forward for a quick kiss. "But I won't complain if you want to play doctor later."

I roll her over, caging her between my arms with a grin. "Is that so?"

"Yo, Cass," one of the other surfers calls to me, interrupting the moment. "Who's your friend?"

It's Brad, a college kid who's spent every summer here for years. He spends all morning, every morning, surfing and then works as a tour guide on a sailboat all afternoon. He's nice enough, even if his timing is impossibly bad.

I roll off her and sit up. If I can't kiss her, at least I can excitedly introduce her to people. "This is Birdie," I say as we stand up and dust the sand off ourselves.

Brad jogs over to us, extending a fist bump her way and setting down his board.

"Nice to meet you, Birdie. You're in good hands with Cass. She's a good teacher. I was on the struggle bus before she gave me some pointers."

"No, you weren't!" I laugh.

"Shhhh," he says, shaking his head. "I'm trying to make you look good here!"

"Oh, you don't have to. I know she's pretty amazing," Birdie says.

I feel the blush spread from my ears all the way down to my toes—a rush of warm not-quite-embarrassment that wraps itself around me whenever our eyes meet. I'm so gone for this girl, it's pathetic.

"Unfortunately, I'm a horrible student," Birdie adds, looking at Brad, who seems delighted by us. He brought his girlfriend here recently too, and before he did, we had a long talk about what a big deal it was for him to do that. Just me and him sitting on our boards in the middle of the ocean talking it out as he decided. I told him I hoped some-day I would be in the same position—caring about someone enough to share this with them—and he swore I would. I know he knows, even if Birdie doesn't fully, that this is a massive deal for me.

"You can't be that bad," he says, peeling down the top of his wet suit and rolling his neck in the summer sun.

Birdie points to the bump on her head. "I mean, if there's

something worse than having your girlfriend rescue swim you out of the water, I don't want to experience it."

I choke on my spit at the word *girlfriend*, and Brad pounds my back, smirking like he knows.

"Hopefully you don't," he says, giving me a wink when Birdie isn't looking. "I'll, uh, let you guys get back to it."

"I'm only going back in that water if she agrees that I only have to paddle."

"Paddling is a start," he says, giving her a thumbs-up before heading over to where his truck is parked.

I pass Birdie her board, and we walk down to the water. I wait till we're paddling out—the water gently lapping at our boards as she precariously balances on hers, while I use big confident strokes on mine—to ask about it. "Girlfriend, huh?"

She huffs out a laugh and looks to the horizon, squinting at the endless water that seems to stretch on forever. "Sorry, it just came out. I don't want to assume, but . . . I would like that."

"I would also like that," I say, feeling like the biggest dork on the planet. *I would also like that?*

She looks at me like she has something else to say, something important, but whatever it is, she must decide to swallow it. "Good," she says, leaning toward me for a kiss and managing to fall off her board instead.

I purposely roll myself off mine too, splashing her in the process, and she splashes me back.

I wouldn't have it any other way.

17

Birdie

I'M LYING ON my bed playing with my iPad, trying to avoid my father, who is currently upset that Cass isn't taking the envelopes of cash he leaves for her every week. Despite saying we were going to tell him, we haven't yet, and I very much *don't* want to explain to him why on my own.

I think he'll be happy about it, honestly. He was the least weird of everyone I told about my bisexuality . . . but I'm still nervous. Besides, I'm working up the courage to ask him if I can stay longer.

I should have asked him last week, when Mom interrupted our dinner—via FaceTime, of course; she still hasn't bothered to come out here to visit—to officially let me know that I would be heading home right after my birthday. I kept glancing at my father, who seemed unusually interested in his chicken Caesar salad, while my mom droned on about being proud of my work ethic, despite the "horrible conditions," and that if

I applied that same grit to our streaming schedule, it would surely be a breakout year.

When Mom finally got off the phone, Dad seemed quiet. Withdrawn almost. (Mom does often have that effect on him, to be fair.) Before I could even try to lighten the mood—let alone ask if I could stay longer—we got interrupted *again* by one of his work calls. This one sounded extra bad—I overheard him saying something about a property deal falling through at the last minute, which has to suck. He was back behind his closed office door before I had even finished my next bite, and no way was I going to disturb him after that.

Should I be able to ask my dad if I can stay? *Yes.* Has he made me feel welcome here every chance he's had? *Also yes.* Does that mean I'm not also still nervous that maybe he's ready to send me back to Boston anyway to at least have one fewer thing on his plate? *No.*

I need to ask at just the right time, when he's in just the right mood, to maximize my chances of him saying yes. Unfortunately, that keeps not happening.

In the meantime, though, Cass keeps showing up to give me rides, and we hang out constantly—if she's not here, then I'm there, or we're both at the Affordable Housing Coalition. I'm finally starting to learn the ropes there. They have me using my internet skills to act as a superspy, ferreting out locations of illegal Airbnbs using Google Image searches or from what I can see out their windows in their listing photos. Then, once we have that, Cass files the paperwork to report them for code violations. The Coalition was able to get some legislation pushed through last year making it a little harder for people to rent out their regular houses short-term, and a lot of shady landlords are trying to fly under the radar. I checked all my dad's listings on my own, just to be sure, but for whatever it's worth, his at least all seem to be on the up and up.

Which brings me to the other problem that has me lying on my bed moping like a Disney Princess in the first act: I haven't told Cass yet that my mom expects me to go back with her after my birthday. I don't want to ruin how good things are going right now. I know deep down a part of her is still afraid I'm just a summer girl, even though I've done everything I can to prove to her that I'm not. The longer I keep this from her, though, the more I start to feel like I am.

I'd be lying if I said a part of me doesn't miss my old life—the swag, the filming schedules, the times Mom brings in actual hairstylists and makeup artists before a special sponsored post. It would be fun if it didn't also mean being stuck under her thumb.

But the thought of leaving Cass, of our time here ending, makes everything inside me twist.

I know we'll both be in Boston by fall, but what will that even look like? I told Cass to stay in the moment with me, but the truth is, I *don't* know what it's going to look like once I get back home. I definitely don't want to break up or keep her a secret or anything, but I also don't want to throw her to the wolves. My social circle isn't exactly known for being warm and welcoming.

I sigh and FaceTime Ada, who picks up on the first ring.

"Hi, babe," she says.

I'm about to unload on her my fears and confusion about going back, when I notice Carly Whitmore in the background, flopped over one of the oversize chairs in the main room of the penthouse. I wasn't aware Carly had even left Newport, let alone made her way to *my* best friend's hotel room. A jolt of jealousy courses through my body, and I try to tamp it down.

Ada moves the phone, setting it on a shelf, and holds up two different equally expensive dresses. I recognize one from her new favorite designer, but the other one, I'm not sure of. "What do you think?" she asks.

She switches them back and forth in front of her as she stares at herself in the full-length mirror, which she had changed to soft globe lighting after complaining to the hotel manager that the harsh fluorescent washed her out. Ada's got on her favorite pink robe with the ostrich feathers, and I try not to seethe at the idea that she's comfortable enough with Carly to hang out with her in pajamas.

I know, logically, I'm not being replaced as a best friend—she wouldn't have answered the phone if I was—but it doesn't help with my confusing feelings about wanting to simultaneously run back to Boston and stake my claim on my old life and *my* old friends . . . and also stay in this cozy town with Cass forever.

"The blue one," I say, pointing to the more glittery of the two.

"Boo, the other one's hotter. Wear the pink!" Carly pouts. I hold my breath, as if whatever Ada picks is going to be some sign about the status of our friendship and not just her following her own sense of style, which seems to shift as often as her moods.

"No, definitely the blue," Ada says, winking at the phone before carrying the dress and, well, me, into the bathroom. "I'll be back in a few," Ada calls to Carly. "If you want to start getting dressed, you can have the room." She closes the door behind her.

"What are you up to tonight?" I ask, trying to sound nonchalant as she positions the phone on the counter just right so I can watch her touch up her makeup.

"The usual. Carly's dad got us into VIP at his club again. It's the worst—they still won't even serve us there! I think he only invites us to keep an eye on her after her last house party fiasco, but still, it's something to do. It's so boring here without you. I can't wait for you to get back home. I'm dying."

"Yeah," I say, trying to sound as excited as I used to feel about home, instead of torn.

"Shit." She leans over the counter so her face fills my screen. "You fell for the monster," she says, like she can see inside my mind. "Well, don't worry, because there's about to be a distraction."

"A distraction is the last thing I need right now," I say, feeling like I already have too much going on.

"I didn't say you needed it!" she protests. "You definitely don't need it and won't want it."

"Great, even worse." I groan. "What now?"

"Mitchell's back."

"What do you mean he's back?"

"I mean, remember when his parents sent him to Italy to

get his head on straight? Well, either they decided that happened or they just gave up, because the boy is back in town."

"Are you sure?" I sigh.

"Positive. I ran into him at the club the other night and overheard him running his mouth about some plan to win you back, which for the record would be an epic mistake on your part. And then he saw me and started fake crying—yes, really—asking if you had someone new and if that's why you aren't responding to any of his DMs, which was obviously bullshit because he *knows* you're not on socials right now. I'm just saying this inevitably forthcoming Mitchell shit show will be a great distraction from the monster disaster."

"Cass isn't a disaster," I say, a little offended. "You didn't tell him I was seeing someone, did you?"

"No. Not exactly. I may have hinted a little, but that was just to get him back for hurting you. That boy deserves to suffer a little."

"Oh my god," I growl. "I wish you didn't do that. You know how fast rumors spread. Everybody's going to be trying to figure it out."

"There are worse things than letting everyone know that not only are you fine, but you've got your very own hot summer fling happening." Ada laughs. "If anything, it's pushing your stock even higher. Half the comments on his TikToks are still hashtag Team Birdie. If it's any consolation, Carly told me that his mom is freaking the hell out over all the bad publicity he's bringing the family."

"I wish Carly would just mind her own business for once," I snap. "None of this has anything to do with her!"

"She's nosy, yeah, but I'm not going to lie. She's been kind of growing on me lately," Ada says, and somehow that upsets me even more.

"Great. Suddenly, now you're besties? What gives? The Ada I knew hated Carly too."

"It's not like you've been around! I know we've been FaceTiming when we can, but you can't be mad at me for wanting to hang out with someone here while you're off living your best summer rom-com life! Until you're out of exile, I don't really have a choice of who to hang out with—unless I want to sit around helping my mom at her office now that she's back, and you know I have my whole life ahead of me to waste doing that."

"Don't do it, then," I say, frustrated. "You don't *have* to be a doctor, you know!"

"Oh, right, says the girl who would rather be imprisoned by her father than risk losing her trust fund. Be for real right now. You're not exactly rocking the boat where you are either."

I look away before I can blurt out something I'll regret. If she even knew half the truth of my situation, the truth of who Cass really is—that she's not some college guy destined to follow in my father's footsteps, but instead a townie *girl* actively trying to work against his interests—she would realize just how much I have been rocking the boat.

"Sorry," she says. "That was mean of me to say."

I look back at her, the truth sitting on my tongue just for a second before I swallow it. As much as I love Ada, I don't know that I'll ever forget how uncomfortable she looked that day I finally told her I was bi, even though I could see she regretted it. Her instinct was shock and discomfort, not genuine acceptance, and it hurt.

Deep down, I wish she could know Cass, the real Cass, the way I do. I wish Ada could see the things I see in Cass; then maybe she would love her too. But even if she could see past the townie thing, I honestly don't know how she'd react to Cass being a girl. I'd like to think she's had time to learn and grow, but . . . what if she hasn't? Do I really want to know?

"It's fine," I finally say, waving her off, even though it's not. Best friends aren't supposed to keep the biggest parts of themselves from each other, right?

And for the first time, I'm wondering, *are* we best friends now? Were we ever? Or have I just been the convenient lifelong friend, the way Carly is to her now that I'm gone. I'm probably being dramatic, but I can't shake the feeling I'm not entirely wrong.

Thankfully, I hear my dad's car pull in before I can spiral about that any more. My dad, who I desperately need to talk to, ready or not. "Hey, can I call you later?" I ask. "My dad just got home."

"Sure," she says brightly, as if nothing ever happened. If there was a queen of sweeping things under the rug, I think Ada would take the crown.

I bound down the stairs, meeting him in the living room. He looks exhausted, more exhausted than I've seen him.

"Is everything okay?" I ask.

"Yeah, honey," he says. "Just a long day. I grabbed takeout on the way home. Why don't you go get us some plates and meet me in the dining room?"

"Okay," I say. I carry the plates into the dining room, setting one in front of him as he opens the boxes of Chinese food and arranges them on the table.

"This is nice," I say, trying to find a lead-in.

"You always loved Chinese food, even as a little kid," he says, pushing the container of beef lo mein toward me.

"Not the food." I laugh. "This. Eating dinner with you."

He smiles, like that's the best thing he's heard all day. Judging by how much he's bitten down his nails, a bad habit that only rears its head during times of stress, that may be true. "It is nice, isn't it?"

"I'm really glad we got to spend this time together," I say, trying to feel him out.

He studies his plate, frowning. "Me too, but I know you're eager to get back to Boston. I should probably be spending a little more time there too," he says, which is not the reaction I was hoping for.

"What if I wanted to stay out here longer?" I ask.

"Doing what? They don't bother with parking lot attendants in the offseason," he says curiously, taking a bite. I try not to be offended that that's all he sees me as. I also try not to think too hard about the fact that he doesn't think of Cass as just a lifeguard. Not ever. She's a future MIT grad who's going to be an asset to *my* family business, and I'm apparently just someone who is going to be able to add "unemployed parking lot girl" to her résumé soon.

I swallow my pride and try to keep my eye on the prize, getting to stay here at least till the end of summer. "I know, but I feel so inspired here! I could start working on designs again, and maybe—"

"Birdie." My dad sighs, pinching the bridge of his nose. "If this is your roundabout way of buttering me up to find out if I'm going to release the trust to you on your birthday, can we skip it? I've had a hellish day dealing with the town over one of my properties that apparently isn't zoned for short-term rentals after all. It must have slipped through the cracks when the regulations changed, and *someone* decided to report it."

The way he says *someone* makes me think he knows who it is. I look down at my plate, trying not to smirk. Looks like Cass finally found one. Speak of the devil—my phone vibrates in my pocket a second later.

Cass: What are you doing?

I smile at her text and glance at my dad, who is already reading emails on his phone, with the same frustrated look on his face as when he walked in. I take another bite of dinner and hit reply.

Me: What, like right now?

Cass: Yes, like right now.

199

Me: Trying not to look too happy that one of Dad's properties somehow got reported for a zoning violation. 😂 But mostly just eating dinner and wishing you were here.

I take a few more bites, waiting for her to reply. It comes an unbearably long few minutes later.

Cass: Good news. Come outside.

Me: What???

"Dad, may I be excused? I think Cass is here."

"What?" he says, looking up from his phone. "Yes, but have her come inside. I need to talk to her about why she's refusing to get paid!"

"Sorry! She's running late," I say, clearing my plate. "Next time!"

I shove my feet into my slides and rush out the door, not even caring that I've already taken off my makeup. She's waiting for me in the driveway, lights on and car still running like we're making a fast getaway. I pull open the passenger door and hop inside.

"I'm not stalking you," she says. "I swear, I really was in the neighborhood."

I laugh, leaning forward to kiss her once, twice, and again. "I don't even care."

18

Cass

"WHERE ARE WE going?" Birdie asks.

Her words seem normal enough, as does the smile she's pasted on her face since we finished kissing, but . . . I know that smile. I've seen it online and in front of her father whenever she's mad. She can fake out her followers, and apparently also her parents, but she's not going to fake out me.

"Is everything okay?" I squeeze her knee, wondering if she was fighting with her dad tonight or if something else is going on.

"I'm with you, aren't I?" she says. "How could it not be?"

She's being evasive, but I respect that she wants me to drop it, even if she isn't outright saying so. If she doesn't want to tell me what's wrong yet, that's fine. I'll just do my best to make it better anyway.

"Yeah," I say, lacing our hands together. "I've got you."

She smiles at me again—a fleeting, but genuine one this

time—and I count it as a win. I squeeze her hand three times, and she does it back, and any worries I had that she was upset with me fall away.

"What are we doing at the office?" she asks, a puzzled expression on her face when we pull up to the Coalition's office a few minutes later.

"Don't worry, my dad knows we're here. I'm not sneaking in or anything. I have paperwork to do, and I was hoping you would keep me company while I did it?"

"Here I thought this was an impromptu date, but you just need a secretary?"

"Can't it be both?" I ask, unlocking the door and holding it open. She starts to walk past me, but I catch her waist, hooking my arm around her and pulling her close. Birdie lets out a startled sound and then tilts her head, looking down at me.

I lean up on my tiptoes to kiss her, wishing once again that I was the tall one.

She meets my lips. "You've got some big moves for someone so small," she teases.

"Hey, I can be as big as I want to be," I say, leading her into the office and kicking the door shut behind us.

"You're perfect." She laughs, her eyes shining, and god, I don't want this moment to end. Just being here with her is enough.

"No, I'm not," I say. "But you're close."

Her smile falters at that, and she ducks under my arm. "What are we working on tonight?" she asks, spinning slowly to take the office in when it's not crowded with people. I hit the light switch, flooding the place in fluorescent white light,

202

and let her change the subject. It's clear that whatever's bothering her isn't going to come easy.

I grab a file and gesture for Birdie to join me at the round table. "I need to finish some supplemental stuff for the Founders' Day Community Improvement Award. The actual application was due a couple weeks ago, but you can turn in additional supporting documents until tomorrow. I told Dad I would polish the organization's résumé tonight so they can see just how much we did. Then, after, we can brainstorm some of those brilliant ideas you have about how to get the public more involved too. Take a break from reporting people to the code office?"

"Oh, I thought my dad's business was getting that award?" she says, looking confused.

"They announced George as Volunteer of the Year already—maybe that's what you're thinking of? But Gordon Development itself was also nominated for the award I'm working on tonight. That one doesn't get announced until the actual dinner," I say, frowning. "George claims he doesn't want it and encouraged my dad to apply as a write-in, but we'll see. We know it's going to be an uphill battle as long as your dad's in the mix," I grumble. "Those people love George for some reason—"

"I thought you did too," she says, studying me.

"I do," I sigh. "It's just, the award is ten thousand dollars, and he knows how much that money would mean to our organization. I wish he would just officially step aside or at least put in a good word for us. Ten thousand dollars isn't *anything* to him. You probably have shoes that cost that much!"

"No, I don't have anything over probably four or five," she says so sincerely I don't even bother to explain that four-thousand-dollar shoes are still ridiculous.

"That ten thousand would help us pay off some of the tax liens and back rent that people have been asking us to help with. Winning would mean people could stay in their homes, Birdie."

"How much do you need?" she asks, sounding incredulous. "Only ten thousand?"

"*Only?*" I snort. "Man, we come from different worlds." I don't miss the way her face falls, so I nudge her with my elbow until she meets my eyes. "It's not a bad thing, Birdie. It's just a fact. But yeah, we need as much as we can get. The award is for ten thousand, though, and that would let us accomplish some life-changing things."

"*Life-changing?*" she says, looking down at the papers and biting her lip.

"That probably seems like pocket change to you," I say, instantly regretting it when her face clouds over.

"It's not all fun and games, you know. You don't under-stand the kind of pressure that comes with the money my family has," she says, and I try not to be offended that I'm talking about saving people's homes, doing *real* work that can help people, and she's talking about . . . being *too* rich or something?

"I think there are a lot of people who would love to have what you have."

"I don't doubt it, but they should be careful what they wish for," she says, standing up as if to leave.

"Are you mad?" I ask, getting up to follow her. She's being ridiculous. "I'm just joking. Like I said, it's not a bad thing, but you can't pretend you aren't privileged beyond belief."

"It's always going to be a joke to you, isn't it? I'm starting to feel like *I'm* always going to be a joke to you. The poor little rich girl and all that?"

"Where is this coming from?" I ask, my heart sinking. How did this perfect night go wrong so quickly? "You know how I feel about you. I've shared things that really matter to me. I took you surfing. I . . . I clearly don't think you're a joke. I care about you, a lot."

"Then why are you acting like I can't possibly understand the concept of money?"

"Can you?" I blurt out, and I know I've stepped in it again. "Sorry, I'm not saying you're not brilliant, or kind, or sweet, or any of the other things I love about you. Please don't take this the wrong way. I'm genuinely asking."

"Of course I can! How could I not?"

"Alright," I say, raising my hands in surrender. "Alright. I'm sorry. I just . . . You don't know what it's like to almost lose your house or wonder where your next meal is coming from. I thought it might be hard to understand if you haven't lived it. Or lived adjacent to it. That's all."

"Did you worry about those things?" she asks, looking concerned, and I shake my head.

"I'm lucky. We always had food in our bellies and a roof over our heads. We had to move around a lot when I was younger, but we always had a place to go. Some of my friends didn't, though. I wasn't trying to make any commentary about you, or make you feel bad. It's more just me thinking about how stupid money is. Like we could all just be monkeys relaxing on sunny beaches, but instead there's this price tag on everything, even living. It makes me so mad sometimes."

Birdie slips her arm around me, tugging me close. "I love your big heart so much," she says, and I almost hear the whisper of *I love you* beneath those words as I melt into her.

"I'm sorry for upsetting you a second ago. I know intent doesn't matter as much as result, but I promise I wasn't trying to make you feel bad. You didn't choose to be born into money any more than I chose to be born into my circumstance. I know you deal with a lot of crap too."

She sighs, her gaze softening. "I'm sorry too. I just . . . I have a lot on my mind."

"If you tell me what's going on, maybe I could help."

"You can't," she says, stepping a little closer to the door, and it makes my anxiety spike inside my head.

We've been having such a good time together; I took for granted that we always would. Or at least that we would rely on each other for the hard stuff and the bad days. But she seems genuinely upset right now, and she's shutting me out. Why is she pulling back, after things have been so good? After she called me her girlfriend. The tiny part of me that stayed guarded—that never could fully trust that she wasn't just another summer girl—whispers in my head, *See? I told you so.*

I sigh, hating that it still exists, but secretly worrying that maybe I need it. That maybe it's safer to keep that part around than give myself fully to her. If she's pulling back, even a little, shouldn't I?

"Okay," I say, hanging my head. "If you're sure."

"I'm sure. There's just . . ." Birdie trails off. She looks conflicted, and it's the only thing making me remotely okay with this situation—like she wants to tell me but can't for some reason. I look at her, really look at her, and decide that her wanting to tell me can be enough, at least for tonight. Let the truth be tomorrow's problem, whatever it is.

I come up behind her, stretching up to set my chin on her shoulder as I wrap her in a hug. "Let me just finish this stuff for my dad, and I'll drive you home."

"Okay."

"Oh, and Birdie?" I say. "Just know I'm here for you, if you change your mind."

She squeezes her eyes shut, and I wonder, *Did I just make it worse?*

19

Birdie

I'M BEING WEIRD.

I know it, and Cass definitely knows it too, judging by how quiet she's been on our drives to and from work these last few days. It's a mess.

The time is ticking down to the Founders' Day Gala. The one my dad has now asked me to give a nice flowery speech introducing him at. Despite whatever he told Cass's dad, he seems pretty enamored with the idea that he's going to get not just the Volunteer of the Year Award but probably also the Community Improvement one too.

Add that to the list of things I haven't told Cass about.

I just don't know what to do about any of that, or about my mom coming for the "big event," or the fact that they both seem to expect me to leave with her after.

How do I tell Cass that everything she's excited for is possibly not happening? Not the award, not me staying the rest of the summer . . . Not to mention that my best friend thinks my girlfriend's a dude. I feel awful about it, especially given how much Cass has incorporated me into her life. She's introduced me to practically all of her friends, both on and off the beach, taken me to parties, brought me to the Coalition . . .

And speaking of the Coalition, I've been helping out there more and more lately after work. They have me editing reels and making TikToks for the staff to try to get engagement up—which is working, by the way.

As much as Cass used to think what I did was silly, she's starting to see how much work goes on behind it all. It feels good to be using my skills to help people, instead of just creating sponsored posts for lip balms or helping my mom set up silly storylines that hardly anyone believes, in between her trying to sell crystals or healing shakes. Everything with my mom feels so fake and scripted and has for a long time.

That's probably why my car accident was so good for engagement—no one saw it coming. Least of all me. It was the first time people saw just how messy our lives are behind the scenes. As embarrassing as it was, it was also the realest thing we've ever shown.

Everything has been building up inside me, and I've been acting so off that it's probably not a surprise to Cass when she catches me wiping my eyes and trying not to cry after getting off the phone with my mother.

I really don't know why I'm crying. We didn't even get in a fight or anything. She was just telling me how excited her team is to have me back. Apparently, the algorithm loves me right now, whatever that means, and her team is dying to have me back on camera driving up engagement.

I'm just so overwhelmed by it all, trying to be the perfect daughter, the perfect girlfriend, the perfect content machine for my mother . . . I can't take it. It's ridiculous. It's too much.

"Birdie?" Cass says quietly. We're in the shady alcove near where she parks at the beach every morning. She knows it's where I always come to hide during my breaks. I'm on lunch right now, and judging by the two salads in her hand, so is she.

"Hey, um, hi," I say, shoving my phone in my pocket with one hand and wiping my cheeks with the other. "That for me?"

"Yeah. I stopped by to see you, and Kiera said you just headed to lunch. I thought I could join you." She passes me the container, light Italian dressing on the side, just like I like it. "I miss you," she adds, following me over to a staff picnic table.

I gently roll my eyes. "You drove me here this morning. You must be really obsessed with me."

"I am, but that's not why I miss you. I kinda was wondering if we could talk."

I hang my head for a second, squeezing my eyes shut before looking back at her. I know she deserves some answers; it's been unfair of me not to give them to her. "Of course. About what?" I ask, like I don't already know.

Cass sits down across from me. "You've been miles away these last few days. I don't want to pry, but I feel like I need to know why. If you can tell me?" She sighs and looks down at her salad. I hate how nervous she looks right now, but most of all, I hate that it's my fault.

"There's just been a lot on my mind lately," I say. I wish I could leave it at that, but I know it wouldn't be right. "I haven't meant to be distant, Cass, I promise. You're my favorite thing about this whole summer. The best thing about it, actually."

Cass smiles at first, basking in the compliment, but then her brow furrows. "The summer?"

I can hear it in her voice—that little hint of worry, that tiny accusation that maybe I *am* just another summer girl. I'm not; I know I'm not. At least, I don't want to be.

"My mom wants me to go back to Boston after the Founders' Day Gala," I blurt out. It's far from being the only problem on my mind, but it's probably the most immediate considering how fast it's coming up.

Cass spears some of her lettuce carefully, not looking up at me as she asks, "And you're going?"

"I don't know," I answer honestly.

She nods to herself, like I just proved something, and then takes a deep breath. "Do you want to?"

And now it's my turn to become intensely interested in my salad. "No. Not really, but it's complicated," I say. "I don't know that I'm really being given a choice in the matter. I've been trying to tell my dad that I want to stay, but he didn't seem to really get it or have the bandwidth to deal with it, and my mom is being pretty adamant about getting me home."

"So we're going to have your birthday together, and then . . . that's it?"

"I don't want it to be."

"And this is why you've been so distant?"

"It's a big part of it."

"What are the other parts?" she asks, like it's that simple.

"Just stuff with my friends. I . . . I can't get into it right now. Okay? Please, I can't." I shake my head. One bombshell is all I can handle talking about today. "I know you were so worried about me being a summer girl. Now here I am being told that I have to go back to the city before the summer's even over!"

"It's not like I didn't know you were going to go home eventually, Birdie. Granted, I didn't think it would be in, like, a week, but I knew at some point you would. I didn't expect you to stay here forever. It won't be too long before I have to head to Boston too, anyway. I just wish you talked to me before you wasted time being weird and beating yourself up for having to leave early."

My eyes snap to hers, confused. "You're fine with me leaving?"

"I still don't want to break up because of it, if that's what you mean. Of course, it's going to massively suck not seeing you every day, but it's not a deal-breaker or anything. We can handle the rest of the summer apart, and then I'll be in Boston and . . ."

"And what?" I ask, my stomach flip-flopping over what that might look like. *Does she have the same fears I have?*

"And then we'll keep handling it." She smiles reassuringly. "You're not my prisoner, Birdie. We can figure this out."

"You didn't think of me as a prisoner in the beginning?"

I ask, holding my fingers up barely apart. "Not even a teeny-tiny bit?"

"The beginning was different. Plus, you were technically your dad's prisoner, not mine. I was a guard at best." She smirks. "Which, speaking of, we really need to talk to him. He's texted me twice today."

"How about we go back to that whole 'staying in the moment' thing we were trying to do before instead?" I say, only half kidding. "I don't feel like dealing with that right now too."

"We can't. He keeps asking me why I stopped taking the money. I've been kind of tiptoeing around it, saying that it hardly seems like work, but he's getting really oddly worried about it. I need to tell him I'm not going to take money to hang out with my *girlfriend*."

I know how much she loves saying that, how much it means to her that I call her that. Just like I know she thinks this is a technicality, like we just have to tell him and everything will be fine. He'll be happy even. I hope she's right, but with everything else going on, I'm not sure the timing's right.

"Can we keep this just for us for a little while longer?" I ask, and she studies my face.

"Why? Are you embarrassed by me?" Her voice sounds teasing, but as I scramble to find words, her eyes go hard with hurt and frustration. "Seriously, Birdie?"

"No! I just . . . My dad will tell my mom, and my mom will try to turn it into content, and then next thing you know, we'll have to do a sponsored post for Bisexual Awareness

Week or something, and I'm so sick of having nothing for me. Everything I've ever had or done in my life was meant to entertain someone else, except for this summer. Except for you! You're mine. And I . . . I don't want to share."

I don't realize how true those words are until they're out of me, until her face softens and she's up moving around the table to slide onto the bench beside me.

"I get it," she says, tipping my chin toward hers. "Hey, look at me. I get it."

"I'm not embarrassed by you, Cass," I say, meeting her eyes so she can see just how serious I am about all of this. "You're so much better than me—you don't even understand."

"None of that," she says firmly. "You're incredible. I'm incredible. We can both be incredible and not at all embarrassing together." She smiles softly, clearly desperate to cheer me up.

Her phone buzzes, ruining the moment. It's Bentley checking on her because she's been gone too long.

"Ugh, I have to go," she says, frantically texting him back. "I lost track of time."

"Go," I say, gently shoving her away. "I'll clean up here; I still have fifteen minutes. It's slow right now, so Kiera told me to take an hour."

"Are you sure?"

"I'm sure. Go keep the world safe, Cassandra Adler."

She grins at that, bending over to kiss me quickly on the temple before jogging out of sight.

I take my time cleaning up and tossing what's left of our salads, thinking about what I should do next, buoyed by how much better my conversation with Cass went than I imagined it would. Maybe I'll get lucky talking with my dad too, if I just have a little courage.

Maybe it *can* all be okay. Maybe I *can* fix all of this after all. Maybe.

Maybe.

20

Cass

THINGS AREN'T GETTING better with Birdie, and I'm losing my mind.

On the outside, things look fine. She's still spending every spare second she can with me, usually helping out at the Coalition. She's fully taken over the social media accounts at this point. She's really kind of a whiz at that stuff.

Our Instagram account has gone from a measly twenty-three followers since we started it (which was composed almost completely of people working at the Coalition) to 3,763 and counting. I know that's still small potatoes in a world as big as ours—even our tiny city has almost 25,000 people in it—but it feels like a real start. And our TikTok? She took it from literally nonexistent to thousands of followers, with several viral videos. Not only that, but she set us up with a website that can take donations using a company she and her mom worked with for a charity drive. While the donations aren't exactly pouring in, they're more than the zero we got before she stepped in.

Birdie has taken our approach and modernized it, made it trendier, and attracted a younger audience who cares deeply about this cause. It's something that none of us really had a handle on before. It's been impressive to say the least.

At the beach, she's been a similar powerhouse. Well, as much as one can be a powerhouse as a parking lot attendant. She's working not just harder, but smarter. She's so confident in her role now that even Kiera is taking some days off, happily letting Birdie train the new people and keep them on track.

Sure, the traffic still backs up like hell for the morning and afternoon rushes, but she stays calm and controlled in a way that she didn't at the start of the summer. She seems happier, more confident than she did when I first met her—or re-met her, technically—in every area of her life. Except us.

When she first told me she had to go home soon, I was relieved. I didn't want her to go, of course, but she had been so distant I thought there might be more to it. But now, several days later, I guess I don't understand why she's become so resigned. She's been throwing herself into work like she's running out of time, and I get that she kind of is, but . . . she hasn't been making time for *just us*. It's confusing. How can I complain about someone who's working so hard volunteering for my family's organization? Like I wish she would help people *less* and snuggle with me *more*. It sounds ridiculous.

Plus, she still hasn't told her dad we're dating. I went with her a couple days ago when she said she was planning to, but she completely chickened out. It didn't help that George started the conversation by letting us know that Verity was unfortunately coming into town a few days early to help get things ready for the gala. I don't know if learning her mom was coming early freaked her out, or if she really is worried Verity will try to "commodify" us or whatever . . . But in the end, the conversation veered into being about how we're "such good friends" now, and *that's* why I feel wrong taking the money. It was so awkward.

I think I left even more confused than when I got there. Of course, then Birdie and I got into a fight about it, and things went back to being tense no matter how hard we've both been trying to pretend they're not. She's just so hard to read sometimes. I wish she didn't keep so many things bottled up inside.

So yeah, professional, work-related stuff, we're golden. Like absolutely golden. Relationship-wise? I don't know. There's been a steady pulling away that I can't tell myself I'm imagining anymore. It's like her walls are closing back up the closer she gets to having to go home, and it's making me feel twitchy and nervous, like maybe mine should be back up too.

As much as I want to believe she's not going to fuck me over like all the other summer girls have in the past, I . . . don't. It's getting hard to trust in that. She swears she's just overwhelmed with her mom coming into town soon and getting ready for the Founders' Day stuff with her dad—apparently he wants her to give a speech introducing him as Volunteer of the Year or something—but it seems like bullshit, if I'm being honest.

She won't even let me plan anything for her birthday. I get that it sucks it's the same day as the award gala, but when I suggested a bonfire the night before or an early breakfast the day of, she shut both down so intensely I almost felt bad for even suggesting it. It's like she wants to pretend it's not happening, or worse, that *we're* not.

"You could just try talking to her," Six says. He's got his head on Bentley's shoulder. They became officially official a few days ago and are so cute and clingy it hurts. It reminds me of how Birdie and I used to be.

The beach is closed today due to a major storm system causing super unsafe conditions, so we're all off. Well, technically you can't *really* close a beach, but they aren't charging for parking. Plus, there are signs everywhere warning that there are no lifeguards on duty and that people shouldn't be in the water. Other than helping to hang the double red flags up on every lifeguard tower and dragging out the signs saying swimming is prohibited today, we weren't needed.

Birdie stayed behind with Kiera to help turn cars away and deal with upset parents who are determined to fit a beach visit in on their summer vacations, even if it's pouring rain and their families run the risk of getting electrocuted by lightning or dragged out to sea in a vicious wave. Given that she volunteered to stay behind and get screamed at by tourists rather than leave with me, I can't help but take it a little personally.

"I already talked to her." I sigh and look at the two guys sitting across from me. I was a little annoyed Bentley brought Six to our best friend date, but now I'm just glad that there's someone else who seems to care what I'm going through. "I thought things were going to be fine after that, and they were for about a day, but now we're right back to it."

"Babe, remember? I told you about that," he says to Six. "But in any other situation, that would be great advice."

Six beams at the compliment, and I fight the urge to vomit, ignoring the fact that not too long ago, Birdie and I were for sure exactly as gross as they are right now.

"I just hope she's not pulling some summer girl bullshit after all this," Bentley adds.

"I don't know what's going on, but it feels big," I say sadly. "She's not just pulling away from me. She's, like, *stressed*. She seems more worried about her mom coming here than she is about having to leave with her after. She says she wants to be together and nothing's wrong, but then she keeps shutting me out. You don't think she's trying to get *me* to break up with *her* so she doesn't have to be the bad guy, do you?"

"Are you guys sure she's even really out?" Six asks, lifting his head from Bentley's shoulder. "I know I was out a lot more on vacation than I was at home for a long time. It's just easier here; it feels like it's not real life. If she's being weird about her dad and now weird about her mom, maybe that's part of the problem."

"She's very out." I laugh. "You've hung around us enough to know she hasn't tried to hide us at all."

"Okay, so . . . she's out *here*," Six says, and my stomach flips when I realize he's right.

Is that what's wrong with us? Is she not out back in Boston? Maybe she's not worried about her family's reaction because I'm some trash townie in their eyes like I was starting to think again, but because I'm a *girl*?

"It . . . it can't be that. Right?" I look to Bentley, desperately searching for some reassurance that I know he can't actually give me. "I mean, I would know. That's something you would tell the other person, wouldn't you? I mean, we didn't talk about it specifically because she was already acting so open about it, but we didn't purposely not."

"She's definitely seemed very out when I've been with you two, but . . ."

"But this isn't her real life," I say, the words hitting me like a ton of bricks. It makes sense, even if I don't want to believe it. How had I never considered this?

I've been out for so long, and so many of my friends are queer, I didn't think anything of it. I might not have been born rich, but I was lucky enough to be born into a family—and a community—that was nothing but loving and supportive when I came out. George never once was weird about me dating girls, but is it somehow different when it's his own daughter? We've been living in this bubble for so long out here, I think I lost sight of the fact that we were even in one.

"I have to go," I say, dropping some cash onto the table and rushing out the door.

If this is what the problem is, I need to talk to Birdie, right now. No more avoiding it. A little spike of frustration wells up inside me as I walk to my car, and I try to shove it down. I know no one should ever feel like they *have* to come out. I know there are a lot of reasons people feel like they *can't*. I can't get mad at her for this.

I just feel like, if that's the problem, if Birdie really doesn't feel comfortable coming out to her family, then that's a conversation we should have already had. I should have known that going in, so I could decide if that was right for me too. We're both in this relationship, not just her. And we *especially* should have had it before she filled my head with the idea of us staying together when we're both in Boston.

She wouldn't be the first person I've dated in the closet. It's not a deal-breaker by any means for me, but it does always put a unique sense of stress on the relationship. Part of making that strain manageable is that everyone needs to be on the same page—they have to be able to communicate.

If you know someone's in the closet, it changes your expectations of them, and changes what you can ask for in a relationship, and how you can act. It's only fair to talk about that before letting things get serious. So no, Birdie being in the closet is not a deal-breaker for me, but her lying about it— even by omission—might just be.

I make it back to the beach in record time, thankful that there's no line of cars. Kiera waves me in when I pull up, but Birdie is nowhere in sight.

I put my window down, yelling over the rain to where Kiera is sitting alone in the guard shack at the entrance to the parking lot. "Where's Birdie?" I ask, and Kiera gestures to the snack bar building.

"Her friend kept calling her, so I told her to go inside and take it. Check the changing rooms maybe? It's pretty dead now. If she wants to head home, can you let her know it's fine with me?"

"Yeah, thanks!" I say, putting my window up before the inside of my car gets even more drenched. I forgo my usual parking spot and pull into a spot as close as I can get to the building just as thunder booms across the sky, making it feel like my very bones are vibrating.

Or maybe that's just how nervous I am to confront her.

I take one deep breath and then another, and then make a mad dash for inside. I get thoroughly soaked in the less than two minutes it takes me to run around the front of the building, up the steps to the snack bar, and into the employees-only area. A miserable day for a miserable conversation.

Vince is in his office and yells, "Slow down, hon!" as I run by, but I can't. *I can't.*

I need to know if this is what's really going on, and if it is, why Birdie felt like she couldn't tell me. Why she didn't feel like she could trust me with that, knowing how important it is, especially since we've talked about continuing things even after she goes home next week, unless . . . unless she really didn't mean that.

Suddenly, I feel cold all over and not because of the storm. I push open the door to the locker room quietly. I can hear Birdie on the phone a couple aisles over. I should walk right up to her, but she doesn't seem to have heard me, or if she did, she doesn't seem to care, so I walk closer, trying not to eavesdrop but failing spectacularly. I recognize Ada's voice right away from all the streams they've done together.

". . . make sure you bring the monster to dinner with us that night," she says. "I can't wait to meet the boy who stole your heart. Can we go out on his boat?"

"I don't know if they're going to be around," Birdie says, and suddenly I can't breathe, my feet frozen in place, just an aisle away, helpless to do anything more than absorb the arrows her words are firing straight into my chest. "They've been so busy lately, we've barely been able to see each other."

Who is she talking about?

"Well, then, I guess it's good I'm surprising you with a visit too, since your new boyfriend is such a flake."

New boyfriend?

"Ada, come on." Birdie laughs. "Just be happy for me, for once, even if you can't meet them."

I feel like I'm going to throw up. This whole time that I've been falling for her, has she been seeing someone else? It feels like my brain clicks off and back on, a total system restart as I try to process what I'm hearing. Before I know it, my feet work just fine and I'm marching over to her, hurt and angry and shivering from more than just the rain.

Birdie glances at me and does a double take, her mouth falling open as she seems to realize what I must have overheard. "Ada, I have to go. It's an emergency," she says. "I'll call you tonight."

She clicks off and sets the phone down, watching me nervously. I stand there, not moving, barely breathing, feeling like my whole world just got turned upside down. "You have a boyfriend?" I manage to grind out, my voice brittle like glass.

"No, no!" she says, jumping up and rushing over to me. She shakes her head again, brushing some of the wet hair that's sticking to my face away and tucking it behind my ear. "I don't have a boyfriend, Cass. She thinks . . . Ada thinks *you're* my boyfriend."

"That makes no sense, Birdie." I shut my eyes, inhaling deeply through my nose. "Why would she think I was a guy?"

"Because she misunderstood, and I let her."

I look at her, nodding to myself. It seems like Six was right on the money about why Birdie has been pulling away so much. "Right, because not only are you dating a townie, but you're dating a townie *girl*, right? You're not out back home, are you?" She looks away, fumbling with the hem of her T-shirt, and that's all the confirmation I need. "Why did you let me think you were, Birdie?"

"Ada knows I'm bi. It's not *exactly* that."

"Then why does she think I'm a guy?"

"Because even though I told people about being bi, I've never been with a girl. They've never seen me with one. My mom and Ada both seemed . . . uncomfortable with it. If I brought a girl home for real, I don't know if my mom would flip out or be planning how to monetize it with a sponsored coming-out post the next day."

"Birdie . . ."

"I know that sounds like bullshit, but it's not. Everything with my family is *a lot*. You don't understand what it's really like. We've been so safe here, and it's been so, so wonderful, but I'm about to be dragged back home, where my life is a billion times more complicated. It's not just *who* you love; it's who they are and *what they can do for you*."

"Right, so back to the poor townie thing, then? Jesus, Birdie, I don't know what's worse—that you let your best friend think I'm a guy while acting like you want to be serious with me, or that you're so gutted by the idea of dating someone who can't afford a yacht that you lied about that too." I shake my head, my heart clawing its way up my throat, and angrily wipe at my eyes. I'll be damned if she's going to see me cry over this.

"It's not like that," she says.

"It's exactly like that!" I shout. "You couldn't even decide what part of me you're most embarrassed by. The money? The townie thing? Being queer? So you just changed every part of me in the stories you told about us. Every part! You made me into some rich guy with a boat, Birdie. She's your best friend, and you didn't tell her one single true thing about me, the person you're supposedly falling for. Plus, George just thinks we're the ultimate besties or something because you didn't want him to know either. I can't believe I fell for that whole 'Can we keep this just for us?' line."

"Cass, it's not that simple."

I hold up my hand, stopping her. "At least you told me the truth about one thing: You're not a summer girl. Whatever you are . . . it's something far worse."

"Cass, wait," she says, wrapping her hand around my wrist as I turn to leave. "I love you."

"Well, you have a really strange way of showing it," I say, spinning back to her. "I let you into every aspect of my life— surfing, my friends, my work with my father—and you just . . . you've just been lying this whole time."

"I was scared!" she says. "Please believe me. I'm sorry I lied to Ada. I'm sorry I didn't tell you what was going on. I felt like I couldn't."

"Why?"

"I thought I would lose you if I did."

"So you made the decision for me."

"No, for *us*."

"That's not how it works, Birdie. I don't care if you're out or not, truly. I don't care if you don't want to tell your parents or your friends. I've been in that situation before with people I cared about, and was it great? No. But was it worth it, and did we make it work? Yes! None of that is insurmountable, but the lying? Keeping all of this from me? Pretending I'm something I'm not to make me more palatable to your closest friends? That's a real problem for me. Like, bigger than the other stuff. You can't love me, Birdie. You're too embarrassed by me for that to even be possible. I can't believe I thought . . ." I shake my head again, trailing off.

"Wait," she says, rushing to get in front of me. "Can we just . . . can we not say anything we'll regret right now? Please, Cass, I handled this so, so wrong. I get it. I hear you. I've been trying to find a way to fix all this these last few days. I've been trying to work up the courage. I was going to the other day, but then my dad started to talk about my mom and—"

"It didn't sound like you were working up the courage on the call just now." I scoff.

"Cass, please. You're absolutely right to be upset. I'm majorly in the wrong here. Just please, don't walk away from us yet. I can fix this. I can."

Birdie seems desperately sad, and my heart breaks even more. She looks as panicked and gutted as I feel right now, but I don't know how to fix this. I don't know where to start or if we even have time. "What's the point?" I ask her sadly.

"The point is that I don't want to lose you," she says, coming closer. "Give me some time to make this right. Just . . . trust me for a little while longer."

"I did trust you, Birdie, and you turned me into some kind of imaginary douchebag guy on a yacht!"

"Don't give up on me. Please. Don't give up on *us*," she says, a distant echo of her words from that first day on the beach. It worked back then. It might even be working now. I'm so weak for this girl. If there *is* some way to fix all this, then . . .

"What do you want from me?" I ask, hanging my head.

She steps forward, putting her forehead on my shoulder and wrapping her arms around me. "I fucked up. I know I fucked up, in a big, huge 'crashing a McLaren looks like nothing now' kind of way, but I love you so much, Cass. Please let me fix this. I understand if I went too far, if you can't trust me. It's no one's fault but my own, but if there's any part of you—"

"Birdie . . ." I try to fight it, to be strong, to remember how mad I am, how hurt I am, but as she trembles against me, her hot tears soaking into the expanse of skin along my neck, none of that seems to matter anymore.

I wrap my arms around her, holding her close until her sobs give way to hitched breaths and I can feel the exhaustion settling deep into her bones.

That's the rub, isn't it? I don't want to give up on her. I don't want to let her go.

But I don't know what the hell else to do.

21

Birdie

IT'S BEEN TWO days since our talk, or really my breakdown, and everything is still a mess. I don't know why I thought it wouldn't be, honestly. The way she held me that afternoon in the locker room, it felt like she was holding me together, like she understood and wanted to be there . . . but yesterday she was different.

I don't want to say cold—that would be too harsh. She still held my hand and drove me to work like normal. She still popped around on her lunch break to see if I needed anything and to make sure Kiera and I had enough water, since parking lot attendants aren't taken care of as well as lifeguards.

Except there's a sadness in her eyes now, a loneliness that I know I put there. I hate that my screwed-up life has made hers worse instead of better. I hate that I don't know how to make it right without blowing up my own life. I hate that I love her so much that I'm actually considering it.

"I'm going to talk to my dad about us tonight, and to my mom when she gets here tomorrow," I say as she drops me off at home after work.

She sighs, and I'm not expecting that reaction. I thought it would make her happy. She looks at me with that same kicked-puppy look that she's had all along. "You don't have to do that, Birdie."

"I want to."

She looks away, and why is even this going so wrong, just when I thought I had figured out the first step to make it right?

"I just don't want you to feel like you have to come out because of me. It's your decision, seriously."

"And I'm making it," I say, desperate for her to understand. "They already know I'm queer anyway, even if they want to pretend they don't."

"If you weren't with me, if all of this hadn't happened, would you still be in such a rush to remind them?"

"What does that matter?"

"It just does! You said that the last time you tried, it didn't go great, and I don't want you to do something you're going to regret. I don't want you to resent me because you feel like your hand is being forced here or something."

"But you deserve—"

"It's not about that," Cass says, finally looking back at me and squeezing my wrist. "This part is only about you."

"But you said—"

"I said I was upset that you lied and that you took the decision away from me, whether I wanted to get involved with you given your . . . situation. I'm still trying to process that, and I'm still hurt that you didn't share that with me. But the answer isn't you rushing to come out again without thinking through what you really want. I don't want you to do it just to prove something."

"I'm not. I'm very sure this is what I want, and I'm very sure about you," I say. If this was any other time, if I could rewind to even just a few days ago, I know she would be smiling at that. That she would be kissing me, or I would be kissing her, and that ache in my belly where the butterflies used to live wouldn't be sending seismic earthquakes of anxiety through my whole body right now. Instead, she just gives me the saddest smile and turns back to look out the window.

"I have to get going. I promised my dad that I would work at the Coalition tonight since I need to take tomorrow off for dress shopping for the Founders' Day Gala."

"I could come with you if you need help," I say.

"Nah, it's boring stuff today. I'm just taking notes for the board meeting so that my fill-in for tomorrow can take tonight off. It's not really a two-person job."

"Dress shopping, then, tomorrow? I don't have my dress either. Let me take you to breakfast first, and then I know a great little place that carries any dress you could possibly want."

Cass shrugs. "Something tells me that the places I shop and the places you shop are really different."

"Don't do that," I say softly.

"What?" she asks, turning to look at me.

231

"Don't focus on the differences between us. Don't look for reasons for us to fail. *Please.*"

"Okay, Birdie," she says, her voice so quiet I almost miss it. "I'll try."

I lean forward and kiss her cheek, because I don't know if a kiss on the lips would be welcome right now given the state of things, and then I climb out of the passenger seat and watch her drive away.

I need to find a way to fix this. Fix *us*. And no matter what Cass thinks, I know coming clean to my father about what's really going on is a solid first step. I know Cass is worried about being the catalyst for me coming out—or, well, coming out again, because what is the life of a queer person if not continually coming out?—but I'm not doing this for her. I'm doing this for me. The fact that me living my authentic life can only help our relationship is just an ideal side effect.

I take a moment before I go inside, knowing that my dad will be waiting for me with takeout from the new restaurant in town. There are only a few more precious hours until my mom swoops in, and he's been trying to make the most of it. He even texted twice to double-check I'll be home in time, so he must be excited. Or maybe he's just lonely. I haven't seen him hanging around with John Adler lately outside of work stuff. I hope the strain between me and Cass hasn't carried over to them.

What I'm not expecting, when I paste a fake smile on my face and push open the door, is to hear Ada and my mom yell, "Surprise!" with Mitchell and my very sheepish-looking father standing right behind them. Mom, predictably, has her phone camera recording my reaction.

I stand there in the entryway for a moment, stunned, my eyes locking on my cheating ex, who is seriously smiling warmly at me, as if he thinks I'd be pleased to see him. My mom puts the camera down as soon as she realizes all she's going to get is this nonreaction. She instantly starts fussing around me, complaining that the sun has fried my hair and "What are you wearing?" and "Now this clip is unusable. You couldn't have at least acted a little happy?" among other things I tune out. I slowly let my eyes drift to Ada, who wasn't supposed to be here until this weekend and who's doing this smile-wince combo that tells me she realizes her earlier timing might not be the best.

Understatement of the millennium.

"Hi, everyone," I choke out eventually, brushing my mom's hands away from where they're tugging on my hair as she groans about how I need a cut and color before I can go back on camera.

"Hi, honey," Dad says, watching me like I'm a volcano that's about to erupt. Maybe I am.

"You didn't tell me they were coming early, Dad . . . or at all!" I add, glaring at Mitchell, whose smile has thankfully begun to slip off his face as he realizes that, no, I'm not actually going to jump into his arms.

"I only found out this morning!" Dad says.

"Yet you've texted me twice since then," I say, forcing a smile.

"Are you okay?" Ada whispers to me. My mom frowns

beside me, clearly displeased not only with the state of me but with my reaction to seeing her.

"I just need a minute," I say, heading to the stairs and the blissful quiet of my room. "Too much sun today maybe."

"I knew you shouldn't have allowed her to work there, George," my mom snaps. "What is wrong with you?"

Instead of answering, my dad slinks away toward his office. Typical. He never could stand up to her; he always just runs off. I never noticed that before, always buying his assertion that he was just away on business, but now that I see it for what it is, it all makes sense. As I hastily make my exit too, I wonder if maybe we're more alike than I realized.

I let my door click shut behind me and flop across my bed. On some level, I know I'm being rude, especially to Ada. I'm sure my mother will be in my face about it later, but right now I just need a second. I spent so long working myself up to tell my dad the truth tonight over a quiet dinner. I never thought I'd be staring down the faces of my best friend, my mother, *and my freaking cheating ex* at the same time.

I groan and bury my head in the pillow, fighting the urge to cry and knowing it won't help anything. A few minutes ago, I was so sure of everything, and now I feel like my world has just been flipped upside down.

A soft knock on the door has me rolling over and wiping at my eyes. I try to make myself presentable as much as possible before calling out "Come in," not knowing if I'm going to be faced with Ada (good), my mom (bad), Mitchell (downright hellish), or some combination of all of them (simply, kill me now).

Thankfully, the door opens to reveal only Ada, who walks over to the bed and sits gently beside me, rubbing my back.

"Sorry for just showing up way early like this."

"What is going on? Why is *he* here?"

She sighs. "Carly texted me this morning that she overheard your mom telling her mom that she was bringing Mitchell out to try to get things squared away between you before you guys go back to filming. I basically got ready as fast as I could, showed up on your mom's doorstep, and insisted she drive me out now too so at least you'd have me here for moral support. She wasn't going to let me, but I told her I would consent to being filmed, and then magically there was room for me too."

"You couldn't have given me a heads-up?" I ask, turning to look at her.

"She threatened to throw me out of the car if I breathed a word of it to you, and—I don't know—your mom is *scary*."

I nod; I know it's true. While I don't *think* my mom would actually throw anybody out of a car, it's not fully outside the realm of possibility—especially if you screw with her filming plans, which apparently somehow still include Mitchell.

"I'm sorry," Ada says. "I know this is a lot."

I want to tell her she doesn't know the half of it, but I don't—not yet. Instead, I ask, "Is he still down there?"

"Yeah." She winces. "Your mom is setting him up in a guest room."

"He's staying *here*, like, in this house?!" I yelp, and Ada blows out a breath so heavy her cheeks puff out.

"Unfortunately."

"Why?!"

"I honestly don't know. She was on a call setting up filming schedules the whole drive. I could barely get a word in to ask her to turn down the AC before I froze to death. I just knew I needed to be here."

"Okay." I take a deep breath. "Okay. Thank you for being here. I don't know . . . I guess if I can't get rid of him, then I need to go talk to him."

"Right now?"

"I might as well get it over with, yeah."

She grabs my arm, looking me in the eyes. "You're not taking him back, are you?"

"No!" I snort. "Definitely not."

"Should I come with?" Ada asks, her hand falling away.

"No. I can handle it. Just . . . if you hear screaming, come downstairs. *He* might need help."

~~~

"Mitchell?" I say, peeking my head through his open doorway to find him already doing push-ups on the floor. "What are you doing?"

"Your mom's filming is out of control; I'm not trying to look like shit when she decides to point the camera my way."

"Wow, you haven't seen me since the crash and *that's* your primary concern? How ripped you look?" I scoff. I can't believe I ever liked this boy.

"Your dad covered the repairs," he says, finally standing up. "Don't worry, we're cool."

I jerk back in disgust. "We are very much *not* cool, Mitchell! You cheated on me at my own family event. Does that part matter to you at all? Not to mention you made a whole TikTok about it being my fault."

He shrugs. "I can see how that would piss you off."

"Piss me off? It hurt me! You were my boyfriend. We were together for a year before you . . . Wait, I bet you were cheating on me the whole time. Weren't you?"

"Is this some kind of trap? Invite me out here just to yell at me?"

"I absolutely did *not* invite you out here!" I stare at him, incredulous. "How could it be a trap when I had no idea you were coming?"

"Our moms wanted us to film together again. That's the whole reason I'm here. I assumed when your mom offered to drive, it meant you were cool with it. You are, right?"

I roll my eyes. "You assumed wrong. Obviously, I had no idea. You being here really complicates an already complicated situation. I have a good thing going out here, Mitchell, or I did. I don't even know anymore. But seriously, why did you come? Are you trying to ruin my life again?"

"Wait, you're seeing someone? That's so messed up! We haven't even been broken up that long and you've already moved on?"

"You moved on while we were still together!" I seethe. "You were literally hooking up with someone *at my own party!*"

"I said sorry!"

"No, you didn't!"

"Fine! Sorry!" he says, crossing his arms. "Look, this wouldn't be my first choice of how to spend my summer either, okay?"

"Then why are you here?!" I yelp, practically stomping my foot. I'm about to lose it on him if he doesn't start explaining, and it's not going to be pretty.

Mitchell lets his head hang for a moment before looking up at me. "My mom *made* me come out here. That's it. I swear. I'm not trying to screw up whatever situationship you have going on," he says, brushing his sweaty hair back and standing up.

"You really never cared about me at all, did you?" I ask. It should hurt to realize this, but instead there's a sense of relief that comes with knowing for sure it was all bullshit. He sucks as much as I thought he did, and that's . . . freeing.

"Of course I cared," he says. "I'm not an asshole."

I raise my eyebrows. "We must have really different definitions of what that word means."

"Fine, I'm not a *total* asshole," he clarifies. "You're nice, and you can be fun to hang out with when you're not a stressed-out pain in the ass. But the filming is a lot, and the whole 'together forever' storyline your mom was pushing on her web series was way too much. I don't want forever. No offense, but I can't even comprehend that. I'm sorry I handled things in a really messed-up way. But I'm barely eighteen—what did you want me to do?"

"I don't know, talk to me first before you shoved your tongue down someone else's throat?"

He rolls his eyes. "Yeah, 'cause that would have gone over well. Your mom would have gone fucking feral if I tried to break up with you, and don't get me started on what my mom would do. Those two work each other up like dogs in a fight."

"I'm not forgiving you just because my mom messed with your life too," I say, because he deserves to know that he really screwed up and he can't keep hurting people like that.

"I'm not asking you to, but a truce might be nice."

"A truce?"

"Our moms decided I had to be here." He shrugs, like it's the most natural thing in the world. "Let's just try to be civil until I can get out of your hair."

"Why did your mom want you filming so bad?"

"She freaked out that your live stream 'hurt our image.' I tried to fix it with my own streams, but all that did was get 'hashtag Team Birdie' to two million impressions." He rolls his eyes. "My mom says she doesn't want future bosses googling me and having my cheating be the top result. Even my dad tried to tell her that with our kind of connections, 'youthful indiscretions' don't really matter anyway, but she doesn't care. My mom threatened civil action against your mom, but then they cooked up this scheme instead where I come here and win you back. A limited-time plotline to save both our reputations. If I didn't agree to it, Mom said she was going to take my condo away."

"I don't want to be with you, though," I say. "I'm not just some prize that you can put up on a shelf and dust off when you need to have the right connections, or someone to look good with at a gala, Mitchell. I don't want that for me. I don't even want that for you."

"I know, Birdie," he says, like I'm still not getting it, and maybe I'm not.

"I'm lost."

"I'm supposed to win you back, show that I've changed, then you dump me later and say we loved each other very much, but it just didn't work out. Then you look like the strong one, and I look like a reformed dirtbag with a newly minted heart of gold, free to go on with my life. Win-win. We wouldn't be the first PR relationship. We just have to follow the script."

"I'm tired of following the script, Mitchell," I say, sitting on the bed. He watches me with something akin to pity on his face. Like I'm some naïve little thing who doesn't know how to play the game, when I'm anything but. Not anymore.

"Meaning?"

"Meaning I'm sorry my mom dragged you out here, but I don't want to film anymore, and especially not this. I . . . I really care about the person I'm with, Mitchell. I won't do this to them or me."

"Wow," he says.

"What?"

"I've never seen you in love before. It looks good on you."

"Yeah." I smile, trying to ignore how sad that is in the context of our relationship. Hell, in the context of my whole life.

He scratches the back of his neck. "Do you really think Verity is going to let you out of all of this, though? I couldn't get out of it, and she's not even my mom! I doubt this will go over well."

"Yeah, I know." I sigh, because I'm sure he's right, but that doesn't mean I'm going down without a fight . . . especially now that I have someone to fight *for*.

22

Cass

I DON'T KNOW why I'm upset that Birdie and I aren't dress shopping together. Especially since *I'm* the one who canceled on *her*. She accepted my decision to blow her off semi-gracefully, telling me that if I change my mind to let her know. I replied with a terse K, and then watched the typing text bubbles appear and disappear about a dozen times before disappearing for good.

Whatever it was she was going to say, she swallowed it down instead. And that's fine, that's fair even. I'm the one blowing things up right now, not her—but it left us even more in this nebulous gray zone. I feel like I'm reading into everything she does or doesn't do a lot more than I probably should, while simultaneously worrying I'm not reading into things enough at all. It's just been . . . a lot.

So fun for me. Seriously.

Bentley and Six are meeting me for coffee later today,

which gives me about an hour and a half to pick a dress for the Founders' Day Gala. I've never really cared much about getting dressed up—I pretty much phoned it in for my own prom a few months back—but this feels special. Even if my dad's organization doesn't win, they'll still read out his and the other board members' names and acknowledge their accomplishments. There will be applause and joy, and I need to remember that.

I really hope we win, though. We've all been working so hard at building the case for us. We've buttoned everything up as tight as it can be, provided about a billion supporting documents, and are feeling good about our chances. Well, as good as can be in a rigged-up place like this. You can do everything right and still get screwed over just because people have more money or better connections, same as anywhere, even if you call it home.

I can't worry about that right now, though. I have to try to hold on to hope, and hope means that I need to find a dress. "Hope for everything, expect nothing" is what my dad always says in times like these, and honestly, it's the only thing getting me through.

That's what I'm *trying* to do with Birdie, despite my decision to blow her off today, and why I'm flipping through all the dresses that I can find in my size in one of the nicest dress stores in town. It has a little consignment area in the back where you can occasionally find deals, which is what I'm hoping for today. All the yacht ladies consign their clothes here at the end of the season, like that counts as donating to charity or something. Their good deed for the "poors."

Naturally, the place turns around and charges prices that most people can't afford—gotta keep the clientele in the right tax bracket and all—but still, sometimes you get lucky. It's taking my dad's budget for the dress combined with a bunch of my lifeguarding money for me to even glance in here, and I'm just praying I find something that feels special but also doesn't break the bank. If not, I guess I'm rewearing my prom dress.

The gala is black-tie, like actual black-tie. Not cocktail attire, not dressy, but actual "Do not pass go, do not collect two hundred dollars if you dare to show up in anything less than an evening gown." I try not to think about how ironic it is that the gala itself definitely costs more than the award they give out to improve the community.

They could save money on all the pageantry, and then just go ahead and give it to the people who really need it. It would make more of a difference than a bunch of people spending one single night patting themselves on the back. That's how I would do things if I were in charge . . . but of course, I'm not.

I slide a hanger off the rack, studying the gown in front of me with a frown. Even secondhand, I feel guilty about the price. We got in a new batch of applications to review this week at the Coalition, mostly tax lien relief requests from people who might lose their houses if we can't help out. And while this gown isn't priced *that* high, I can't help but feel guilty at the idea of spending a couple hundred dollars on a dress for myself to wear for one night, when some of those tax liens are barely over a thousand dollars. Buying a dress that could get them a quarter of the way to paid off is an outrageous privilege.

Even though I can't imagine having the kind of money Birdie's family has, or what it must be like living in her shoes, I also need to stay aware of my own privilege. We have enough money to have carefully set some aside for this event. I'm going to one of the best colleges around—yes, because their institutional aid lets me go there basically for free, but I wouldn't have had the grades to get in if my parents hadn't been incredibly involved or if I had been too busy trying to work to help out my family instead of studying for all those AP tests, which *also* cost a lot of money.

Compared to Birdie, we barely have a toehold on the mountain of lower-middle-class financial stability. One emergency could land us right back where we used to be—where the people sending in relief applications to the Coalition are *now*. But that doesn't change the fact that we have it better than a lot of people. Sometimes with Birdie, it's easy to forget that. When I see her wealth, how easily she moves through the world, I get a little jealous. I forget to be grateful for what I *do* have. I hate that.

In fact, it's probably irresponsible for me to even be here. I should be saving my money for college in the fall. I should be thinking about the unexpected expenses instead of how bad I want to wow my girlfriend with a dress worthy of her. I don't even know if she is my girlfriend anymore. God, it's so stupid.

I slide the dress back in place with a sigh, flipping through the rest of the rack and wondering if there's a way to make do with what I have at home. To somehow dress up my old prom dress so it looks a little more sophisticated while still holding on to most of my money.

I lost sight of myself here, just for a minute, walking into one of the places I knew *she* would likely shop. Only thinking that I want to look hot for Birdie, that I want to prove that I'm on her level. Prove that I belong in her circle even once we're both in Boston. Prove that I'm one of them, or I will be soon, after I graduate and her father helps me land a dream job.

Except I won't be, a fact that was proved to me when I found out she had lied not just about my gender and sexuality, but about where I'm from and how much money I have.

No matter what I do, I won't ever truly be one of them. And god, why would I even want to be? All that extravagance? All that waste? I already feel ridiculous standing here literally contemplating spending a week's wages on a dress just so I can show off for Birdie and her family. What is wrong with me?

I squeeze my eyes shut and take a breath, trying to calm the warring factions in my head. It's my own insecurity getting in the way right now. My own insecurity that has me standing in this shop instead of tearing through my own closet or the real thrift stores in the less nice part of town, where you can find a dress for dozens of dollars instead of hundreds or thousands.

I shake my head, leaving the dress rack behind and stepping out into the fresh summer air. I need to call Birdie. I need to stop spiraling. I need to—

Wait, is that Birdie driving by *in her father's car*?

I stand there, stunned, as she parks in the little lot beside the store. It's definitely Birdie, along with Ada—*when did she get into town?*—and there's a guy in the back seat whose face I can't see. It must be Ada's boyfriend or something. I can tell they're smiling at something the boy said, and haven't noticed me yet, but from what I can see, Birdie looks relaxed. She looks *relaxed*.

I step back, debating whether to try to slip inside the store and hide, but then I see her hold her phone up and talk into it. I don't know if she's live streaming herself right now, or just recording for later, but either way my stomach drops.

She told me she was done with that, that she didn't want to do that anymore. That was *the old Birdie*, not the girl I fell in love with this summer. The girl I fell for said she *hated* working with her mom and was trying to get her dad to let her stay. Birdie said filming for the Coalition was the closest she would ever come to going back to that. But now here she is with her old friends, in her dad's fancy car, returning to her old ways?

It feels like all the wind gets knocked out of me, like my heart is caving in, like I've forgotten how to breathe, as Birdie laughs, actually laughs. Like she's fine, happy even. Like she doesn't care anymore that things are so messed up between us. I know, I know—I canceled on *her*. I don't get to be mad that she's out having fun, but I can't help it. I want her to be as torn up as I am.

I turn away, ready to—I don't know—bolt down the road or hide or disappear, something, anything to get out of this situation, to unsee the old Birdie, the one I couldn't stand, the one I thought was gone for good, but they're right behind me as I push open the door and any hope of disappearing into the racks dies right along with my pride.

"Um, excuse me," Ada says, clearly trying to push past me to the fancier racks lining the edges of the store. I step back, letting her pass, staring at the floor as the boy and Birdie walk by me too. At first I think Birdie's trying to ignore me, but the way she jumps when I tug on her sleeve makes me realize that she was just too engrossed in her recording to notice I was even there. I'm not sure which is worse, honestly.

"Oh! What are you—" she starts, her surprised face meeting mine. Her eyes widen, and she quickly glances at her friends.

"Hey," I say. "I see you're filming again." She clicks her phone off and slides it into her pocket, a guilty look on her face.

Her friends have gone on ahead, thankfully, and we have a moment alone. I'm not expecting it when she grabs my hand and pulls me into the dressing room area, but I'm not mad about getting her to myself a little longer. I tuck into one of the stalls, and she shuts the door behind us.

"Sorry, I don't really have a choice on the filming thing," she says. "My mom showed up last night. She was waiting for me after you dropped me off. She's making me do this stupid recording stuff for her episode about the Founders' Day Gala."

"You could say no." I shrug. "If you really wanted."

"I . . . I turned her down about something else, and she's furious with me. She basically threatened to drag me back to Boston last night if I didn't get content for her."

"You've got to get out from under her thumb, Birdie," I say, like it's the most basic thing in the world, *because it is*. How does she not understand this?

"Right, you try telling my mom no and see how well it goes over," she says.

I roll my eyes. "You really didn't look that torn up about it when you were walking in."

Birdie looks away, a blush rising to her cheeks. "What, were you watching me or something?"

"No, I was leaving when I saw you getting out of your car. I just . . . What's even the point of this?"

"Of what?"

"All of this! Us! If you're just going to go right back to who you were when you get home."

"That's not fair!"

"Isn't it? One night, not even a full twenty-four hours with your mom, and you're already acting like the old you again! Did you care when I canceled on you today? Or were you relieved?"

"Cass," she says, "I just need you to be patient a little while longer."

"For what?" I ask. "So you can drag this out and hurt us both even more?"

She bites the inside of her cheek, looking so sad it's taking all my willpower not to reach out and tug her into a tight hug. I know she doesn't want things to be this way any more than I do—I know that—but it doesn't change the fact that *things are this way.*

"I should probably let you get back to it," I say, sounding more stoic than I feel. "You seem . . . busy."

"Wait," she says, but I don't. I flick the lock and march out of the dressing room area, running right into Birdie's friends, who have clearly been looking for her.

"Birdie?" Ada says, looking behind me. "You good?"

"Yeah, Ada," she says, coming up beside me.

The stupid hope-for-everything part of me wants her to introduce us, to prove that I'm important enough to meet her friends, that I matter, that I'm wrong about this situation we're in. The expect-nothing part of me suspects she won't.

"I heard yelling. Do you know this girl? Should I get the cashier, or—"

"No!" Birdie yelps. "I know her. This is . . ."

My stomach twists as her words trail off.

"Hope for everything, expect a kick in the gut" is what my dad should have said, because that's exactly how this feels right now. Birdie flung the word *girlfriend* around so casually before, but now it seems stuck in her throat, choking her. The boy tilts his head, waiting, and I realize who he is.

He's not Ada's boyfriend, or even one of Birdie's many Boston friends. It's Mitchell—the piece of shit who cheated on her. If she's hanging out with him again, then screw it.

"I'm her assistant," I say, understanding exactly where I stand now. My heart shatters into tiny, jagged pieces, each shard slicing into my softest parts and reminding me why this could never work. Why I was right to have my guard up this whole time and should have had it even higher.

Birdie and I could never be more than stolen kisses on moon-drenched beaches. We weren't inevitable, ever. We were transient, always, a liminal phase. A worthless wish on eyelashes and shooting stars.

"You never mentioned you had an assistant," Ada says, narrowing her eyes. "The only assistant you ever mentioned was—"

"I do!" she cuts Ada off, glancing back at me. "My dad brought her on to help with the, uh, Founders' Day stuff," Birdie continues rambling. "I was supposed to meet her today to look at dresses, actually, except you were both here. But, yeah, she's, um, she's great."

"I wish my dad would get me an assistant," Mitchell complains. He raises his hand as if I should high-five him or something, and I glare at him with a tight-lipped smile.

"Well, I see my *assistance* isn't needed today," I say as cheerfully as I can while trying to hold it together. "I'll leave you to it."

I'm out the door before Birdie can say anything else, my stupid stubborn heart dragging behind me, trying to claw its way back to her even though she doesn't want it. Doesn't want *me*. How could she, if we're finally being honest?

I'm not like them. I don't know why I ever thought I could be.

23

Birdie

THE NEXT HOUR passes in a blur.

I text Cass, but she doesn't reply. I'm a jackass, like certifiably. For a split second, when Cass called herself my assistant, I thought everything was going to be okay, like she understood how complicated things are and was trying to be there for me. Like she was being patient like I asked.

But the way her face fell when I agreed with her told me I was wrong—dead wrong. Thus, the texting and calling her repeatedly after she ran out. I know the direction she headed, but not where she went, and even if I did know, it's not like I could just run out and ditch my friends.

Well, *friend*. Ada. I don't know what Mitchell is. Not quite a friend. I'm still furious with him. But he's been weirdly cool since I told my mom we weren't going to film. He even backed me up, saying if I was out, so was he, leaving my mom double mad. I appreciate the united front in the face of that horror, but I can't just let him off the hook.

My mom eventually stopped yelling long enough to tell me that if I agreed to provide content in the lead-up to the Founders' Day Gala, she could "rework the rest of the season." I took the bone she decided to throw me and left, not telling her I was done filming for good after that, and not touching the "Oh yeah, I have a girlfriend now" talk at all. (Which I don't even know if I still do. I'm such an asshole.)

I'm still deep in my head about this as we walk by the coffee shop on our way to the jewelry store that Ada wants to check out. I glance in the window, utterly relieved to see Cass inside. It makes sense she would go there, especially if Bentley is around. I don't know why I didn't think of that. They're in their usual corner, with Cass's back to me and Bentley facing outward. When he meets my eyes, he scowls. So much for a warm welcome, not that I was honestly expecting one.

"Guys, go on without me," I say, heading for the door. Ada scrunches up her brows and tries to follow, but I hold up a hand. "I have to talk to somebody. I'll meet you there soon, okay?"

Mitchell starts to say something about needing coffee anyway, but I shake my head, looking at Ada with pleading eyes. She stares at me for a second, and then grabs Mitchell's arm, locking it in hers and tugging him along beside her, clearly realizing I need a minute.

I take a deep breath, steeling my nerves and pushing inside the coffee shop. Bentley *and* Six, who I didn't even notice sitting on the inside of the booth, lean back in unison, crossing their arms as they watch me walk up. I wonder if they practiced this protective big-brother thing or if it just comes naturally when your best friend is a girl.

Either way, Cass straightens and turns toward me. Her eyes are red-rimmed as she wipes at her nose and studies my face. She lets out a watery sigh and turns back around, effectively dismissing me. Or rather it would be effective, if I paid attention to it instead of walking right over and planting myself in her line of sight.

"I need to talk to you," I say, crouching in front of her. She looks at her friends and then slowly back at me.

"No."

"Cass, you can't just throw away—"

"What can't I throw away? My job as your assistant?" She scoffs.

Across from us, Bentley rolls his eyes, and Six leans forward and puts his elbows on the table, daring me to fuck this up even more.

"Yeah, we heard all about that," Bentley says, a sneer on his lips. It seems I've gone from being a coworker he genuinely likes to his bitter enemy all in one go.

"You said that first," I point out, turning my attention back to Cass. "Not me."

"You were so quick to agree with it! God forbid your boyfriend finds out, right? Did you guys even break up? Or was I just your side chick for the summer?"

"Come on, let's go," Bentley says, stepping around me to

254

offer his hand to Cass. "You don't need to see her any more today."

My heart sinks. She's got the wrong idea—an even worse idea than what's really going on. I might not be able to fix everything, but at least I can fix that.

"Mitchell and I are not together! I hadn't even talked to him once since that night at the villa. My mom brought him here with her yesterday to surprise me. It's all for a stupid storyline; it's got nothing to do with me." She looks at me like she doesn't believe me. "I love you, Cass. I swear to you, Mitchell and I are very, very over. I only agreed to film today to get her off my back because I'm refusing to do the rest of the season the way she wants. Please," I say, my voice cracking at the neutrality in her eyes. "I'm telling the truth. I love you. I love you like breathing."

I want her to react—I need her to. If she says she loves me too, or even if she says she hates me, those are things I can work with. But this distant, detached look? Her pain framed by eyes that have cried real tears—tears that are my fault? It makes all of this feel like a lost cause, like I've ruined something special.

"You don't love me, Birdie," Cass says quietly. "And it's okay. You don't have to make yourself try anymore."

"It's not about making myself do anything," I insist. "Don't say that!"

"Nah," she says, taking Bentley's hand and standing up. "Even if we forget everything else, you wouldn't be running around filming with your ex if you loved me, especially not without talking to me first. What do you expect me to do when it's posted? Sit around with all my friends and family, watch you laughing with that guy, and say, 'Oh. It's okay. It's just knockoff reality television'?" Her words sound mad, but her voice is monotone, so far away. "'I play her assistant'?"

"The only reason I'm filming today is to get out of something a million times worse. Trust me, I did this for us!"

"Keep telling yourself that."

"Cass," I say desperately.

"Congratulations, Birdie Gordon. You're the summeriest summer girl to ever cross my path. You win."

"Win? What did I win if you're telling me I ruined the only real thing I've ever had?"

"Maybe real's not what you're looking for," Cass says, squeezing my shoulder as she walks out. Bentley shoots me a glare as they leave, his arm around her, while Six stays back, seemingly taking pleasure at the way I slowly stand up beside the now-empty booth.

"What?" I ask.

He stares at me a moment longer, his eyes squinted in disgust. "Stop texting her."

I rear back like I've been hit. "You barely know her. You don't get to—"

"You're right. I barely know her, but I *do* know Bentley, and I know when she hurts, he hurts. Which means when you hurt her, you *also* hurt the person I love. Bentley's a really great person, and so is Cass. They don't deserve any of this. Stop. Fucking. With. Them."

"Oh, spare me," I say, and he takes a step forward, forcing me to step backward out of his way.

"You should know, Birdie, that I'm *not* a really great person. So I'll tell you once more—back off. If you can't be everything to her, then be nothing. Go away. Because if you keep messing with her head? If you keep hurting her? We're going to have problems."

"Are you threatening me?" I ask, incredulous.

"No," he says, smirking. "Just giving you a nice little lifeguard warning. There are a lot more people at the beach who love Cass than there are who give a single flying fuck about you and your little princess life. We can make the rest of your time here very uncomfortable. Just save everyone the trouble and leave her alone."

"I can't," I say, taking a shaky breath. "I love her."

The tiniest bit of anger slips from his face, replaced by something that looks more akin to pity. "Then either get your shit together immediately or let her go," he says. "Anything else is just cruel."

I stand there, stunned, as he walks away. The waitress eyes me warily, probably trying to decide if I'm going to order something, or if she can wipe the now-empty table in her busy café. I don't know how long I'm there before a hand reaches out and gently wraps around my forearm. I spin around, hoping it's Cass, but it's Ada instead.

"Birdie?" she says, looking worried.

"Sorry," I say, wiping at my eyes. "I didn't mean to ditch you. Jewelry store?"

"I'm all done. We came back to find you," she says, gesturing to where Mitchell stands ordering at the counter. "Are you okay?"

"No," I say honestly. "Not at all." Because I know Six is right. It's beyond time to take some action, or I'll lose Cass forever.

24

Cass

I'M SITTING IN my room wallowing when my phone rings. I pick it up, hoping it's Bentley coming to put me out of my misery now that his shift is almost over—they had to call in Mika today to cover my hours since I'm faking sick—and drop it in surprise when I see the name *Gordon* pop up.

It's not Birdie, though; of course it's not. She's all settled back into her nice life with her rich bitch best friend and her horrible (ex?) boyfriend. I mean, why wouldn't she be? You can't fault her for going back to her old ways any more than you could fault a flamingo for not being happy in the Arctic. It's where she belongs.

Which means it's George on the phone. George, who, according to my dad, needed to spend today getting things organized for the Founders' Day Gala. Apparently, one of the sponsors couldn't send their volunteers out, so his company is stepping up even more to ensure it goes off without a hitch.

This is probably the final nail in the coffin of my dad's chance of winning tomorrow, but nobody is mentioning it, so I'm not either.

I hesitate before answering the phone, but *it's George*. He never calls me unless he really needs something; he always goes through my dad for regular stuff like asking what he should bring to dinner or double-checking birthday party times. If he's calling me, something must be really wrong. *Is Birdie okay?*

I click accept quickly before it can go to voicemail. "Hello? George?"

"Cassandra?" he says, worry in his voice, and oh boy, if he's going to ask me about his daughter, we're both going to have a bad time on this call. "You okay?"

And oh. *Oh.* Did Birdie tell him about us? Did she tell him what happened? Is that why he's on the phone, not out of worry for her but out of concern for *me*?

"About as well as can be expected after everything, I guess," I answer honestly.

"Did something happen?" he asks, sounding surprised.

I backpedal, realizing nearly too late that I've almost said too much. Birdie definitely did *not* tell him, then. "No, just tired, and . . . I don't have a dress yet," I say, grasping at straws.

"Yes, Birdie mentioned that you couldn't take her to work today. She said you called out sick. I hope you're okay."

"I'm fine, just needed a day off."

"Well, I can't help with that," he says. "But I might have a way to get around the dress issue, actually. That's kind of what I'm calling you about."

"Really?" I sit up, wondering if he's about to somehow offer up his wife's closet to me, or even Birdie's. I'm sure she has just as many beautiful gowns as her mother. She'd have to with how often they film events.

"Yes, I don't know if your father told you, but we're scrambling over here with all of the missing volunteers we had been expecting. I just got off the phone with the catering company, and they don't have any extra waiters to send us. That part was supposed to be covered by some children's organization or something. Can you believe the incompetence? Anyway, I told the Founders' Day Committee that I would reach out to some people I've used in the past to see if they have any interest. So? What do you say? Do you think you could round up a couple of friends to pitch in the way you did for the Gordon Development Gala?"

"You're asking me to be your waitress? I'm supposed to be a guest."

"I'm asking you to be a volunteer, technically, but I'd pay you and your friends off the books for the trouble. You really turned Birdie around this summer. I owe you more than just gas money for that.

"Besides, your dad was telling me how worried he's been over that housing deposit you need to make for college, so why don't I take care of that today too while I'm at it? Can't have my future intern missing out on her big chance, right?" he says cheerfully, like he didn't just prove that he doesn't see me as anything more than a commodity to be bought and sold.

I can't believe how badly I've misjudged that entire family. He wants me to waitress on a night my family should be being honored. He doesn't even see how screwed up that is. He genuinely thinks he's being helpful.

"I don't think I can do it," I say. "I want to sit with my father in case he wins."

"Hmm," he says noncommittally. "Think about it and ask your friends. Five hundred for the night for each of you."

"Five hundred each? Are you serious?"

"Plus, your housing deposit," he says happily. "Is that not enough? I'm in a tough spot. Name your price and it's done."

I almost want to say something outrageous, like ten thousand dollars, just to see what he'd say, but I stop myself. "No, that's very generous of you. Can I think about it for a minute, though? I'm a little wiped out right now."

The truth is, I feel backed into a corner. It's one thing for me to turn down the money, but to turn it down on behalf of my friends? That's a whole other thing. Some of them could really, really use it. Not to mention the fact that apparently my father is stressing over my housing deposit, something I didn't even know about until right now.

"Sure, sure. I have to get going anyway. Verity is running us all ragged. I think Birdie went to work just to escape from her." He laughs. "Will you please check in with me by tomorrow morning either way? If you and your friends aren't available, I'll have to reach out to my connections in

Boston and import some real cater waiters unfortunately."

I resist the urge to say *Like the one that made out with Birdie's boyfriend last time?* instead choosing to say, "Good night," and ending the call.

I need to talk to my dad.

〰

"I thought you were staying home today 'resting,'" my dad says, complete with air quotes.

"Hey, I needed it," I say, walking over to the round table and dropping down beside him. It's mostly dead in the Coalition office today, just me and my dad and a couple of the volunteers over by the photocopier.

"Uh-huh," he says, looking at me. "I'm sure it has nothing to do with the fact that Birdie hasn't been around to volunteer lately either."

I narrow my eyes. "What do you know about that?"

"Know? Nothing. Suspect? Plenty," he says with a sad smile. "I've seen enough broken hearts in my life to recognize one. Do you want to talk about it?"

"Not really."

"You came all the way down here just to say hi to your dear old dad, then?" he asks suspiciously.

I wince. My dad always could read me like a book. I don't know why I thought today would be any different.

"George called me today. They need waiters for the Founders' Day event." I take a deep breath. "He's offering me and my friends five hundred each for a night's work if we do it."

"Weren't you just dress shopping yesterday?" He frowns. "I thought you were going to be my plus-one?"

"You know Mom is your plus-one, right?"

"I can have two plus-ones! I'm a popular guy!" He laughs, leaning back in his chair. "Let me guess, you're considering it because you know your friends will jump at the chance to make that kind of money in a night."

"Something like that."

"You don't have to do it, you know. The whole world is not your problem to solve, even though I probably have given you that impression. Let me talk to George. Maybe he'll still hire them on without you there to wrangle them. It's not like they aren't perfectly capable of handing out fancy snacks to rich assholes without you holding their hands."

"It's not just that." I bite my lip. "He also offered to pay my housing deposit. He said you've been really stressed about that. Which is weird because you made me think you were all set on that front."

"Why would he tell you that?" My dad sits up, his leisurely position in the chair instantly ruined. "That's not for you to worry about."

"I have enough saved from this summer and doing odd jobs for George, if you need me to cover it. I didn't realize—"

"You need that money for expenses during the semester. You're not going to be able to work once classes start. It's a rigorous school."

"I'll work at one of the Waffle Emporiums at night like

Mom did when she was in school. I'm sure they're all over by campus. I don't want you stressing out about me on top of everything else. I can figure it out."

"You shouldn't have to figure it out," Dad grumbles. "I owe you an apology. Your mom wants to kill me, and you should probably let her for what I did."

"What do you mean *what you did*?" I ask, growing concerned. "Did something happen?"

"You know Mrs. Alba? The one who has that little apartment over the bodega she owns?"

"The grandma lady who's, like, two hundred? What about her?"

"Watch it, Cass," he says. "She's not *that* much older than me. She's only seventy-eight!"

"You're barely fifty!"

"Regardless! Respect your elders," he says, his fake outrage giving way to laughter.

"So, Mrs. Alba?" I ask, prodding him to go on.

"She had been ignoring some pretty important bills. A social worker got involved and recommended she get a little more care. Mrs. Alba came to me frightened. I reached out to her daughter, and together we've been helping to get everything organized. Her daughter might even be staying a little more permanently to make sure things stay on track."

"Okay?" I say. "Why would that make us mad?"

"George was trying to buy the place from her. He offered to cover the tax bill and then gave her a lowball cash offer on the property itself. She didn't want to, but she was desperate."

"George was trying to take advantage of a little old lady?" I wince.

"To him, I'm sure it just looked like a good deal," Dad says. "In the end, I loaned her the money to cover her back taxes and past-due bills so she wouldn't have to take his offer. It was several thousand dollars, and the Coalition didn't have enough in the coffers to cover it. We usually can't spend that much on one person when there's only so much to go around." He looks down. "I gave it to them as a personal loan instead of running it through the Coalition. They've already started making repayments, but—"

"But you dipped into the little bit of money you had managed to set aside for my college to do it," I say, trying not to be frustrated. I probably would have done the same thing, even if it does suck, and I completely understand why Mom wants to kill him. It's just as much her money as it is his.

"Yeah, unfortunately," he says. "She's good for the money, but things are going to be a little tight for the next few months. We may have to cosign a loan for this first year of school with you now, but we'll pay it off for you as soon as we're repaid."

"Got it," I say, wondering if that will actually happen. A tiny, run-down kosher convenience store isn't exactly the most lucrative business in a tourist trap like this.

"Do you want to kill me too?" he asks. "It would make me feel better if you did."

"No," I say, and I mean it. "Your heart was in the right place."

"I'm sorry, Cass. I honestly didn't realize how much I was withdrawing at the time. Things just kept popping up with her, and I was trying to help. I wouldn't have dug into our personal finances if we could get this Coalition a little more firmly in the black. If we win this Community Improvement Award at the gala, it's going to take a lot of pressure off me to keep hunting down funding." He holds up his hands. "And don't worry, I've already promised your mother that I won't be dipping into our personal funds again. I know that was a mistake," he says. "I hope you can forgive me."

"I do," I say. "What you're doing is important. Mrs. Alba is important. I'll cover the housing deposit, even if I don't take George up on his offer. We'll get the loan to cover my other expenses. It'll be okay."

"Still," he says. "I'm sorry. I was impulsive and unfair."

"I just wish I didn't hear about it from George, you know?"

"Yes, and that makes me want to kill *him*, so I guess we're all in this murder club together now." He smiles, catching my eye. "Cass, try not to be offended by his offer. Sometimes George doesn't realize that what he thinks is a neat favor is really an insult. It's kind of a hallmark of people with wealth like theirs. It makes them all a little weird like that."

"How do you stand it?" I ask, and his face softens, probably realizing I'm not talking about George at all anymore.

"I don't always. That's the great thing about George. I can call him out on it, and I fully intend to call him out on this. You are not his personal TaskRabbit, and he needs to—"

"No, I'm gonna do it, I think. The money's good, right?

And I'll still be there, kind of. Plus, he's right—I won't have to worry about finding a stupid dress anymore."

Dad frowns. "Are you sure that's what you really want to do?"

"I'm sure," I say, because what else is there?

25

Birdie

MY MOM IS fussing with my hair while her assistant films us getting ready.

The goal is for her to look like a doting mother, but judging by how frustrated she's getting that my hair won't behave (blame it on the ocean air) and that I'm not smiling enough (hard to when there's a hollow cave where my heart used to be), I doubt she's getting the footage she wants.

It's my birthday today, and Cass is still not returning any of my calls or texts, and my mom is furious that I won't go along with her plan for me and Mitchell to fake date or whatever she was thinking. Happy birthday to me.

The only thing going right is my father told me officially that, considering the maturity I've shown this last month, he's going to be releasing my trust to me today, just as originally planned. Oh, and I can have my car back. I should be jumping for joy, but instead I just want to take a nap and pretend none of this is happening.

"Why are you moping now, Birdie?" Mom asks, utterly annoyed. She shoos out her assistant, which means she's gearing up to yell at me and doesn't want any witnesses. I decide the smartest thing is to head her off at the pass.

"I don't feel like filming any more today," I say. "You know I don't want to do this."

"Don't act like this is something I forced you into. You loved filming; you used to beg for it."

"It's all I knew, Mom." I look in the mirror, studying my newly finished face. I don't even look like myself anymore. Gone are the freckles that Cass loved to kiss all summer, covered up under tons of concealer because Mom says freckles are "common." My nose and cheekbones have been contoured within an inch of their lives, making my features look sharper, tinier, the way the old me used to be desperate for.

I want to wash it all off.

"It gave you a good life," she says, sweeping some of my hair back.

"Did it? I think Grandpa's money did that." I snort, and she tugs on my hair a little too roughly. "I don't want to do it anymore."

"Do you really want to leave our fans thinking you grew up to be an irresponsible crybaby who got cheated on and then disappeared forever in embarrassment?" She sighs.

"Jesus," I huff, horrified at the words coming out of her mouth. "Is that what you think of me?"

"What else am I supposed to think when it's completely

in your power to change the narrative, but you'd prefer to sit around acting sad instead?"

"I'm not sad about Mitchell! I'm upset about—" I cut myself off, not sure I want to do this now.

"If you're nervous your father is going to somehow go back on his word about the trust, don't be. He sent the papers to the lawyers this morning. Happy birthday, the money is yours. The seed money for your designs will be waiting for you when you return to Boston with me in the morning. It's going to be an amazing storyline for the—"

"I'm not filming anymore after today." I turn to look at her. "I don't even care about the money right now. I mean, I do, but not because of purses or your storyline!"

"What happened out here? You spend a month with your father, and you're suddenly filled with the starry-eyed optimism I've been drilling out of his head for the last two decades?"

"I fell in love," I blurt out, anger overriding my better judgment. "Caring about people isn't a bad thing! Trying to make the world better isn't a bad thing!"

My mother puts her hand over her heart, like this is some kind of horrible shocking news.

"Oh god," she says, rolling her eyes as she finally walks over to the vanity to pick up my fake lashes. "Who is it?"

"No one you know."

Her eyes meet mine in the mirror. "Then say his name, Birdie."

For a second, I think about lying again.

Part of me wants to keep Cass hidden, to shield her from

this machine that is my mother and her stupid YouTube show, but another, louder part of me knows that denying Cass again will break me in a way that nothing else ever could.

Despite my mother's accusations, I'm not a starry-eyed optimist. I know there's probably no hope for us. If Cass wants nothing to do with me after tonight, then I'll respect it, of course. But it won't be because I'm lying, and it won't be because I'm a coward.

"It's Cass, Mom."

"Cass?" She says the name like it means nothing to her at first, and then her eyebrows arch up. "Cassandra Adler?" She sounds incredulous. "The girl your father paid to be your friend all summer?"

"She didn't take the money," I grumble, like that makes it all better somehow.

"She's a clever one—I'll give you that," Mom says, passing me the lashes before going back to touch up her own.

"What's that supposed to mean?"

"It means she's got your father wrapped around her finger, obviously—he hires her for all his little events, has dinner with her family. She's been his little pet for years, but she's much cleverer than I realized. Getting you to fall in love with her is an even better plan than waiting for your dad to give her a job. She can start enjoying the benefits early. Kudos to her."

"She's not like that."

"Everyone is like that, sweetie." My mom pats my cheek. "I don't blame her! She wasn't born in the best circumstances, and obviously she's bright and good at going after what she wants." Mom looks up for a moment, squinting like she's thinking really hard. "We can work it in. This might even be better. Yes, yes, I like this more."

"You like what more?"

"We'll get Mitchell to play it like he came here to win you back, only to find out you'd already moved on, and with a *girl* at that. Then we'll capture the whole story of you and your beloved rough-around-the-edges local as she drags her way out of poverty on your coattails."

"That's disgusting, Mom."

She rolls her eyes, waving her hand. "Everybody loves a good Cinderella story. I know I told you to stick with boys before, but queer is trendy. It'll give us a little edge the other shows don't have. We can follow you two as you start to make your little purses or whatever. She can help you. It'll be cute."

"She's not trying to help me or use me. She's doing just fine on her own. She got into MIT! MIT!"

"Yes, of course, I'm sure your father had nothing to do with that at all."

"When did you become this person?" I ask. "You were nice once. Do you remember? When I was tiny, you used to play with me all the time. We had so much fun! Then all of a sudden, you started filming everything. I became your little doll instead of your daughter. Why? What happened?"

"The world happened." She laughs. "It'll happen to you too."

"That's bullshit."

She tilts her head. "You'll understand when you're older, Birdie, believe me."

"God, I hope not," I say. "Not if it means turning into you."

Fury flashes across her face, but only for a moment, before she slides her mask of indifference carefully back into place. "Text your little friend. I'll have my manager reach out to some LGBTQ designers, and we'll get you two outfitted. We could probably do a quick shoot next week. Maybe I could even get it sponsored. I probably should have done this earlier. We could have captured that demographic from the start."

"My coming out is not sponsored content, Mom," I say quietly, but she doesn't hear me, already calling her manager to make plans.

~~~

Ada and Mitchell are thankfully ready to go by the time I get downstairs. With my father nowhere to be found, I make the executive decision to grab his car keys off his desk. There's a fifty-fifty chance he's going to be mad about me taking the Audi without permission—he did *just* lift the driving ban yesterday—but I don't have time to stick around and find out.

If Mitchell and Ada are surprised that I've stopped filming, or that I insist we need to be at the event a half hour earlier than expected, they don't complain. Ada asks me twice if everything's alright, and Mitchell cracks some joke about how maybe he should drive given my history with fast cars, but other than that, we ride in silence.

I scan the already-forming crowd as soon as we're inside, hoping to see Cass in the mix. My heart twists at the idea of seeing her all done up. I love her in her hoodies and shorts, but I bet she'll be truly stunning tonight.

I catch the back of her father's head and follow him through the crowd to what I assume is her table. My heart sinks as he takes his seat beside his wife and I realize Cass isn't there. *She didn't come.*

I'm attempting to make my escape when her father notices me. "Birdie?"

"Hi, Mr. Adler," I say, turning back around with my best "parents, please love me" smile fixed into place. His eyes narrow, like he sees right through it.

"Birdie, hello," Mrs. Adler says, not looking especially happy to see me either.

"Did your father need something else?" Mr. Adler asks.

Something else?

"No, I haven't seen him yet. I was just looking for Cass. I came here early hoping to catch her. Is she . . . is she not coming?" I manage to stammer out.

Mr. Adler eyes me for another moment. His expression softens before he gestures with his head behind me, toward the corner of the room. I spin around, expecting to see Cass walking toward me, no doubt looking radiant, but instead see . . . a bunch of waiters?

I'm about to turn away when I realize that one of them looks like Bentley, and there's Six too. *What is going on?* The door to the kitchen area opens, and Cass walks out with a tray of salmon mousse canapés. *What. The. Hell?*

I snap my head back to her father. "Cass is working tonight?"

"Your father made her an offer she couldn't refuse." He sighs, like he's disappointed. My stomach flips. This was *not*

275

part of the plan. What was my father thinking? He knew tonight was special for her. How could he even ask?

"I see," I say, not really seeing at all. "I'll go talk to . . . Thank you," I mumble.

I glance behind me to see that Ada and Mitchell are watching me closely from their table near the Adlers. Mitchell whispers something to Ada, and she shakes her head. I wonder if they've figured out what's really going on yet. If they haven't, they will soon enough.

"Cass," I say, reaching out my hand gently to stop her from walking right past me.

"Canapé?" she offers, pushing the tray between us to create more space. Her eyes are hard, cold pools of amber, as if all the warmth they once held has been drained out.

"No, I'm good," I say, realizing a moment too late that she wasn't actually asking. "Can we talk, please?"

"I'm working." She sidesteps me, and I follow her. It's immature, I know, but I need her to hear me out. If she's still done with me after we talk, that's fine. But I can't let her go without her truly understanding how much she means to me and how much she's changed my life for the better. I need to fight for Cass. Now. Tonight.

Blurting out that I love her didn't work last time, so I scramble to think of a better opening. "Why did you say yes to working?" I ask, which is possibly the worst thing I could have said, given the scowl that takes over her face.

"Because not all of us were born rich, Birdie. I know that's really hard for you to understand."

"That's not what I mean, and you know it," I say softly, trying not to piss her off any more than I already have. "Your dad is up for an award. I *saw* you dress shopping. You were supposed to be a guest, not a . . ." I trail off.

"Yeah, well, I guess the fancy dress and all that was just a dream. I know where I belong now. Don't worry."

"Cass—"

"Did you know that your dad was trying to buy a property that was being foreclosed on, a bodega with an apartment over it, run by a little old lady who's owned it her whole life?"

I shake my head. "No, but that does sound like him."

"It does, doesn't it? Guess what? My dad blocked it. He paid the back taxes and got her all set up. But we're not like you, are we, Birdie? We don't have an unlimited amount of money. We can't crash a McLaren and then escape to our summer home."

"That's kind of a low blow," I say, even though I might deserve it.

"You know what's a low blow? My dad having to use the money he set aside to pay for the balance of my first semester of college to save that woman's house from *your* dad. That's why I'm working tonight. Because I need the money, and because your dad knows that and offered to help if I played my part as a little waitress tonight. It's kind of funny how we came full circle, though. Now I get to wait on you and all your little friends again, just like I did at the start of the summer."

Cass looks like she's about to cry, but before I can say anything, Ada comes up behind us. I don't know how long she's been eavesdropping, maybe a little too long, judging by what comes out of her mouth next.

"You should be grateful for Mr. Gordon," Ada says. "He keeps getting you jobs, and now he's helping you with college too? You're not going to stand here and make my best friend feel like shit when her father is bankrolling your whole life. Show a little respect."

"Yes, my lady," Cass says, glaring at us as she curtsies and bows her head. "Forgive me. It won't happen again."

"Ada, what is wrong with you?" I ask as Cass rushes away.

"That girl was being a mega bitch to you! Was I just supposed to stand there and let her talk to you like that? Why do you even care?"

"Because I love her," I admit, and Ada's eyes go almost comically wide.

"What?" she asks, her mouth hanging open. "But she's—"

"You knew I was bi," I say, frustrated about having to come out *again*. "Can you try to be, like, five percent less biphobic right now? I need my best friend."

"I'm not biphobic," she says. "Seriously! I don't care if you want to date a girl!"

"Then what were you going to say?"

"That she's a townie, obviously. And what about the monster? Your dad's assistant that you were dating all summer?" I don't think her eyes can get any wider, but they do. "Oh my god, she's the monster? *That's* Cass?"

I nod sadly.

"She wasn't ever really your assistant, was she?"

I shake my head.

Ada squeezes her eyes shut. "Is there any chance this is just a weird little summer fling?"

"No," I say quietly. "Not if I can help it."

"Damn, you *really* screwed up at the dress shop, then," she says, pulling me into a hug. "Is that who you needed to talk to at the coffee place?"

I nod, my eyes starting to water. "I don't want to lose her."

"Well, I just made everything even worse." She sighs, shaking her head. "When I saw her talking to you like that . . . I didn't know this was the one time someone had a good reason for it. I owe her a huge apology."

"Welcome to the club," I say, trying to catch the tears threatening to spill before they screw up my mascara.

"How do we make this right? What can I do to help?"

"I have an idea, but it's going to really, really piss off my parents."

"In that case, you should definitely do it." Ada laughs.

I bite my lip, fighting a smile. It's a long shot that this will work, I know, but I still can't help the tiny tendril of hope blooming up inside me. I'll either get her back tonight or go up in flames, but at least I'll know I did everything I could.

26

Cass

MY HEART IS hammering in my chest as I walk away from them. *Show a little respect.* Ha! I guess I was just stupid enough to think that I might deserve a little respect in return. God, I hate summer girls. There's a reason I made it rule number one. I should have never made an exception.

"You okay?" Six asks, looking genuinely concerned. I've emptied my tray already, and I'm back at the server station for a reload.

"I'll be fine." I smile.

Six is good for Bentley. *He* should have been the only exception. Or rather, the rule should never have applied to him. His grandma has a house here. She used to be free summer child-care when he was little, and now he comes to stay with her on every college break. He's mostly like us, working all summer here to pay his way through college. If I'm going to hold that schedule against him, I'd have to hold it against me too after this month.

"I don't think I would be fine," Six says honestly, restocking my tray for me.

I shrug.

"You don't have to always have it together, you know?" he says, and I shake my head, watching him load all the tiny treats that I thought I would be eating instead of serving tonight. If I look up at him right now, I'll break, and I'm not going to do that in front of Birdie and her friends. I won't give them the satisfaction. I won't be the townie who cries over a summer girl.

"I just need to survive this last night, and she'll be gone forever anyway. Not my circus, not my monkeys, right?"

Six frowns at that but then seems to decide to drop it. He gives me a smile and squeezes my shoulder before lifting his own neatly refilled tray. "Thanks again for getting me this gig," he says. "This is really going to help this semester."

"No problem," I say, my smile genuine this time as I watch him walk away.

I take a deep breath and try to steady myself. I have to head back out into the main dining room, but I hope I at least missed Birdie's speech. She's supposed to be introducing her father for being recognized as Volunteer of the Year. Gross.

If I can just see Birdie for the absolute least amount of time possible, maybe I can survive this night.

Naturally, I step into the room just as she steps up onto the stage, no doubt fully prepared to kiss her father's ass. She has a trust to win back today, after all. Why would I expect anything less?

The clapping dies down as Birdie takes her place in front of the microphone, and I roll my eyes. I duck back into the dimmest lighting I can find, my platter now full of fancied-up pigs in a blanket, since apparently canapé time is over. I try not to think about how literally and metaphorically appropriate this is right now—Birdie's exactly where she's meant to be, up on the stage, and I'm where I'm meant to be too, in the shadows grinding away for my next paycheck.

"Hi, I'm Bridgette Gordon. You might know me as Birdie, since that's what everyone has called me my whole life." The crowd politely chuckles.

I catch myself tracing her skin with my eyes, missing those beach freckles I used to kiss back when I was delusional enough to think she was really mine. My eyes dip to her collarbone, and my fingers twitch to touch it. I hate how much I miss her. I hate that I still have her birthday present—a tiny seashell necklace I made myself with a shell I found when I tried to take her surfing—tucked above the visor in my car. I couldn't bring myself to toss it.

I lean back against the nearest wall, my heart thumping uselessly at the sight of her in her beautiful dress. It's simple pink silk, the overly basic cut somehow highlighting the curves of her body. It's probably more expensive than it looks.

I squint, trying to make out the faint echo of the girl I loved—love still, if I'm being honest—underneath all that makeup. My eyes sting with emotion, and I force myself to blink rapidly. I straighten up and push back into the crowd, trying to drown out her speech by focusing on the task at hand.

It works for all of two minutes before I hear Birdie's voice crack. My eyes snap up to hers, and I realize too late that I've wandered close to the stage in my travels. I have no idea what she just said, but I wish I did, when she continues.

"So, you see, it wasn't my choice to be here tonight or this summer, really," she says. "I learned a lot these past few weeks, some of which I owe to my dad and some I owe to others." Birdie takes a deep breath, scanning the crowd. "I learned about what it means to show integrity and good character. My dad is great at that stuff—he's built a career on being reliable, helpful, and trustworthy, which is probably why you're naming him Volunteer of the Year. Unfortunately, that stuff doesn't come as naturally to me.

"See, when I came here, I was worried about two things: getting back to Boston and getting access to a trust fund my grandfather set up for me when I was born. I had grand plans of using it as seed money for this silly purse company that literally no one was asking for."

There's a polite round of laughter as Birdie nods. She's got the audience eating out of the palm of her hand. I look around, and everyone looks just as entranced by her as I am. A tendril of possessiveness curls up my spine, but I blink it away, choosing instead to feel proud of her for getting up there. Despite how things ended, I know tonight is hard for her, but she still showed up.

"It seems laughable now," Birdie continues. "But I really did think I was going to change the world as the latest trust fund baby turned designer entrepreneur. What I learned from spending a summer living here with my dad is that there are many ways to change the world. In fact, there are people in this town right here who are changing lives.

"I met someone really special about a month ago. Her name is Cassandra Adler; some of you might know her. Her dad's organization is up for an award tonight, and I really hope he wins—or if he doesn't, that whoever does win finds a way to acknowledge and honor his contribution to this town anyway." I follow her gaze over to George and Verity and her friends, who are all shifting uncomfortably or fiddling with their napkins.

"Cass hated me at first, and rightly so. I was kind of a jerk." She bites her lip as she finally finds me in the audience, and I smile. I can't help it. "She didn't give up on me, though, and I started wanting to prove both to her *and myself* that I wasn't just a 'summer girl.' I wasn't just here to use up this beautiful town and give nothing in return.

"I must have pulled that off at least a little, because eventually she trusted me enough to take me to visit the Affordable Housing Coalition her family and neighbors all work so hard for every day. They're all about saving people's homes and helping them get back on their feet when they need it. They're preserving our neighborhoods in a way that deeply matters—you can google it, if you haven't heard of them. I'll wait. Feel free to clap when you do—I did a really good job on their website," she says, fanning herself.

I roll my eyes good-naturedly when she smiles down at me. There's a smattering of applause then. Mitchell yells out,

"Woo, Birdie," and everyone laughs and claps a little more. Birdie shushes them with her hands, swallowing hard before continuing.

"Listening to Cass talk about their mission was incredible, but getting involved myself was life-changing—even though I'm kind of the enemy thanks to my dad's evil Airbnbs, which somehow keep getting reported." I glance at George, who is definitely *not* laughing along with everyone right now.

Where is Birdie going with all of this?

"Cass is actually here tonight, working for all of you instead of being the guest she was supposed to be. That's how much she cares about this place. When someone is in a pinch—whether it's someone needing help with a property tax lien or the Founders' Day Committee forgetting to hire waiters—she's there to help, always.

"It's just one of the things I love about her," Birdie says, her eyes shining in the light. She wipes at them, licking her lips before standing up a little straighter and looking back out to the crowd. "If I had to list *all* the reasons I'm in love with Cass Adler, we'd be here for years. I'm sure anyone who knows her can probably relate." Six lets out a whoop from somewhere in the back, and Birdie grins. "I messed up in a big way recently. I was presented with the opportunity to go back to my old life, and I almost made the wrong choice. I had to dig deep these last few days to remember who I really am now and who I want to be in the future.

"I know that, regardless of whether I permanently blew it with the person I love or not, I want to dedicate myself to making real change—not performative bullshit on social media or donating five cents from every purse I sell to some random cause, but real, actual change. I know my father does too, as does Cass and her family, and the entire Affordable Housing Coalition.

"That's why I'm pledging the first ten thousand dollars from my trust to their organization while they get their fundraising feet under them. I've heard that will cover most of the outstanding relief applications they've received. It isn't charity, though, so please don't see it that way. It's a token of my gratitude for giving me a chance and for showing me grace when I didn't deserve it. Thank you to Cass and the Adlers for that," she says.

The crowd goes uncomfortably silent, not knowing what to do with any of this. Birdie seems to sense it, lifting her chin and holding her arm out toward her father, who is rising out of his chair. "Now without further ado, I'd like you to meet the man who made me who I am, both good and bad, your Volunteer of the Year, George Montgomery Gordon."

The crowd might not know whether to clap or leave horrified, but I do. I set my tray down and clap my ass off as I run over to hug my father. Ten thousand dollars! We're going to be able to help so many people with that money! Bentley and Six run over to join in the hug. My father, caught in the middle of us, starts weeping happy tears.

My mother eventually pushes us out of the way, hugging him to herself while I turn back. Birdie is still stuck onstage as her father walks up to join her with her mother. Both of them look a little concerned but like they're trying to cover it up. Birdie ignores them, her eyes fixed on me, even as her dad approaches the microphone. I scan the crowd to find her friends, worried that they might be upset too. Except Ada is smiling so wide that it almost makes me hate her a little less. *Almost.* Even Mitchell sports an expression that can only be called befuddled amusement.

"What are you going to do now?" Bentley whispers, coming up behind me.

"I would personally run up there and kiss her senseless," Six helpfully supplies, joining us on my other side.

Bentley scoffs. "You better not be making out with anyone onstage unless it's me."

"You know you're it for me," Six answers, puppy dog eyes in full effect. God, they're gross, but man, do I kind of love it.

"Seriously, Cass," Bentley says, using his "grown-up" voice. "This doesn't have to change anything between you two, if you don't want it to. It's extremely generous, and that speech was . . . well, it was a little weird in places." He laughs. "Her heart seems to be in the right place, but if you feel like she's just trying to buy you with that donation—"

"I don't," I say, surprising even myself. "I really don't. I think she means it."

Bentley bites the inside of his cheek, studying my face. "We're here for you, no matter what," he says, pulling me into a one-armed hug while still balancing his tray in his other hand.

"You better be." I laugh, wiping at my eyes.

I've been on the verge of tears all night, but I never expected that when they finally spilled out, they would be the happy kind.

"In that case," Bentley says, shoving me in the direction of the steps Birdie will shortly be walking down. "You should tell her how you feel."

"And maybe kiss her," Six says.

"Yeah, and maybe kiss her," I agree.

27

Birdie

I'M GOING TO throw up right on this stage, in front of everybody.

That's literally the only thought going through my head as the president of the Founders' Day Committee comes onstage at the end of Dad's speech to announce that my dad is actually not just getting the Volunteer of the Year Award but also the Community Improvement Award—the one with the cash prize that Cass and her family were hoping for. Dad's acting surprised, but a quick glance at my mother tells me she knew it was coming, which means he did too.

I can only hope that my pledge to donate to the Affordable Housing Coalition offsets some of the sting of Mr. Adler not winning.

I scan the crowd for Cass, but I don't see her. Beside me, my mom squeezes my hand painfully hard. Her public persona smile is still on her face, and to any outsider she probably just looks like she's excitedly, or maybe even proudly, holding my hand. The bones in my fingers that she is currently grinding together know the truth, though. She is seething. I don't know if it's because I embarrassed them by donating my own money, or because my announcement takes away her chance of making spon-con for my coming-out story, or because I just officially blew up her plans to have a spin-off about me and my purses.

I don't even care. I really don't.

I force myself to keep looking for Cass in the sea of people staring at me, swallowing hard to force down the anxious bile trying to creep up my throat. I find Mitchell first. He's hard to miss being six foot four. Plus he's standing up, for some reason. He smiles and gives me a little thumbs-up, trying to be supportive, I guess.

I thought he would be pissed at me for blowing up his whole redemption arc, but maybe he's just looking for an escape hatch too. Maybe we all are. Maybe that's the thing about the summer after high school—we're all just trying to figure out what comes next as best as we can.

I find Ada standing beside him. She's looking at me reassuringly, her face kind and proud. Whatever weirdness was between us the first time I tried to tell her I was bi seems to have been washed away with today's fresh revelations. She's smiling so big, like it all makes sense now. It kind of does. Or it would, if I could find Cass. I need to know if my speech was the first step in winning her back or the last step for us to have closure.

I take a deep breath and turn to my father, watching him uncharacteristically stumble through a whole other acceptance speech now. The normally poised and elegant man is clearly thrown off by the giant check in his hands, and the fact that his daughter suggested someone else might be more deserving of it, while donating an equal amount.

I kind of put him on the spot with this. He would be right to be mad at me too. I wonder if later his hand will also be squeezing mine too hard on the walk back to our table. Except when he glances back at me, he nods and gives me a small smile.

"What's so extra special about this," he says, gesturing for me to come forward, "is that I get to share this moment with my daughter."

I take the few steps toward him, suddenly feeling like every thread in my dress has turned into one collective vise, and I wonder if I'm walking to my doom.

My father puts his arm around me. I still can't tell if this is an act or if he really means it, but if I ever needed a hug and reassurance before in my life, it's now. *Where is Cass? Did she leave?* I lean into him, shocked to realize he's legitimately beaming down at me.

"Tonight, Birdie has inspired me. She opened not just her heart to this town but also her pocketbook. She put her money where her mouth is in a way that should make all of you as proud of her as I am. In fact," he says, holding up the giant check, "I'd like to also donate this prize to the Affordable Housing Coalition, as well as provide a company match from Gordon Investments. Birdie is right, John." He points to Mr. and Mrs. Adler's table. "You're doing good work out there."

The crowd erupts into applause as I stare at my father,

stunned. He's going to give them the award money and provide a match on top of it? That's thirty thousand dollars that will be heading to the Coalition! Cass said ten thousand would be life-changing for some; I can only imagine what they can accomplish with triple that.

"I love you, kiddo," he says, hugging me tight before turning back to address the audience. "Now, unless anyone else has any other surprise announcements to share with all of us, let's eat!"

I turn to walk down the side steps of the stage, mostly just trying to escape my mother . . . and there she is.

Cass. I finally found her.

Her eyes are wet and a small smile tugs at her lips as I rush over to her. I stop a little short, not sure what the rules are, or if she's still willing to break them for me anymore.

"Hi," she says, blushing. "That was quite the speech you gave."

"Cass, I—"

"I'm sorry," she says, shocking me.

"For what?" I ask, confused. "I'm the one who should be sorry! I treated you horribly. I shouldn't have lied about you. I shouldn't have lied about what you mean to me. I'm so sorry."

"That's true, but that doesn't mean you owed me your coming out," she says, stepping forward to run her thumb gently along my jaw. "I loved your big grand romantic gesture, but I hope I didn't make you feel like you had to tell everyone about yourself, about us."

I catch her hand and pull it toward me, giving it a gentle kiss. "What if I want to tell the whole world? I'm done hiding from people, especially myself. I want everyone to know that I'm in love with Cassandra Adler." Cass blushes and looks away, and it makes my stomach do that weird swoopy thing it does whenever I'm around her. "I owe you an apology, Cass, several actually."

She shakes her head. "I shouldn't have immediately thought the worst of you. I didn't even hear you out."

"I wasn't forthcoming with what was going on either."

"It's safe to say neither of us handled things perfectly," she says, her voice lilting up, and my stomach twists. I want to hug her so bad, and I have no idea if she wants me to.

She takes my hand and smiles. Her grip is the exact opposite of my mother's—it's warm and firm, like she's holding me up instead of tearing me down. We're practically falling over ourselves in a race to apologize to each other, to not let the world and its stupid rules tear us apart.

I follow her down the steps, not letting her hand drop for a second, and praying she's going to lead me right out of here. Ada walks up behind me once we're halfway across the room, and we pause, Cass studying her with narrowed eyes. Ada drapes her arms around me, putting her chin on my shoulder. She looks at Cass for a second, and then reaches out her hand.

"Ada Burke," she says. "World-class asshole. I'd like a do-over too, if you're still handing them out."

Cass reluctantly shakes her hand. "Cass Adler," she says, "and we'll see."

"In my defense," Ada says, "I thought you were hurting my best friend. I didn't understand the situation, and I'm sorry."

"I get it," Cass says, looking toward Bentley. He's stopped

handing out food. Instead, he stands a little way behind Cass, his tray tucked under his crossed arms as he watches us. "I wouldn't expect *him* to forgive you anytime soon, though."

Before either of us can respond, my mother appears, frustration practically radiating off her. "A word?" I'm tempted to say no, but then she looks at Cass and Ada, dismissing them with a curt "If you'll please excuse us, both of you, I need to speak to my daughter. Alone."

The girls look at each other, clearly not sure what to do, but I won't let my mother direct any of her ire their way.

"It's fine," I say, even though I don't mean it. "Cass, I'll text you in a little bit? If you're not still here? Ada, why don't you go help Mitchell find the dessert table before he starts sneaking bites off other people's plates."

I can tell neither of them want to leave me with her, but reluctantly they nod. I turn and follow my mother into a little room off the main dining room. It serves as a greenroom of sorts during events like this, complete with little trays of snacks and bottles of water lining a table. One of the board members grazes the offerings before scurrying out.

I'm surprised to see Mr. Adler in here, already shaking my father's hand. His eyes are shiny with gratitude as he tells my dad how much this means to him. He rushes to shake my hand too, as soon as he notices me.

"Birdie!" Mr. Adler says, turning our handshake into an awkward hug. "Thank you so much. That was such a brave and lovely thing to do. I can see my daughter is in good hands with you."

"If she'll have me back," I say. I know the conversation with her was a start, but nothing is set in stone. Not yet anyway.

"Maybe I really am the hopeless optimist your father keeps insisting I am, but something tells me you two are going to be okay."

"Thank you, Mr. Adler."

He pats my shoulder and then heads for the door. "I'll let you all have a moment. I have some celebrating to do."

My parents smile and wave at him, but the second he's out of the room, the entire mood shifts. "What were you thinking?" my mom snaps. "I was willing to work with you on not wanting to film with Mitchell, but—"

"Enough, Verity," Dad says, gently pulling her back from me. "This isn't about filming or any of that other nonsense! What Birdie did tonight was very special. You should be proud of her the way I am."

"Thanks," I say, relieved that he has my back again. "I can't believe you're tripling it. I wondered if you genuinely supported their work. Mom said—"

My dad waves his hand. "It is an excellent tax write-off, Birdie. Let's not get too carried away."

"Dad," I say, my stomach sinking.

"I need to send the money somewhere; it might as well go to them. I *do* mean well, honey. I do," he says. "You certainly put me in an awkward position, though! You really didn't leave me any choice."

My face falls. "You said you were proud."

"I am." He laughs. "You were shrewd! You backed me into a corner. You're the first person who's knocked me off my game in years. You have more business sense than you think, and I can't wait to see where it and that big heart of yours take you."

I smile and give him a quick hug. Is his donation the genuine commitment to social change that I had hoped? No, but it's a start and hopefully, with a little luck, we can build off it.

"I *am* going to hold you to donating that portion of your trust, though," he says. "Your mother thought we should edit out your speech for her show and cover the donation ourselves to maintain her storyline, but I think you need to learn the importance of keeping your word."

"I wouldn't let you cover it," I say. "I meant what I said. It's important to me to give back. If I let you pay for it, then it negates all of that. What about the other stuff, though—the me and Cass stuff. I'm sorry for keeping that from you. I did tell you I was bi, but I'm sure seeing it can be—"

"I couldn't think of anyone better for you, Birdie. If she makes you happy, that's all that matters. Although in retrospect, I'm glad I wasn't actually paying her to date my daughter."

"Yeah." I laugh, feeling like a weight has just been lifted off my chest as he puts his arm around me and squeezes.

"I'm glad for you, kid," he says.

"Well, I'm not sure I am," my mom says. "I *just* scheduled a coming-out post for her for next week. There was going to be a photoshoot! A photoshoot! What am I supposed to tell the people we asked to sponsor the reveal, now that everyone's already hashtagging 'bi icon Birdie' on all of their posts about tonight? You're blowing up our plotlines left and right!"

"Mom, I'm not filming anymore. I don't want to, and I don't want to go back to Boston with you."

"Do you mean that, Birdie?" my dad asks, studying my face. "If you're not filming or working on the purses, what are you planning to do?"

"I'm still figuring everything out, but I know it's not any of that," I say, giving him a weak smile. "Is that . . . okay?"

"Absolutely, it is," Dad says, giving me another squeeze before turning toward my mother. "It's settled. You do what you want to do in Boston, Verity, but leave Birdie and me out of it. Our daughter can stay out here as long as she wants, and I'll be doing the same."

"What does that even mean, George?" She sneers . . . and that's my cue to leave.

I flash my dad an apologetic smile and dip out the door. I grab my purse off the table and round up my friends to drop them back at the house before firing off a single text to Cass, who is no doubt off somewhere in this room celebrating with her family and the board.

Me: Meet me at Chair Five in an hour?

Cass: Wouldn't miss it. Bentley and Six have already banned me from working any more tonight. Apparently my only job now is to "celebrate."

Me: I like the way they think 😊

28

Cass

THE HOUR NOTICE is barely enough time for me to go home and change out of my stained server clothes and into something a little cuter, but still, I don't rush.

Tonight was a lot, and I need a minute to collect myself.

I can't believe the Gordons are collectively donating thirty thousand dollars to the Coalition. The people we'll be able to help now, it's awe-inspiring. I try not to think about the fact that George could have done this all along. It doesn't matter, I suppose. He's doing it now.

My parents follow me out when I leave, but Dad's only home for about fifteen minutes before he excitedly heads off to the Coalition office to start going through the applications. He wants to get a jump on organizing them in order of urgency. Mom knows better than to try to dissuade him, simply giving him a hug and packing up some healthy snacks for him while still in her evening gown. We both know he won't be back until at least dawn.

After he's gone, my mom tries to talk to me. I'm not ready, though. She has questions about Birdie, questions about what this all means for me and her, and the truth is, I don't know yet. She relents, hugging me too when I come back down freshly changed into a hoodie and some leggings. She also gives me a healthy snack—two actually, one to share—and I can't help but see the parallels.

I make my way to the beach, parking on the street and jumping over the long-closed parking lot gate. There's a little chill in the summer air. It would be a great night for a bonfire party, and I suspect we would have had one if I hadn't invited most of my friends to work at the Founders' Day Gala with me.

Which means right now it's just the ocean and me as I walk through the sand toward Chair Five. The sand mutes my footsteps, the waves erasing any clues that Birdie is up there, waiting for me. I'm desperate to prove to myself that this whole night wasn't just a dream; it still doesn't feel real.

I take a deep breath beside the chair, preparing myself for whatever comes next. The wood is cool under my hands as I drag myself up the rungs, little splinters poking into my soft, meaty palms. My heart thunders in my ears as I climb higher, finally peeking over the top. The relief I feel as she comes into focus has me nearly slipping down a rung before I haul myself up onto the chair. Matching grins split our faces as I move toward her.

Birdie's wedged herself up into one corner of the big bench seat, wrapped in a soft blanket I stowed up here for her in case she ever came back. I couldn't bear to see her in that scratchy discarded one she picked up last time. I didn't know if she would ever have a reason to find it up here, but I'm so glad she did. She's still in her dress, but her shoes have been discarded, hastily tossed in the corner of the chair.

"You came," she says quietly, her voice a little awed. It hurts me that she thought I wouldn't. It hurts me that I wondered the same thing about her.

"So did you," I say as I tuck myself up on the other side of the seat. I want to sit closer. I want to feel her arm pressed against mine. I want the waves and wind to wash us clean as we sit here above them.

We're in an unknown, awkward space, and I hate it. It was easier when I thought we were done. It's one thing to want to hold someone—to ache for them and miss the feel of their skin under your fingertips—when you know you can't, shouldn't, wouldn't be allowed to touch them. But to be beside them, to know the possibility exists that you're going to get everything you've been dreaming about, but not yet . . . it's torture.

She looks at the space between us, and I wonder if she's thinking the same thing, wanting the same thing.

"I was scared you weren't going to show." Her words settle between us, cutting through the silence.

"I was scared of the same thing," I admit, looking toward the ocean, overwhelmed by my desire to hold her and reassure her. *Not yet,* I remind myself, but that doesn't mean *Not ever.*

"Even after what I said on that stage?" she asks, her words

an accusation. It feels like we're letting each other down again, without meaning to.

I tear my eyes away from the water and find hers in the moonlight. I study the emotions flitting across her face: concern, maybe a little hurt.

"What you said onstage was incredible," I say, daring to slide my hand closer to hers. "It was everything . . . but I know things can change in the space between sentences. I know your mom can be a lot, and when you left with her—"

"I'm done letting my mom—or anyone, for that matter— come between us. I'm done with the people who make me feel like I have to hide or do what they tell me unquestioningly." She walks her fingers toward mine, linking our pinkies. "I'm done filming for good, by the way. My dad even has my back on that. He's letting me stay here as long as I want, even if he was confused about some of the other things."

"The coming-out stuff? That had to be hard."

"No, actually he didn't care about that at all." She scoffs. "He was mostly confused about what I'm going to do now."

"What *are* you going to do now?" I ask, my heart pounding as I slide closer, pulling her hand into my lap.

"I'm not sure." She shrugs. "Something important. Something big. I'm going to stay here with my dad while I figure it out. Hopefully they'll still let me show my face around the Coalition."

"I'm sure that won't be a problem," I say, studying her face. She looks more relaxed than I think I've ever seen her.

"What?" she asks, wiping beneath her eyes. "Is my makeup messed up or something?"

"No, you're perfect," I say, scooting closer. We're within kissing distance now, if we both leaned in a little and met each other in the middle.

"I'm finally free," she says, a smile splitting across her face.

"Yeah, you are." I laugh.

"I can even drive now."

"Wow," I say, inching even closer. "Wherever will you go?"

"I don't know," she says, tapping her chin. "I was hoping you would let me pick *you* up for once."

"Oh yeah?" I say, leaning closer.

"Yeah," she says, finally closing the gap between us.

Her lips are tacky with the layers of color and gloss she's wearing tonight, but I don't even care. Beneath it all they're still perfectly warm and inviting, perfectly Birdie. We break apart to catch our breaths, and she burrows into my neck, pressing a gentle kiss along the edge of my jaw.

"I got you something," I say, pulling the necklace I made out of my hoodie pocket. "For your birthday."

She smiles, leaning forward so I can put it on her. I run my fingers over the delicate shell that sits perfectly on the chain, feeling luckier than I ever have before.

"I love you," I say, meaning it with my whole heart. I never said it back to her—I wouldn't let myself—but now I want to be free too.

Birdie looks at me, her eyes filling with tears as she nods, and whispers, "I love you too."

EPILOGUE

Birdie

One year later

MY FATHER WAS right.

I can be a shrewd businessperson when I want to be. I do get it from him, I think, although my mother is certainly not lacking in that department. Either way, it's this shrewdness that has me weaving through his busy Boston office this afternoon. There are two cups of coffee in my hands as I head to my most important meeting of the day.

I curve around a copier and make my way to where the intern cubicles sit, eager to get to the one farthest back on the left. It's deserted, like I was hoping it would be. I put the coffees down and set to work stapling up the little banners and arranging the small bouquet of flowers that I had hidden in my giant tote.

A few of the other interns look over curiously before going back to typing on their keyboards. I smile politely at them, and then I drop into the chair, satisfied with a job well done in record time. I check the time on my phone.

I don't have to wait long.

Less than five minutes later, Cass comes bustling around the corner, her arms full of folders and the work tablet that my dad calls "the office lifeline." It's been ever present in the corporate apartment my dad has put her up in for the duration of her summer internship here.

Cass stops short when she sees me, a puzzled smile crossing her face. "What are you doing here?" she asks.

I stand up and take her folders before passing her a coffee. "Surprise," I say, kissing her on the cheek, which promptly curves up into a smile. "Happy other one-year anniversary."

"You're such a mush." She laughs, glancing around us to see who's watching. I know she got a lot of crap for dating the boss's daughter when she started this internship—they didn't know she already had it secured long before I came into the picture.

"Only when it comes to you," I say, pulling out the chair for her to sit down. *One year.* We really made it. Granted, the year hasn't been the easiest. We've had our ups and downs, struggling to find middle ground and learn from each other, but we made it, and we're stronger for it. If anything, I think I'm more in love with her now than I was when we first got together.

"Didn't we already celebrate this a couple weeks ago?" she asks, taking a sip of her coffee.

"You know we have two." I laugh. "I told you I wasn't letting it go." Cass had wanted to pretend that our semi-breakup never happened, that our anniversary is the day we first got together and not the second. She called our fight a blip, but it didn't feel like a blip to me.

It felt like an earthquake, a nine on the Richter scale—something devastating that forces change. I want to honor the work we did to rebuild. It wasn't easy for either of us. Who knows where I would be today had she not said, "This isn't okay," and meant it, or had I not risen to the occasion in a way that no one had ever let me before.

"Birdie," she says, her voice going a little wobbly as she looks at me. "This is nice. This is really nice."

"I love you too," I say, hearing the words she's not saying. "Which is why I also scheduled a meeting for us with my father for right now. Come on." I check the time again and then scoop up our coffees. "We're going to be late."

"A meeting? For what?"

"You'll see."

She follows me as we head down the labyrinthian hallways of my dad's office building, ending up in the C-suite area. I wave to Dad's assistant, Milton, as we pass by. He nods, knowing better than to interrupt me when I'm on a mission. There are not a lot of places my name holds any weight, but thankfully this is one of them.

"What are you up to?" Cass asks, linking our hands.

My dad looks up from his computer and smiles as we push open the door. "Birdie! I thought I saw you on the schedule."

"Hi, Daddy," I say, settling in across from him.

"And Cass!" he says, finally noticing her. "Back again so soon? Don't tell me you've finished summarizing the data and comps I sent you with. It's barely been twenty minutes."

"Hi, George," she says, taking the seat beside me, shifting slightly at his question. "I'm afraid not. Birdie appeared at my cubicle out of thin air and informed me we had a meeting with you I was going to be late for."

He laughs, flicking his eyes between the two of us. "Should I be worried?"

"No," I say. "I come to you today with a simple business proposition."

Dad groans. "John sure is getting his money's worth out of you."

I snort. I'm spending the summer working at the Affordable Housing Coalition, interning there the way Cass is for my dad. The only difference is my position isn't paid, which my father knows. It's strictly for college credit. Yeah, college credit. I applied to a small business school just off the island—a spring admit since I'd already missed all the fall deadlines. I wrapped up my first semester just about a month ago and have been working at the Coalition ever since.

I still do some influencer stuff on Insta and TikTok too. It turns out, I did miss it after a while. The difference now is that my focus is on promoting ethical businesses and highlighting young people like me and Cass who are trying to change the world.

Some of my followers left when they realized I wasn't going to be posting drama anymore, and more than a few accused me of "going woke," but I don't care. I'm proud of what I'm doing now, and while my numbers aren't quite what they were, I'm finding my new audience just fine.

Cass, meanwhile, has been holed up here in Boston all summer with my dad. She's working in his newly created Ethical Acquisitions Department—which is just a fancy way of saying that he wants to make sure he's not *fully* screwing over every new neighborhood he starts to develop, just *kind of* doing that.

He uses Cass mostly to check numbers, summarize reports, and give her opinions. She's kind of my dad's conscience, for lack of a better term. I thought she would get sick of it or see the mess underneath my dad's shiny exterior and run away screaming, but to her credit, she's thriving. I think she loves the fast-paced work environment and is proud of changing things from the inside out. It helps that she's not afraid to call my dad out on his bullshit.

Cass nudges my foot, and I realize my dad is still waiting for me to speak. I sit up a little straighter, readying my opening volley in this crucial negotiation.

"Dad, as you may or may not know, today is Cass's and my second one-year anniversary."

My dad raises an eyebrow. "And this requires a meeting with me because . . . ?"

"Because she needs a three-day weekend to come back home with me for a little R & R and a visit with her dad, who misses her greatly. He reminded me twice to tell you that last part. I think he was afraid I was going to leave it out."

"I was just home two weeks ago!" Cass yelps, turning back

to my dad. "George, I promise I didn't have anything to do with this."

"Don't worry, this has Birdie's fingerprints all over it," he says, narrowing his eyes at me. "Anything else?"

"Also, a half day today so we can leave now, and . . ." I hesitate. "I think you should come out on Saturday so we can all do a family dinner together—you, me, and the Adlers. Mrs. Adler's making goulash." I instinctively slide my fingers up to feel the seashell necklace Cass gave me exactly a year ago today. It's become a good luck charm of sorts, and I know I can use all the luck I can get if I expect my father to actually go along with all this.

"I see," he says, clearly amused. "What do I get out of this?"

"Besides a wonderful home-cooked dinner by Mrs. Adler?"

He opens his mouth to speak, probably to tell me the terms aren't good enough because he can have that anytime he wants. I hold up my hand to stop him because I already anticipated that part. I'm not finished.

"You should also know that I just cleared a new press release with the Affordable Housing Coalition. We're finally going to announce the recurring donations your company has pledged. We'll line up a press conference with the local media while you're in town as well. In addition to the press release, we'll include a PR document highlighting the families your generous donations have personally helped as well as information about your new Ethical Acquisitions Department. We'll also pass all of this on to your in-house PR team, for their further distribution and posting on your corporate website."

He narrows his eyes. "In exchange, all I have to do is give Cass a three-day weekend?"

"Three-and-a-half," I point out, because I'm still hoping to leave right after this. I glance at Cass out of the corner of my eye and see she looks delighted. "Plus, you have to meet us there Saturday too. Don't forget."

"Birdie, the timing right now isn't—"

"That part's nonnegotiable," I say, knowing he hasn't taken a day off in a while. A weekend with all of us in Newport sounds so, so good. I know my dad needs it, especially with the way Mom is fighting him on this divorce—something that was definitely a long time coming.

"You drive a hard bargain," Dad says, leaning back in his chair.

I grin. "Some might even say I'm shrewd."

"They might." He bites his cheek at that; it's become a running joke with us. "Alright, Birdie, you have a deal."

I jump up and give him a quick hug, before tugging Cass out of her seat. "Love you, Dad, but we have to go. The train's in a half hour, and Mr. Adler's picking us up in Providence."

Cass laughs, running after me. "How did you know your dad would say yes?"

"I gave him a pretty sweet deal," I say, dragging her into an elevator that whisks us to the lobby. "Plus, he hasn't been to the summer house once since he let me repaint it last month. I've refused to send him any pictures. I know he's dying to see what I did. If nothing else, I thought that would help lure him out."

We step onto the street, where our Uber is already pulling up. I couldn't have timed this all more perfectly if I tried.

"Your ride, my lady," I say, pulling open the door for Cass with a bow. It's kind of been my mission to spoil her as much as she'll let me since that night on the lifeguard chair, even if she thinks it's ridiculous.

"You're my favorite person." She laughs, sliding across the seat to make room for me.

I don't let her get too far, pulling her back against me as soon as I shut the door and kissing her—because now she's *my* summer girl, and I'm never going to let her go.

ACKNOWLEDGMENTS

Huge thanks to my agent, Sara Crowe, for her support, advice, and enthusiasm; to my editor, Stephanie Pitts, whose insight and encouragement help make my stories the best they can possibly be; and to my family, who've been on this roller coaster with me from the start.

I'm also incredibly lucky to be surrounded by such a talented and truly wonderful team! My sincere gratitude: To the delightful Matt Phipps, who has been an ever-steady presence that keeps the train rolling on time. To Brittani Hilles at Lavender for being such a passionate cheerleader as we bring this book into the world. And to everyone at Penguin, including my publisher, Jen Klonsky, and publicist, Lizzie Goodell, along with Felicity Vallence, Shannon Spann, Alex Garber, and everyone at Penguin Teen! To my very patient copyeditors and proofreaders, Cindy Howle, Misha Kydd, and Lana Barnes.

Also, an indescribable level of gratitude goes to Jeff Östberg for perfectly capturing the story in yet another incredible cover illustration, and to Kelley Brady for creating such a stunning design.

And last, but never least, thank you to all the readers, bloggers, Instagrammers, BookTokkers, teachers, librarians, and booksellers who make this community the type of place I never want to leave.

© Amber Hooper

JENNIFER DUGAN is a writer, a geek, and a romantic who writes the kinds of stories she wishes she'd had growing up. She's the author of the graphic novels *Coven* and *Full Shift*, as well as the young adult novels *Playing for Keeps*, *The Last Girls Standing*, *Melt With You*, *Some Girls Do*, *Verona Comics*, and *Hot Dog Girl*, which was called "a great, fizzy rom-com" by *Entertainment Weekly* and "one of the best reads of the year, hands down" by *Paste* magazine. She lives in upstate New York with her family, their dog, a strange kitten who enjoys wearing sweaters, and an evil cat who is no doubt planning to take over the world.

JLDUGAN.COM | @JL_DUGAN